THE DEBT

GEOFF MAJOR

Grosvenor House
Publishing Limited

All rights reserved
Copyright © Geoff Major, 2025

The right of Geoff Major to be identified as the author of this
work has been asserted in accordance with Section 78
of the Copyright, Designs and Patents Act 1988

The book cover is copyright to Geoff Major

This book is published by
Grosvenor House Publishing Ltd
Link House
140 The Broadway, Tolworth, Surrey, KT6 7HT.
www.grosvenorhousepublishing.co.uk

This book is sold subject to the conditions that it shall not, by way of
trade or otherwise, be lent, resold, hired out or otherwise circulated
without the author's or publisher's prior consent in any form of
binding or cover other than that in which it is published and
without a similar condition including this condition being
imposed on the subsequent purchaser.

This book is a work of fiction. Any resemblance to people
or events, past or present, is purely coincidental.

A CIP record for this book
is available from the British Library

Paperback ISBN 978-1-83615-389-4
Hardback ISBN 978-1-83615-502-7
eBook ISBN 978-1-83615-503-4

Other books by Geoff Major

DEADLINE

HELL HATH NO FURY

To Lucia, and to my girls. Love you all.

Becky Banning – you will always be a star.
Twinkle in the night sky and be at peace.

Jon Taylor – your time and dedication in helping to improve all three of my books cannot go without a special mention. They are *infinitely* better than they would have been, thanks to your detailed and objective feedback which is of the highest quality.

Mum – yes, I'll also start on the book
I promised you, next.

ALSO:

Iain Clark – thank you so much for once again offering your support, insights, and critique.

My thanks to everyone who contributed their knowledge. Any mistakes, misinterpretation of their expertise and advice is my fault, not theirs, and is a liberty I've taken to support the plot.

To the real Gary Hibberd – without your insights, this plot would simply not have been plausible.

Erika Jurgaite – your knowledge (and willingness to share it) was gratefully received.

Daniella Wainwright, for making sure my numbers added up.

James Turner of Turner Little Limited, for sharing his experience of shell companies.

Ross Aubrey – appreciate the fraud and financial crime insights.

Cover design by Howard Rushfirth (www.rushfirthcreative.co.uk)

Author photo copyright of Mark Skeet Photography.

This book was produced entirely from my brain. A.I. has no place in my creative process.

All rights reserved.

A MESSAGE TO MY READERS

This is a sequel to HELL HATH NO FURY.

It is hopefully written in a way that means you can read this book as a stand-alone story, if you so wish. It does however contain spoilers for 'HELL' from the very start, so I'd encourage you to read that first, if you haven't done so already.

One thing to note is that the main story takes place in 2019 and 2020, which is why I refer to the social media site as 'Twitter', not as it's now known, 'X'.

Geoff

Prologue – 2017

The meeting took place at a five-star private dining room on Pall Mall, in London. The man fidgeted in his seat as he awaited his dining companion, who was already 10 minutes late.

"Another water, sir?" asked an immaculately dressed waiter.

"No, thank you, I'll wait until my..." at which point, Robert Kendrick marched up to the table and stood next to him, slightly out of breath.

"We'll take two Perrier, please," Kendrick instructed the waiter, before smiling down at his host. "Sorry. I forgot just how tortuous London public transport can be."

"It's alright," lied his host, still irritated that he had been kept waiting. Kendrick saw his discomfort.

"Relax. No one here knows either of us. It's the sort of place people meet their wives for lunch to find out how expensive her shopping trip to Selfridges was, or to meet their mistresses and complain about how much their wives spend when they go shopping." Kendrick chuckled at his own joke, but the humour was lost on his dining companion, so he moved on from the small talk. "So, what's so important I had to drop everything and fly over?"

The man subtly glanced around the room, aware of the surreptitious nature of their conversation, before pulling a folder from a satchel by the side of his chair. The cover said *Market volatility report: Chilean copper mining*, but that's not what the contents were.

"I thought this might be of interest," he said. Kendrick opened the file and couldn't decide whether to be surprised or disappointed. The document appeared to be a student's thesis, entitled *Fighting Data Security in A Digital World, Where Data is More Valuable Than Money*, but the name of the author had been redacted. The man could see the quizzical expression on Kendrick's face, so he lowered his voice and explained, "I think Mr Ruiz might find this of some interest. It's a fascinating read and opens up a fantastic opportunity."

"I'll review it and decide if it's worthy of his valuable time," replied Kendrick, quickly flicking through the document. "Why are two pages missing?"

"You think I'd give you pure gold, for free?"

"And how much do you think this 'pure gold' is worth?" Kendrick asked nonchalantly. He didn't want to get his host over-excited about what might be a useless report.

"Read it and then let's talk."

"If it's so valuable, how did you come across it?"

"A friend and I have swapped reports and insights for years. He came across this, but kept it locked away until recently."

"I see." Kendrick nodded. "I'm assuming, though, that if your friend found it, others could," but his host smirked in response.

"I don't think anyone else except the author or my friend had seen this."

"Okay, I tell you what: let's save some time and posturing, shall we? You and I will continue to grow our business relationship in the coming years, so how about I give you £1m for the report plus the missing pages. If the report isn't worth it, I'll take the hit," Kendrick said, placing the folder in his own bag. "I can even transfer the money here and now, if you're interested?"

"No. If it's worth what I think it is, I want 'in'."

"What do you mean, 'in'?"

"I want to be a partner in whatever you do with it."

Kendrick shook his head as if the man had asked for either the impossible or the ridiculous.

"I can't do that. Mr Ruiz is very..." and he mulled over what words would best describe the demanding, egotistical, dictatorial and ruthless Ruiz, before adding, "... particular about who he does business with. I'll take the idea to him and see whether he's at all interested, but don't hold your breath." He then stood and was about to walk out when his host gently but firmly took hold of his sleeve.

"This is a golden opportunity. Don't blow it for both of us," he said.

Robert Kendrick reached down and took hold of his hand, pressing gently on his median nerve to force him to release his grip, before leaning a little closer and whispering, "If you're serious about getting involved, be careful you don't overstep the mark. It can be a long and painful fall." His steely glare was then replaced with a broad smile and, as he walked out of the restaurant, he reached into his jacket pocket and turned off a small anti-snooping device. He was a wily operative, and as part of every conversation, he always had one of the devices with him. Whether it was law enforcement or a rival gang, it was best to assume that someone was always trying to find out what was being said. He wasn't wrong. Outside, two MI5 operatives sat in a fake British Gas van and had been trying to monitor the conversation inside the restaurant.

"Forseti to base," one of them said, speaking into a microphone on his headset.

"Go ahead, Forseti."

"Audio interference spoilt the concert. We do not have the virtuoso on record. I repeat, we do not have the virtuoso on record. Over."

"Roger that, Forseti."

Five days later, Kendrick sent the man a cryptic text message:

The captain has said no, but the first mate has decided the ship needs to set a new course and he needs a crew.

They arranged to meet a few days later, and this time the tone of the conversation was very different.

"I don't understand, if he doesn't want to play, what's your plan?" the man asked.

"I've read the thesis, and if the missing pages are as good as you say they are, I have a proposal."

"Go on."

"Interpol are investigating Ruiz, correct?" checked Kendrick.

"They are, but they're making slow progress."

"What if they had enough evidence to identify a red thread from some of the criminal activity, up to Ruiz himself?"

"You mean you'd be willing to provide sufficient evidence to incriminate Ruiz?"

"I would and I can. Of course, we'd need to leave the BOrg infrastructure in place, but if you were to come across some information, you'd be revered by everyone in the security services: even the Parliamentary Minister for Cyber Security."

The man guffawed. "I'm not bothered about that pompous prick, but yes, I'm in."

"Okay, I'll get you the incriminating information. In the meantime, I might be going dark for a couple of months. If Ruiz suspects someone is trying to undermine him, he'll hunt that person down, and I don't want to be the one he finds. After that, I'll find a suitable investment partner. Someone new to cybercrime, but with an ego as big as Ruiz's."

"And I know just who to give the incriminating information to," said the man.

PART 1:
LET THE GAME BEGIN

Chapter 1

The teenager was starting to tire, but the three men chasing her were getting closer. Her lungs felt like they were going to burst, and the lactic acid in her thighs began to burn, but she'd been lucky to escape and had no intention of letting them catch her again. They had held a knife to her throat when they dragged her into a derelict warehouse near the club she'd been working at. The taste of blood in her mouth reminded her just how savage and unforgiving they had been when she had initially tried to resist their groping hands, the tugging at her skirt, and subsequent ripping of her blouse. Her left breast was now partially exposed, with the torn fabric flapping as she ran, but it was the least of her worries. As she turned a corner, she could see a car sat at some temporary traffic lights. She pushed herself harder and screamed at the top of her voice for the driver to help.

The streetlights had been unable to penetrate the damp mist that hung in the air that night, so the driver had been concentrating on the road, given the unusual route his navigation system had taken him to head home. It was thankfully clearing now, and as he pulled up at some temporary traffic lights, the music on the radio – Mussorgsky's *Night on the Bare Mountain* – was building to a crescendo. His wife wasn't in the car, so he allowed himself the joy of turning up the volume until the dashboard vibrated with the bass tones, and he was now enveloped by the music. He hadn't seen the teenager, nor could he hear her shouting as she raced towards him; her face contorted in both fear and hope. The first he knew was when she slammed into the side of the car, hammering on the roof and window. His heart jumped, and he stared at her, wide-eyed. She pleaded with him to unlock the door and let her in, as she pulled repeatedly at the door handle.

"Please, please," she implored. *"They're coming. Hurry!"*

The driver hesitated, startled and unsure what to do. Who was she, and why was she imploring him to let her into his car? Then, his peripheral vision caught sight of three burly men running towards them; their faces contorted in anger. He glanced at her and then back at the men, who were now less than two hundred metres away. She became increasingly frantic as they thundered towards her, and he thought he could see a knife in the hand of one of the men.

"Get in," he instinctively shouted, as the central locking on the door clicked open. She pulled at the door handle, but her fingers slipped, before she grasped the handle and pulled again, crying out in panic. This time, the door opened, and she jumped in, slamming the door shut. The driver then pressed a button, and the comforting clunk of the central locking system provided a moment of calm, but the men were now less than 50 metres away.

"Drive!" she shrieked. With the temporary traffic lights still showing red, and a vehicle heading towards them from the opposite direction, there was a split-second hesitation before the man slammed the car into

gear and jammed down on the accelerator. The tyres squealed and the car shot forwards, horn blaring to warn the oncoming car. The other driver honked back in anger, but as the cars closed on each other, the oncoming car swerved into a ditch where workmen had been laying a pipe. As they sped away, the girl looked back at the car in the ditch and then at the men who had been chasing her. She sighed in relief, turned to face forwards, and closed her eyes as she whispered a prayer of thanks.

The three men came to a halt and watched as the car disappeared into the night, breathing hard from the chase. One of them retrieved his mobile phone and dialled the person who had recruited them.

When the call was answered, he said, "She's in."

Chapter 2

Arlo and Alessia McCleary first met in the 1960s. He was a data analyst for the British government, on assignment in Malta as part of its move to independence, and she was the feisty young Maltese woman who had politely but firmly refused him entry into the Grandmaster's Palace. In a country where girls were largely precluded from secondary education at that time, her self-confidence and air of authority were rare, and he was spellbound by her. Five years after they first met, they got married at a Catholic ceremony, given their deeply religious beliefs. Five more years, and he persuaded her to move to England, where they had remained totally and wholly devoted to each other, even given their growing eccentricities and foibles.

Today, over 40 years later, they sat in the garden of their house in the village of Barwick-In-Elmet. Their cottage was hidden from their neighbours, with a copse on one side of their property and a small hillock on the other, affording them a degree of privacy. Alessia was pouring their regular afternoon cup of tea while they waited to hear from their son, Mike. He had moved to Canada a few years earlier and always spoke to them at noon on Sundays.

"Must be fascinating," she said with a touch of sarcasm, breaking the silence between them.

"Hmm? What?" replied Arlo, clearly still distracted.

"Whatever's on that new phone of yours must be fascinating because I've been talking to you for the last two minutes and you don't seem to have heard a word." Arlo looked at his wife before shaking his head as if to clear his train of thought.

"No. Well, yes, actually." He turned the screen towards her. His interest had been piqued by a tweet that had recently arrived. His son had bought him a new phone, a smartphone, after he had accidentally trodden on his father's old Nokia the last time he was home.

"Here, give it to me," she said as she put her reading glasses on. On the screen was a photo of a pile of books, some boxes, and a variety of bric-a-brac, all stacked in an attic. Below the photo, it said:

You could literally have money in your attic.
A client recently sold a vase they'd bought at a car boot sale for £1 for £4000! Maybe you have an old painting that's worth millions, or a toy car that your grandad gave you that's actually a collector's dream?
Contact us now, before it's too late!

She scrunched up her nose, passed the phone back to him and asked, "What's it for?"

"Dunno," he said. "It was on my Tweeter feed. It's the third random one I've had recently."

"Twitter," she replied.

"What?"

"Mike said it's called Twitter, not Tweeter. You get or send tweets, but it's called Twitter. Did you click on anything, or like a tweet that you'd seen?"

"I '*liked*' one about saving money, that's all." Arlo shrugged to indicate it was all a little confusing. He was

7

intrigued, however, at the concept of possibly having something of value in the attic. There was a website listed on the bottom of the tweets he'd received: *youdbemadnotto.info*. Maybe he'd check it out tomorrow? Maybe there were more money-related ideas? Alessia read his mind and smiled warmly at him.

"We'll be fine, you know. The bank will sort out the mix-up." He smiled back, grateful for his wife's comforting words, but it had been over a week since the bank had informed them that access to their savings account was frozen, and no one wanted to explain how or why their money was inaccessible. Now, as they sat and sipped the tea she had poured, he wondered whether the website might be able to deliver the kind of income or savings it promised. '*You'd be mad not to*', he thought to himself.

Chapter 3

The man was slammed against the dining room wall. It knocked the wind out of him, and a family photograph that hung on the wall fell to the floor. Slumping to his knees and grimacing in pain, he wanted to beg them to stop, to reason with them, but all he was physically able to do was hold up a trembling hand to indicate he'd had enough. The two thugs, called Tom and Jerry, clearly thought otherwise. Tom lifted him to his feet, and Jerry crashed a sweeping left fist into his solar plexus, sending the man reeling across the room and crying out in submission.

"It's not a difficult decision, but you're making it difficult," said Tom, as he knelt next to the man. "All you have to do is say 'yes' and this can stop. And think of your family," he added, as he looked over his shoulder at the woman and two small children cowering in the corner.

"Maybe you want us to talk to your wife next?" taunted Jerry. The man shook his head vigorously, because when the thugs had burst into the house, they had said that's all they wanted to do with him; just talk. Wincing in pain, he waved his hand frantically, begging them to leave his terrified family alone. His wife began to scream and kick out as Jerry stooped and took hold of her arm. The two children began crying out incoherently, and the small boy slapped his thick, muscular arm, which made Jerry laugh. He wagged a finger at the child, but that only infuriated the little boy, who sank his teeth into the wagging finger. Jerry yelped, releasing his grip on the woman's arm as he prepared to lash the child across the face.

"Not the children!" shouted Tom. "You know the boss will be mad if you hurt either of them."

With the tiniest amount of blood seeping from the superficial wound, Jerry gritted his teeth and lowered his face to within inches of the boy's, snarling at the child. When the boy then tried to slap his face, Jerry caught his arm and squeezed it hard enough for the boy to realise just how powerless he was. When he finally released the boy's arm, the boy turned and buried his head in his mother's lap, as she put a protective arm around him. The boy's younger sister hadn't moved from her mother's side, with her face buried in her own hands.

"Alright, yes," wheezed the man in submission, blood dripping from his face. "I'll do it. Just leave my family alone." The thugs smiled at each other for another job well done, as they both stood and took a step back. They really did enjoy their work.

"Someone will be in touch in a couple of months," said Tom. "Don't make us come back. You really wouldn't like it if we had to come back." The man nodded, fearful of what such a visit might mean.

"Enjoy your Sunday roast," jibed Jerry as he looked at the plates, food, and cutlery that had been swept onto the carpet during what they would playfully refer to as 'the interview'.

As soon as the front door closed, the little boy leapt to his feet and ran over to hug his father, which made his father wince with pain. His wife then ran across to help him stand, and they made their way over to a comfortable chair in an adjoining room. As he sat back and groaned in pain, Steve Morris reflected on what he'd just agreed to. Everything he'd worked so hard for in the last 20 years, building his knowledge, his credibility and a profitable business, would be destroyed if anyone ever found out.

Chapter 4

"But that's not even my email address," Stephen Attwell explained, exasperated.

"I'm sorry, Mr Attwell, but your application passed all the necessary security checks, and we received an electronic signature from you when requesting the credit card," replied the call centre agent.

"I need to speak to someone in your fraud department. I can't just leave this."

"I'm afraid all their lines are busy at the moment, but I've put an immediate hold on the card, so no further transactions can be made," she explained.

Attwell sighed. "There's no credit limit left for anyone to spend on anything, anyway," but the call centre agent either didn't hear the comment or chose to ignore it.

"Can I take the best number to call you back on? I'll make sure they call you as soon as possible." He gave the woman his mobile number. "And is there an alternative number? A landline, perhaps?" she asked.

"No. Who uses a landline nowadays?" he replied, sarcastically. The call ended with a promise to pass the details to the fraud team. Attwell flopped into an armchair as he gathered his thoughts.

"What the hell?" he said to himself, looking at the seven recently arrived credit card statements that were laid out on the coffee table; all of them showing a credit card in his name and all already used up to their limit. It totalled £30,000 worth of debt. Next to them were printed copies of two loan applications that had also been made in his name, equating to another £20,000. Although he had a sizeable mortgage, he would probably have been able to scrape enough money together to make the minimum monthly repayments, which he assumed was why there had been no flag on his credit rating. The problem was, given the divorce proceedings his wife had recently instigated and yesterday's news that he was included in a departmental redundancy process at the export company he worked at, the financial pressure was starting to build. He checked his bank account via his banking app, but quickly tossed the phone back onto the settee in disappointment.

"At this rate, if I lose my job, it's all gone in three months," he concluded after looking at the account's remaining balance. As he continued to stare at the screen, a text alert popped up. When he'd upgraded his phone last month, he had accidentally deleted his entire contact list, so he was unsure who it might be. He opened the text:

Answer your phone.

As he wondered who might have sent him such a message, his phone started ringing, startling him. The caller ID was the same number that had just sent the text. *If it's someone I know, they'll leave a message*, he thought to himself as he turned his attention back to the paperwork spread out in front of him. The phone eventually stopped ringing, but five seconds later, another text arrived:

I told you to answer the phone. You have one last chance.

Almost immediately, the phone started ringing again. After a moment of deliberation, he pressed 'accept' and put the phone to his ear. "Hello?"

"Mr Attwell, I hear you have a financial predicament that we might be able to help you with."

"Is… is this the bank?" he asked, hesitantly.

A low, scoffing laugh could be heard at the other end of the line. "Not exactly."

Chapter 5

Dr Mark Pickett had been a lecturer at Oxford University for three decades. He was in his early seventies before he finally decided to retire; the onset of mild dementia visibly dimming his razor-sharp mind once too often. During his time there, he had scores of articles published by both the university and in several prestigious external publications. Since his retirement, he dabbled in the stock market and continued to work on his lifelong passion of drafting a book on the life and times of Frederick the Great of Prussia. History hadn't been his vocation, but it was a passion.

The sun streamed into his study through two large picture windows that looked out onto the expansive and beautifully manicured rear lawn, and the sheer curtains rustled from a soft breeze that whispered through the French doors that were ajar. A shadow loomed behind him as an assassin slid silently into the room through the open doors.

The force of the initial blow was enough to fracture Pickett's skull and cause a catastrophic brain haemorrhage. The blows that followed were pure adrenaline, rather than a necessity for the kill. As his body slumped forwards, blood seeped onto some papers that were spread out on his desk. The attacker dropped the lead bar he'd used and, as his racing pulse slowed and the bloodlust craving subsided, he looked down at the layers of latex gloves he was wearing. Such was the frenzy of the attack, he'd dislocated one of his fingers, which would make it difficult to pull a piece of paper out of his pocket, and impossible to manoeuvre the dead man's head so he could place it in his mouth.

"That will do," the assassin grumbled as he placed the piece of paper under Pickett's hand.

When he stepped back, a cheque for £20,000 caught his attention. It was partially covered by Pickett's other hand and was stapled to the top of a thin, brown folder that had *Stocks and Shares* written on it. He carefully took the folder from under the man's hand and placed it on a nearby chair, so he could easily open it and take a look inside. The folder contained several charts that tracked the rise and fall of a number of share prices, as well as bank statements: the most recent of which showed a total of just over £476,000 in an account under his victim's name. Of more interest, though, were some handwritten notes on a piece of paper stapled to the inside cover of the folder. As he studied them, he realised they were a bank's website address, an email address, and what might be a password. He wondered if the old man had become so forgetful that he needed to write down his online account details.

The unexpected sound of a key sliding into the front door broke the attacker's concentration. He stared, wide-eyed, before abruptly snatching the bank statement and the slip of paper from inside the file. He was about to leave when he turned and ripped the cheque from the cover, hurriedly tossing the file back onto the desk.

As a woman's voice called out, "Dad, where are you?" he quickly but quietly stepped back through the open French doors and ran onto the lawn. By the time he heard the scream from the house, he was already over the wall at the back of the garden and onto a deserted country lane that ran behind the property.

PART 2:

WEAVING THE WEB

Chapter 6

Matthew Berry, known among the criminal fraternity as The Broker, had built a fearsome reputation among London's gang leaders and illegal gambling syndicates: his usual clientele. They hired him when they needed a debt recovering or a gangland judgement delivering. His family knew nothing of his real career, believing he was an import-export specialist who used his expertise to help the police, who seemed to frequently want to talk to him.

Six weeks ago, he watched Detective Inspector Steve Denton announce the closure of the 'Lottery Ticket Murders' investigation, and was grateful there was no link back to him through the client who had funded the murder campaign. Once the press conference was over, he had turned his attention to the high-level proposal two men wanted to discuss with him. One of them was called Robert Kendrick.

Kendrick had worked for a cybercrime organisation, called BOrg. When he was presented with an opportunity a few years ago, he anonymously provided the authorities with enough information to arrest the leader of BOrg, a man called Dennis Ruiz, so Kendrick could take over the infrastructure and BOrg operation. What he didn't have, though, was enough working capital, which is why he and another man had courted The Broker.

Today, Kendrick was alone with The Broker and had already spent hours poring over a detailed operational plan, with its key milestones, monthly financial model, and risk mitigations. Although the overall idea appealed, there were still several significant risks.

"I know your model forecasts huge profits, but I'm an enforcer, not a cyber-criminal. For all I know, all this could be complete bullshit," The Broker reminded Kendrick.

"I understand your concerns, but I know what I'm doing."

"And you're sure you've not missed anything?"

"We have all the information we need. Anyone so much as sneezes, we'll know before they reach for a tissue," replied Kendrick. "So, are you happy to commit to the initial investment of £64m?"

"Talk me through the set-up, again," requested The Broker.

Twenty minutes later, Kendrick had explained that to help hide their various ownership stakes, he had set up several offshore shell companies. Many were based in the British Virgin Islands, but some were in other locations, like Panama and Dubai.

"Unlike in the UK, where anti-money laundering legislation requires a director's proof of identity and a statement about the company's purpose, none of the countries we're using has any of those controls," Kendrick confirmed. "If agents from Her Majesty's Revenue & Customs turn up at any of the registered offices to ask questions, all they'll find is a plaque on a wall outside the building. It's a veritable ball of regulatory spaghetti."

"£200m is a lot of money," The Broker replied, still assessing the option.

"So is your share of £20bn," Kendrick said calmly. "What's your hesitation? I've fulfilled every promise I committed to so far, haven't I?" he added, referring to the work he and the third man in their scheme had already delivered. The Broker nodded. Everything Kendrick and his business partner had said would happen had happened, and he did have enough for the initial investment of £64m that Kendrick and his partner were looking for, but he'd need to borrow from others in order to raise the remaining £136m. He exhaled loudly and sat forwards.

"You can have the £64m when I'm convinced your pilot is running as planned."

Kendrick smiled. "I thought you might say that, which is why I put a clause in the contract about how the release of the money is tied to the pilot's success, but you needn't worry because everything is going to plan." He pulled the contract out of his courier bag and slid it across the table, then watched in silence as The Broker worked his way through the seven-page document.

"Any final questions?" Kendrick asked when The Broker had finished reading the last page.

"Just one. Are you sure *you* want to commit to this?" It was a threat rather than a question, given the ultimate penalty for failure would be Kendrick's execution.

"I've signed it, haven't I?" replied a confident-sounding Kendrick.

"Okay, let's take this to the next stage," confirmed The Broker, signing the document and sliding it back over to Kendrick. "Anything else?" he asked.

"We just need to be patient now. I've tried to buy my way into one of the companies we need, but the CEO isn't biting, yet. I'll try to convince him one more time; otherwise, if I can put someone else in charge who is more... easily influenced, I will. The CEO probably needs replacing, but that will take a little time because..." Kendrick was explaining, but The Broker interrupted him.

"What's his name?"

"Haruhisa Sakamoto, why?"

The Broker turned to face his computer and typed in the name on his search engine. He scanned the results and then clicked on an image, before turning the screen towards Kendrick.

"Is this him?"

"It is... yes," came Kendrick's hesitant answer.

"If you want my investment, you have 48 hours to get him to comply. Otherwise, I'll remove him, permanently." He turned the screen back towards himself and stared dispassionately at the image.

"I'm sure there'll be no need for violence," said Kendrick, in an attempt to sound assuring.

"Let me help you understand something. If I commit to your plan and he gets in our way, I'll want my money back with interest, or I'll bury you under six feet of concrete. Understood?" explained a stony-faced Broker. Kendrick nodded, although killing someone was never part of his plan.

"Very well," The Broker said. "Is that everything?"

"Yes, I believe it is."

The Broker, satisfied his message had been received and that the meeting was over, gestured towards the office door with his open hand, indicating it was time for Kendrick to leave.

Shortly after he'd left, The Broker printed out the image of Sakamoto and buzzed through to the thug sitting outside his office. He had no intention of risking his proposed £200m investment on Kendrick's skills of persuasion, and felt the only choice was to remove the man from the equation.

"Get Tom and Jerry up here."

"Yes, boss."

When they entered the office, he handed his loyal thugs the printout.

"This man, but not yet. Leave it a couple of days, and then make it look like a tragic accident. I don't want the police sniffing around this any more than they would for any other accident. Understood?"

"Yes, boss," they both replied.

Chapter 7

"What have we got?" asked the detective as she climbed out of the car.

"Victim is Dr Mark Pickett, aged 82. Found by his daughter. She's been popping in twice a week to make sure he's taking his medication and eating properly, but, beyond that, she's too traumatised to answer any more questions right now, Sarge," replied a uniformed officer, as she checked her notes.

"Er, SOCO confirm the back of his skull was crushed, so it was more than just a single blow to the head, and the assailant or assailants probably escaped through the French doors, which we found wide open."

"Any other members of the family we can talk to?" asked the detective.

"His wife's abroad at the moment, speaking at a conference in Egypt. We're trying to get embassy officials in Cairo to break the news and make the necessary travel arrangements."

"Where did you find him?" she asked as they walked into the house.

"The body was in the study, with a blood-stained piece of lead piping on the floor."

The detective paused and tried to suppress a smirk as she said, "I thought you were going to add that you suspect Professor Plum, or Miss Scarlett."

There was an awkward silence before the uniformed officer, looking genuinely confused, asked, "Who?"

"Doesn't matter," sighed the detective, realising that the person she was talking to was probably too young to know what Cluedo was. Her peripheral vision registered some movement off to her left. It was the lead SOCO, which meant she and the police officer could both walk away from what was a short but increasingly embarrassing moment.

"Afternoon. Got anything for me?" the detective asked the lead SOCO.

"Nothing definite, I'm afraid," he replied. "But there's a folder on the desk that looks like it's been moved after the attack."

"What makes you think that?"

"The pooling pattern of the blood is inconsistent, with more blood underneath the folder than one might expect to see compared to if it had simply seeped under. That also fits the hypothesis that the assailant or assailants moved the folder, which is why we found tiny drops of blood smeared on a second chair in the room, but it's just a theory," he explained.

"Wouldn't the assailant or assailants have noticed the drops of blood?"

"Probably not. We only found them because we used a UV light. Without that, they're virtually impossible to see with the naked eye."

"Have you had chance to look inside the folder?"

"We have. There's a lot of financial charts about investments, some old bank statements, and there's a staple on the front of the folder, but it only has a small scrap of paper still attached to it. Looks like CBS1, but we'll need to get it back to the lab to validate that assumption."

"What's CBS1?"

"It's the approved standard of paper they print cheques on."

"I wonder if the victim had pulled it off, or whether it was something the assailant took?" she mused, out loud. "And you said the folder was all about investments?"

"Yes. His daughter said he loved to dabble in the stock market. Apparently, he told her he was very successful at it, although she told me he suffered from early signs of dementia. I wonder whether he thought buying a lottery ticket was 'dabbling', and he'd won some money on that?"

"A lottery ticket?"

"Yes. We found a copy of one under his right hand."

Chapter 8

"I'm thinking of moving to Canada," Mike McCleary had blurted at the end of a party three years ago, held to celebrate his master's from MIT. "Not for good... well, I don't think for good, but there's an amazing opportunity to join an electronics company out there. They came to MIT to talk to a few of us. I know I've been away a lot what with university and all, but this is exciting!" He didn't know how they'd take the news.

"When... when are you thinking of going?" his mother, Alessia, had asked.

"Erm, well, quite soon, I expect," he answered nervously. "It's just... I promised I'd let the company's HR director know as soon as possible. But hey, if you are not okay with it, I can stay here. I guess I've been away quite a lot." He'd watched his parents' glance at each other, and Arlo spoke first.

"You got a first with honours for your degree, and now you've achieved a distinction for your master's. I'm not surprised you're wanted, son," said Arlo proudly. Mike blushed. "And that acceptance email is going to write itself," he added, winking at Mike, who jumped up, barely able to contain his excitement. He ran around the settee to give his mother and father a hug before racing to his room. He didn't see his father then gently and protectively embrace his wife.

"Are you alright?" Arlo asked softly.

He heard her sniff before she replied in a wavering voice, "Of course not. It feels like we've only just got him back from MIT and now he's going away again?"

"Our boy is a man now, and if he needs to unfurl his wings and fly, we need to let him," Arlo had replied. She had known it was true, but it still broke her heart, and she had sobbed quietly in his comforting arms. Now, three years later, Alessia called out to her husband, who was gardening.

"Don't forget, it's almost noon," she said, as she placed a tray with a teapot, two cups and a small milk jug onto the table on the patio. Every Sunday for the last three years, Mike called them just after he'd woken up on the east coast of Canada. Arlo pulled off his gloves and walked over to the patio, taking his smartphone out and squinting at the screen.

"Where are your glasses?" she asked.

"I don't need them," he replied, squinting a little harder as he flicked through some tweets. Over the last few weeks, he'd received a lot of adverts from the money-saving account whose tweet he had initially 'liked' – @youdbemadnotto – as well as some direct messages.

Scammers don't always personally contact you. Sometimes, they use what's known as a bot, designed to mimic human interaction. Spam of this type can be programmed to suit different scenarios.

A small payment to us can protect you.

Warn family & friends about the Top 10 Twitter scams by sharing the article below, Arlo.

Report scammers to Twitter or the police, but don't report us. We know things about you that your wife doesn't. Yet.

The previous ones had seemed quite random, but the latest one – the seventeenth – was the first one that had included his name.

"*Arlo?*" demanded his wife. He looked up and saw her glaring at him. "You know, sometimes I think you pay more attention to that phone than you do to me," she grumbled, holding the milk jug in mid-air. "More milk, or not?" she asked him for the fourth time.

"Yes, please," he replied, as he typed a reply. It was the first time he'd replied to anyone on Twitter, so he didn't know what to expect.

I don't know who you are, but I'm not interested. Stop sending me this rubbish!

Moments later, as the clock in the hallway struck noon, the phone rang. It was Mike.

"Hey, Mum, and hi, Dad," he said brightly. "I've got some news."

"Oh really? Well, don't keep us in suspense, Mike, what is it?" his mother eagerly asked.

"I'm coming home. I have a job offer at a small disruptor in the semiconductor industry, based in York... and..."

"And?"

"Well, you know I've been seeing this girl for a couple of weeks, right?"

"The one called Tania?"

"Yes, Tania. Well, she's coming with me. We're both moving to England!" The excitement in his voice was obvious. Him having a girlfriend hadn't been big news, but the fact this Canadian woman was willing to move to England with him, especially after such a short relationship, seemed a surprising step. He waited several seconds before his mother's slightly hesitant voice broke the silence.

"Well, that's... that's wonderful, darling. We're both so pleased, aren't we, Arlo?" Alessia replied a little nervously as she looked up at her husband.

"Is she pregnant?" blurted Arlo.

"No, Dad," chuckled Mike. Alessia slapped Arlo on the arm and gave him a disapproving look. "We're happy together, and she has some research papers to complete for Imperial College, in London. She's been working on it remotely so far, but she's excited about being closer to campus and collaborating in person, rather than over a video call. Also, her uncle is apparently a big deal in venture capital, so not only is he happy to see her over there, but he's already joked that if I turn out to be a complete loser, she can move into one of his properties until she's finished the research."

"Oh, that's wonderful, Mike. When are you coming back?" his mother asked.

"We fly in two weeks," he replied. "Can't wait for you to meet her."

"And, just to confirm, I'm not pregnant," came Tania's soft and silky Canadian voice, as her bright, beautiful face appeared just on the right of the screen. Alessia stared at Arlo, wide-eyed. He glanced back at his wife, blushing, but Tania said, "It's okay. I love that you're so protective of Mikey, and I promise you, if you don't like me, you can ship me straight back to Canada," she chuckled.

"Well, I'm sure you're absolutely lovely," said Alessia, as she glared once again at her husband.

"So, what's new with you?" asked Mike, realising just how embarrassed his parents would feel right now, given his father's faux pas.

"Your father's an idiot, but I'm not sure that's really news," replied a newly assertive Alessia, still shaking her head.

"And your mother's not at all embarrassed by me, even though I do still open my mouth before I put my brain into gear from time to time, Tania," Arlo said apologetically.

"No problem," she replied warmly. "Looking forward to meeting you both."

Chapter 9

As arranged, Attwell's mobile rang at precisely 8am. Yesterday, they had told him he had a way out of his financial situation, but that he'd need to complete a few tasks first.

"Hello?" Attwell said. His tone was one of resignation, rather than asking who was calling.

"Why do you sound so glum, Stephen?" asked the voice, with a mock tone of sympathy.

"Can we just get on with it?"

"Patience is a virtue. This will be easy, but it might not be quick, and we don't want any mistakes made, do we?" Attwell felt like a bird under a cat's paw: escape felt impossible, and the cat had only just started to play with him. "And don't forget the magic word... which is?"

Attwell sighed. "Can we just get on with it, *please?*"

"Good. There's no need for this to become unpleasant, but let's remember who's in charge, and we don't want anything bad to happen to Emma, do we?" Emma was Attwell's estranged daughter, and although they hadn't spoken for several years, he still felt very protective towards her. The caller assumed that Attwell's silence meant he understood and would be compliant. "Now, how about we get rid of one of those credit card debts for you?"

"What do you need me to do?"

"Firstly, I want you to open a new current account with an internet bank. We'll let you know which one, and we'll send you a 'refer-a-friend' code so your application is directed to someone we have inside the bank. That way, they can make sure you pass the security checks. You'll only use that account for a month, but leave it open to avoid flags being raised. You'll need to deposit £500 of your own money and, once it's open, we'll deposit £500 as well. After that, you'll receive small deposits from a variety of people, which you'll need to send to an account we hold, every day. *Every* day! Understood?"

"Yes," Attwell replied, hesitantly. "But *you're* going to deposit £500?"

"We are, yes. You can't keep it, but let's call it a gesture of trust in our partnership. You've got enough available in your savings account to be able to deposit the £500, haven't you?"

It didn't feel like a question, and Attwell assumed they knew more about him than he had originally imagined. "Complete this, and we'll write off the debt on card ending 4494." Attwell shuffled the papers that lay on the table in front of him until he found a statement for that card. It was the smallest of the debts at just £3,000, but it would be a start.

"Understood."

"Good," the caller replied. "We'll check in with you again next week."

"How do I contact you if there are any problems opening the account?" asked Attwell.

"If there are any problems opening the account, you won't need to contact us, Stephen, because we'll be on our way to find you," came the ominous reply.

Chapter 10

News about the murder of Dr Pickett had reached DI Steve Denton, who was now slumped in his chair. He was stunned.

Over the previous six months, he'd led an investigation into a series of murders where the police had found a copy of a lottery ticket at every crime scene. The media was quick to name it the Lottery Ticket Murders. His team eventually realised that there was a pattern to the deaths: the first victim's house was the first number of the ticket, and their postcode started with 'A', and the second victim's house number matched the second number on the ticket and their postcode address started with 'B', and so on.

There had been two lottery tickets and twelve crime scenes before Denton's team eventually identified the killer and avoided the two final murders that would have completed the fourteen numbers on the tickets. Denton was satisfied that the person behind the murder spree had also coincidentally been murdered, but was Jones now briefing him on a murder related to a third lottery ticket? A copy of it had arrived just as he had finished a press conference announcing that the murder spree was over, but he had assumed the killer had sent the ticket to taunt them, before they had died.

"… with an Oxford postcode," she concluded. She paused, waiting for questions, but he just sat with his arms crossed as he stared at the board where a photo of the new victim was now pinned. "What do we say to the media? This will get out somehow," she added.

"I have no idea," he sighed, before checking, "No trace, no suggestion of a motive, and no link between the new victim and any of the previous lottery-ticket victims?"

"None, sir," she replied. She'd already told him this, but it simply confirmed what she already knew: he hadn't really been listening. "Exactly the same MO as all the previous murders. Well, with the exception that this ticket was found under Dr Pickett's hand, not in his mouth," replied Jones.

"Is that relevant?"

"Reporting officer said the assailant or assailants perhaps fled the scene after being unexpectedly disturbed, so perhaps the ticket was put there in a rush."

"So no, it's probably not relevant," grunted an increasingly frustrated Denton.

"No, sir, probably not."

"Bloody brilliant," he mumbled, as he shook his head in exasperation. He swivelled his chair away from her and stared out of the window. He had shading under his eyes from a lack of sleep, and this latest news only added pressure for the newly promoted detective inspector. *He looks ready to explode, or implode*, she thought. She walked over to the whiteboard on the wall and wrote the numbers from the ticket onto the board.

Postcode:	<u>OX</u>	<u>P</u>_(6*)_	<u>R</u>_(3*)_	<u>S</u>_(15*)_	<u>T</u>_(8*)_	<u>UB</u>	<u>W</u>_(9*)_
# on ticket:	4	19	27	32	35	44	6

* = number of different postcode cities/areas that start with the primary letter.

Denton puffed his cheeks out and exhaled slowly in exasperation, as he looked up at the board. As he was doing so, Jones checked her watch.

"Sir, sorry to bring this up, but may I be excused? I've got my selection interview for the vacant detective sergeant position in an hour and would really like to..." she started to explain, but without looking at her, he just waved his hand to indicate she could go. As she walked out of his office, another detective was about to walk in.

"Good luck," the detective said, knowing that Jones had the interview.

"Thanks, but I think you're going to need it more than me," she replied quietly, as she gestured towards Denton with a slight movement of her head. As the detective knocked and entered the office, Denton stood and, without saying a word, headed for the door.

"Sir?" asked the detective, holding up an incident report Denton had asked for, relating to a separate investigation.

"It'll have to wait," Denton shouted back. Someone had to tell the DCI what was happening, and if anyone was going to let her know that he might have made a mistake closing the Lottery Ticket Murder case and holding that press conference, he'd rather it be him.

Chapter 11

"How's the plan progressing?" The Broker asked Kendrick.

"All on track. We intend to make an offer for a minority shareholding in Kintaro Semi-Conductors, in exchange for a £50m investment."

"Do you think they'll bite?"

"Oh, they'll bite. They're on the verge of bankruptcy, and I know their current CEO declined our second offer, but I'm sure we won't have any problem," said a confident Kendrick. "We'll have the ability to mass-produce the amended chip to host our secret software."

"Do you have a new CEO lined up?"

"I do."

"What if they find out about our scheme?"

"He won't be a problem if your team play their part in the overall plan. We'll have more than enough leverage," Kendrick replied with a malevolent smile.

"So, if we buy the minority shareholding in Kintaro for £50m, what's the other £14m you want for?"

"We'll be purchasing a 75% shareholding in a small software company, Centro Simio. That's who'll produce the new software. We're placing key employees in there right now, and they will write and test the new code," explained Kendrick.

"And then, at some point, you'll want the balance of £136m?"

"Yes. The majority will fund a second £50m carrot for Kintaro."

"What triggers the second investment?" The Broker asked.

"They have to deliver against the targets we'll agree in the initial offer we'll put to their new CEO and, if the company decline the second capital injection, we'll make sure they're bankrupted. At that point, as the largest minority shareholder, we'll look to convince the rest of the investors that our plans represent a better future for the company and for their dividends. If they're not interested in that proposal, we'll send Kintaro into administration, and one of the many shell companies I've set up will offer them all a fair price to buy their worthless shares. Either way, we invest the money and we win control," said a confident Kendrick.

"And the remaining £86m?"

"We'll purchase a third company, called Anakart. What's left over will be used as contingency for the expansion of BOrg."

"Anakart? They're the assembler, right?"

"Yes. They'll receive the fraudulent software from Centro and the amended chips from Kintaro. Anakart is the key, as they'll distribute the finished product at such a low cost, we'll eat into market share, and no one is likely to question the final product, because all three companies involved will have independent verification from external assessors: ISO 9001 and ISO 27001 certification is guaranteed."

"How will you manage that?" questioned The Broker.

"All three companies are allowed to select from an approved list of certification assessors, and we already have an assessor in our pocket, so he'll deliver the right outcome. He'll do exactly as we want, to keep his family safe."

Chapter 12

It was strange feeling like the new boy, but Mike McCleary was as excited as he was anxious. He had flown over to England to make sure everything at his prospective employer's was as he expected before he and Tania moved here permanently. His new boss, Haruhisa Sakamoto, or 'Harry' for short, walked out of his office and beamed.

"Mike, really pleased to see you again," he said, effusively.

"It is an honour, Mr Sakamoto," Mike replied. Harry laughed lightly at the respectful formality.

"Please, call me Harry," he said. "We are a close-knit team at Kintaro, and while people must always be respectful to their colleagues and the management, we do not ask them to follow what we consider outdated formalities."

"Understood, Harry," Mike said.

"Let me take you around the building and introduce you to some of the team." He gestured for Mike to follow him. "I can't tell you how excited I am to have an MIT alumnus join me here, especially one with such a brilliant mind." Mike blushed a little.

"Brilliant?" he asked, pinking in the cheeks.

"Yes. Your thesis was brilliant, but it's purely academic theory, whereas we now get to benefit from your real-life experience. I hear the work you were doing in Canada was very good too." That was the moment when they almost literally bumped into Bob Hall, the operations manager. He was hurrying around the corner, checking some paperwork on a clipboard and muttering to himself.

"Oh, sorry, Harry," he offered.

"Hello, Bob. Busy sorting out today's scheduling?" It was a rhetorical question, and before Hall could react, Harry gestured towards Mike. "This is Mike. He'll be joining us as the head of our new research and development team."

"Pleased to meet you," Hall replied, shuffling the paperwork he was carrying so he could hold out his hand.

"And you, Bob," Mike said. As they shook, Mike could smell a faint body odour. Not so unpleasant it made him recoil, but noticeable. He assumed Hall was self-conscious about it, which was probably why he seemed a little reticent to make eye contact.

"Sorry, got to get back to the planning office. Seems we've got a short shift, again," Hall explained to Harry.

As he strode away, Mike looked at Harry, who smiled and said, "Don't worry, just a minor operational issue, but we have an important deadline to meet."

"I assume you're running a JIT production, to keep inventory costs down?" asked Mike.

"Yes, but our Just-In-Time approach has its challenges. Our client understandably expects on-time delivery, but we seem to have a spate of prolonged absences."

"Want me to take a look?" offered Mike. Harry smiled, but shook his head.

"Not today. I'm sure Bob and the production team can resolve the issue. Please, this way," and he resumed the tour. A little further down the corridor, Harry opened a door which had a name plate on it: 'Quality Assurance'. Inside the room were two desks, one of which was occupied.

"Let me introduce you to our lead analyst, Penny Büggs. She'll talk you through our assurance and testing protocols. Penny, this is Mike, who will soon be joining us as the head of our new research and development team. Mike, I'll be back in a few minutes to rescue you," said Harry, and a mischievous, elfish grin spread across Büggs' face before he marched out of the office, leaving the door wide open.

"Alright?" Büggs asked rhetorically, in her Bristol accent. "Mind shutting the door? Ruddy freezing in here when it's left open." Mike nodded and closed it. "Grab a chair," she said, pointing to a spare one behind her. "Here," and she pulled it closer to her. "I don't bite."

Mike took his seat, and she turned one of her computer screens so he could see it.

"He's alright is Harry, but he's always rushing everywhere," she said. "Just needs a bit of a break."

"A break?" queried Mike.

"Yeah, things are tight financially. Cashflow's a bit of a problem, but he says there's an investor who's interested in putting millions in. Might even get a Christmas party this year," she joked.

"So, what is it you do, exactly?" asked Mike, making a mental note to query the financial issue.

"It's my job to analyse and report on samples of all the incoming goods and test the components for our outgoing orders," she explained. "For example…" and, for the next 20 minutes, she talked Mike through the intricacies of her role.

Harry returned, thanked her and gestured that Mike should follow him.

"My apologies for leaving you there for so long. I had some urgent business to deal with."

"Not a problem," replied Mike.

"I was going to take you through our production process, but I think we'll leave that and the other introductions for your formal induction. I'm sure Bob wouldn't thank me for taking up any more of his time today." As he and Harry walked back to the reception area, Mike decided to ask about the financial challenge.

"No need to worry, Mike. We've received a second financial offer from an investor this morning. I'm still not happy with the conditions surrounding the proposed deal, so I rejected it, but I'm confident we'll have plenty of other offers very soon."

Chapter 13

The online bank Attwell had been told to use hadn't raised any questions and didn't seem to have any concerns when he asked about opening a new current account. Their online team took him through the standard security process, and, within an hour, there was a contract in his inbox, ready to be electronically signed.

The same week he had opened the account and passed the details to his mystery caller, students like Gwen Dier had seen and responded to an online advert that offered a quick return for some simple work. The advert said:

Earn up to £500 a week while you study

The Elpinsk Property Group (EPG) was established in 1987 and operates in over 20 countries around the world. We are now expanding into the UK and urgently need support from some exceptional candidates to collect deposits from our eager house-buyers. We are an industry disruptor and firmly believe that tomorrow's organisations will work best as a virtual team, not by making people sit behind banks of desks for 40 hours a week. It's how we keep our costs down and our ability to respond so high.

The demand for our services has skyrocketed, so to help meet that demand, we are looking for students in higher education who are confident with numbers and with a few spare hours every week. You must own your own computer: no abusing college or university hardware and software, please. In return, we offer 1% of each deposit as reward for your time and flexibility (so, on a typical £5,000 deposit, you'll get to keep £50 just for collecting and processing the payment). Just forward the net payments to our super agents once a week and see your bank balance grow.

"Yes, of course I researched them," Gwen lied. "Elpinsk Property Group is legit." The truth was she had only undertaken a cursory search online. It was true, their website was very impressive and professionally designed, with scores of recommendations from homeowners and payment agents. Besides, her mounting debt was a higher priority than spending time on research, and fresh food was a luxury she'd almost forgotten the taste and texture of. She'd been living on stale pizza and pretty much anything she could recover from the abandoned trays in the university's refectory. It hadn't taken long to get approval from the team at Elpinsk and, just a few days later, she and her three close friends were lying on her bed, stuffed with Kentucky Fried Chicken and beer.

"Shit, that was good," said one of them, as he dropped the remnants of a drumstick back into the takeaway bucket.

"I need to get me some of that," said another, referring to the scheme.

"Sounds dodgy, if you ask me," said the third one, as she wiped the crumbs and grease from her lips.

"Enjoyed your food, did you?" asked Gwen, frowning at her friend's scepticism. Her friend held up her hands in admission of the double standards. "Look, people want to pay a deposit for a house. I'm just earning some money by helping bring their dream to reality. What's your problem?" Gwen had challenged.

Six days after opening the account, Attwell sat at home transferring the final deposits from Gwen Dier's account and a dozen others when his phone rang.

"Hello, Stephen," said the familiar voice.

"Hello," he replied flatly.

"Why the miserable tone? You've just finished your first assignment, and if you log on to your credit card apps, you'll see the first account has been paid off in full, as promised."

"This feels wrong. I'm still uncomfortable with the whole scheme. Who are the people putting money into my account?"

"Why does that matter to you?"

"Because, for all I know, they're in the same position I am."

"They're not, I promise, Stephen. There, does that make you feel any better?" Attwell still had questions about the scheme, but it did feel good to see the first account paid off.

"So, what now?" Attwell asked.

"Wait a couple of weeks and then use the £500 float to open another current account: same internet bank, but for a different purpose this time. Perhaps a savings club? Once our contact inside the bank has set up your new account, we'll bump you up to super-agent status, and you can start to process bigger fees and clear a bigger credit card debt. I hope that's alright?"

"I suppose so," Attwell said. "I'm just having a bit of a moral dilemma, that's all." There was a deep sigh from the caller, whose tone turned slightly threatening.

"I'm your only dilemma, Stephen. Piss me off and we'll come looking for you and your daughter."

The man ended the call, and Attwell took a deep, uneasy breath. He had never done anything illegal in his life, and he had no idea what else this could be other than a money-laundering scheme, but he knew he'd have time to think about how to get out of this situation legally, once he had opened the second bank account. Right now, though, buying himself some more time and protecting his estranged daughter were his priorities.

Chapter 14

The interview with Dr Pickett's widow had been delayed because when the British Embassy official had broken the news of her husband's murder, she had collapsed. After a day under observation in her Cairo hotel suite, she was cleared to fly home. Denton sent Jones to Oxford to participate in the meeting.

"Were you aware of any concerns your husband had, Professor Pickett?"

"Please, call me Eileen. No, he... he seemed happy in his retirement and filled his days with reading, listening to BBC Radio 4, and his hobby of dabbling in stocks and shares."

"How much do you know about his hobby? Your daughter said your husband often talked about his success, but she didn't know if he was successful or perhaps just thought he was. I'm sorry if that sounds insensitive." Eileen Pickett looked as if she was about to crumble, but she closed her eyes for a few seconds and held a handkerchief against her nose as she sniffed back a few tears.

"Do you want a minute to yourself, Eileen?" Jones asked.

"No, it's... it's alright. Sorry, I'm... just still in shock."

"That's totally understandable," said the lead detective. "Please, take your time." After a few more seconds to compose herself, Eileen continued.

"Mark had a brilliant mind, even at his age. I don't know how he did it, but he turned the £25,000 he started his hobby with into a sizeable sum: he was into six figures the last time we discussed it. He never invested too much, though, as he'd always say if the stocks and shares crashed, he wanted to be sure he could stand the loss." Jones turned to the Oxfordshire detective and frowned briefly, but even though it was a split-second glance, Eileen noticed.

"What?" she asked the detectives. The lead detective nodded to Jones, who turned to the woman.

"Does the company name 'Ashton, James, and Proctor' mean anything to you?" asked Jones. Eileen shook her head.

"Should it?" she asked.

"Eileen, I'm afraid it looks like your husband might have invested all his money in cryptocurrency," explained Jones.

"What? No! No, Mark wouldn't do that. We always discussed and agreed what he did. He's... he's been suffering with early signs of dementia, but he knows he's not supposed to do anything without my agreement," she protested.

"A single transfer of £475,000 was made from your husband's bank account to that company. We've tried to speak to the company on numerous occasions, both through their Panamanian and Dubai-based offices, but they seem quite elusive. We hoped you might know of a contact there?" Jones asked.

"I've never heard of them, and I really can't imagine Mark doing anything like that. He wouldn't!"

She was now becoming visibly and increasingly distressed, so both detectives decided it would be best to end the interview.

"We'll look into the offshore company a little more, Eileen, and we'll be in touch," said the detective.

Once the woman had been collected by her daughter, Jones drove back to the London Met headquarters to brief Denton.

"So, his wife knew about his hobby and his success?" checked Denton.

"She did, yes, but she seemed confused about him dealing in crypto and transferring all the money, even given his growing dementia," she clarified, but there was a touch of doubt in her tone.

"What is it, Jonesy?" he asked, recognising her quizzical expression.

"It doesn't sit easy with me, boss. I know his wife and daughter have both mentioned his dementia, but everything else suggests he was a balanced risk-taker. Until that point, no single withdrawal or transfer was for more than £20,000. Why would he suddenly invest everything with an offshore crypto-broker?" She then noticed him smiling softly to himself.

"What's cheered you up?" she asked. Denton's cheeks pinked a little at being caught out.

"Just enjoying my job," he lied. He was actually enjoying working with her again. They had been a good team on the Lottery Ticket Murders, thinking along the same lines, finishing each other's sentences, and drawing the same conclusions. *Just like old times*, he thought to himself, and he suddenly missed being a detective sergeant in the thick of it, instead of attending committees, reviewing budget reports, and all the politics that came with his current role.

"So, what now?" she asked.

"We follow the money and keep digging into the offshore company, I guess?" suggested Denton. She smiled and nodded. She loved doing research.

"You're like a pig in muck, Jonesy," her colleagues would joke when she had research to do for an investigation. On this case, the muck was about to become knee deep, and she was going to love it.

Chapter 15

The target for Kendrick's fraudulent software pilot fell into three categories. Firstly, there were people with a reasonably high income but a surprisingly mediocre credit rating. The data suggested they had a natural inclination to rely on credit cards, but it wasn't because they couldn't make ends meet, so creditors were reasonably tolerant of the risk. Stephen Attwell was a prime example.

The secondary group were pensioners with a moderate lifestyle, but who could easily be tipped into needing short-term loans or high-interest credit cards to bridge the occasional gap if they didn't have a lot of savings. Arlo McCleary was an example of this now they'd hacked into the bank and cut off access to the joint savings account, although he'd also been selected for a different, very specific reason.

The final target group were known within BOrg as 'insecure peacocks': those who had a history of wanting to feel part of something bigger, and to be liked. It never failed to amaze him just how much information these people shared on things like Facebook, and how a few simple 'fun questions' could harvest vast quantities of valuable and personal information. His favourites included *Tell me what year you were born without telling me*, which recently drew tens of thousands into sharing their year of birth. When their profiles were subsequently mined, the vast majority also had a post celebrating their actual birthday. Combine those two pieces of data, and you had pure gold. More surprising was the volume of people who replied to *Your porn star name is your middle name plus the name of your first pet* which helped identify passwords, or answers to security questions. A survey in the United States showed that 39% of pet owners used their pet's name as part of a password for an online account. In another recent data harvest, over five thousand people had responded to the question, *I want to see how far this post can reach. Tell me what city you're saying hi from.*

Although Kendrick's initial conversations were to assure The Broker that the pilot had started well, in truth, Kendrick was worried. The accountant he'd recruited had found a flaw in the spreadsheet's algorithms, but of even greater concern was that one of the core assumptions in the model wasn't playing out in real life. It assumed an average life expectancy, but three of the 50 fraud victims in the pilot had unexpectedly died. When he remodelled the assumption on deaths and he corrected the algorithm, the benefits of the fraudulent scheme almost halved. Despite this news from the accountant, Kendrick tried to rationalise the latest results.

"It's a tiny sample, so three deaths are just unfortunate and create a disproportionate glitch."

"That might be so, but I now need to check all the tolerances in your model. After all, that same tiny sample was used to validate the forecasts, and your investor is about to commit £64m into the scheme, based on them. If I were you, I'd..." but Kendrick cut across him. His tone was assertive, bordering on aggressive.

"You're not me, and I don't want this model altered, nor do I want you to share a revised version. Do you understand?"

"Wait, are you asking me to cover up the change to and impact of the revised forecast? I know who your investor is, and his reputation, and I don't want to give him any reason to question either my credibility or trustworthiness." Kendrick was about to explode at the response, but he needed this man on his side, not as an adversary. He sighed, as if admitting he was wrong, placing an assuring hand on the man's shoulder.

"You're right. I understand your predicament," he said in a softer tone. "But can you understand mine? I can't show him a revised set of figures this early, and I just know that this is a temporary anomaly that will even itself out as the numbers grow. I've invested my time, my blood, even my marriage to get this close. I just need a couple more weeks." The previous look of incredulity and scorn at Kendrick's request slowly dissolved, and the accountant softened.

"I don't want to deceive him, but what I can do is produce two reports: one that shows a revised forecast due to the algorithm error, and one with the error corrected *and* the potential impact of the incorrect assumptions. You'll have to explain the algorithm glitch to him because I'll be amending that in both, but how you handle the two reports is up to you," he explained.

Kendrick nodded in both understanding and appreciation, while thinking about what he'd be willing to do to save his own life. He had never thought about killing anyone, but if it was a straightforward survival decision, he would have no choice.

Chapter 16

Arlo was sitting in his potting shed at the bottom of the garden, where he'd hidden a notebook behind a stack of brown plastic plant pots. Over the last few weeks, he'd received a total of 21 tweets or direct messages and, given his years working as a data analyst, he had finally noticed a common pattern in all of them. By following the pattern, he now had 21 letters underlined – one from each tweet or message – and while the letters were not sequential, he'd already started to rearrange them. The arrival of the twenty-second tweet earlier that morning added another letter.

Joining Cubs and Scouts was always exciting. Sean Dooley, a past Macaoimh (Scouting Ireland) youth leader, has taken on the challenge to revive the fortunes of the once proud movement, despite his own checkered past.

With a quivering hand, Arlo wrote the message in the notepad and underlined the key letter: 'o'. Just as he finished, Alessia called out from the top of the garden, breaking his contemplation.

"Arlo, where are you?" He hurriedly pushed the notebook back into its hiding space when he heard her call out again.

"Arlo? *Arlo!*" She was starting to become impatient.

"*Coming,*" he cried out, as he put the plastic pots back in place. He took a moment to gather his composure before opening the shed door and waving at her.

As soon as she saw him, she shouted, "Mike will be back from his visit soon. Can you please help me prepare the dinner table, rather than sitting down there like Alan ruddy Titchmarsh?" Before he could respond, she turned on her heels and disappeared back into the house.

"Yes, of course," he replied with a broad fake smile on his face, even though his wife wasn't looking anymore.

Twenty minutes later, Mike returned. As they sat eating, Alessia asked him about his visit to Kintaro.

"It was fantastic," enthused Mike. "There's so much to do, but it's such an amazing opportunity. My boss, Harry, has some amazing tech ideas that he wants me to develop. It's leading-edge stuff."

"Harry?" checked Alessia.

"That's not his real name, but he prefers to be called that rather than Haruhisa. That's his Japanese birth name: Haruhisa Sakamoto."

"Will you get an office and your own team?" she asked, as Mike stuffed a fork full of food into his mouth.

"I don't know about an office, but, yes, I'm running the research and development team," came the animated if muffled reply, given Mike was still chewing the mouthful of food.

"And when do you start?"

"In a week, but I need to get Tania and I settled here before I throw myself into work. She's been looking at properties to rent and found an old farmhouse in a village near York. She flies in on Sunday, and we can move in straight away. I can't wait for you to meet her!"

"How exciting," Alessia replied before glancing over at Arlo, who seemed to be focused on his own thoughts. "Isn't it, Arlo?"

"Hmm?" Arlo responded, still consumed by the message he had been decrypting.

"Mike, starting work: exciting, isn't it?"

"Oh, er, yes, of course. When do you start?" he asked, still not truly focused on the question or the conversation. Mike chuckled under his breath at his father's lack of attention, but Alessia was clearly irritated.

"Next year," she replied.

"Well, that's not long," Arlo mumbled, before suddenly looking up in surprise as his brain registered what his wife had said. "What? Next year? I thought…" he started, but she interrupted.

"It's next week, but you're clearly not interested in being part of this conversation. What's wrong with you?" she probed, trying but failing to hide her irritation.

Arlo stared back at her, feeling momentarily frail and fearful, before his anxiety burst into anger. With tears forming in his eyes, he exploded: *"Nothing. Nothing is wrong with me. I just didn't hear, that's all. Why must you talk to me like I'm an imbecile?"* and he threw down his knife and fork, splashing gravy and scraps of food onto the tablecloth, before storming out of the room. Mike sat in silence, unsure of what had just happened. His father was usually the meekest, kindest person he knew. After a short period of silence, he glanced over at his mother to see how she was, but she saw the question coming.

"I'm fine and, in answer to your next question, I have no idea," she said, not looking up. She tried to sound strong and calm, but a slight waver in her voice belied the truth. She, too, was stunned. Arlo had never reacted like that in all their time together, no matter what the situation. She slowly and deliberately put her cutlery down on her plate and stood. "You finish your meal, Michael, and just leave your plate there. I'll clear it up later. I'm just…" but she had to leave the room, as she could no longer hold in her emotion.

Sat alone at the table, Mike didn't know whether to go see how they were or whether to leave them in peace for a while. He decided to clear the table, taking all the plates and bowls into the kitchen, sweeping the leftover food into the bin, and then putting the crockery and cutlery into the dishwasher. As he put the final plate in it, the kitchen door opened slowly, and a remorseful Arlo stepped in. He looked at Mike, and then down at his own feet.

"Sorry about that," Arlo said. "Things are a little tense at the moment, that's all. Total over-reaction on my part, and I'll go see your mother in a minute."

"What's going on? You and Mum always seemed so easy-going," Mike queried.

"Oh, there's a problem with the bank. Well, at the bank, really. They can't or won't give us access to our savings. Some glitch, apparently. It's all just a little awkward, that's all. It will blow over in no time."

"How long has this been going on?"

"About six weeks," replied Arlo.

"Have you spoken to them?"

"Yes, yes, but they tell me they're working on it."

"Do... do you need..." Mike started to ask, but Arlo shook his head vigorously.

"No, we don't need any help, thank you, son. We can get by on our pensions."

"Then, how about I go down to the bank with you, to try to sort it out? They won't talk to me if I'm by myself, but perhaps I can ask some technical questions that you might not be familiar with? And, if they still won't play ball, I could always talk to my friend at the newspaper? That would scare them into action, I'm sure."

"That would be helpful, thank you. It's all a bit like talking Martian, to me." Arlo forced a smile. "We can discuss it later, but I really should go talk to your mother."

Mike nodded, so Arlo walked out of the kitchen and into the hall. As soon as the kitchen door was closed, he stopped at the foot of the stairs and pulled out his mobile phone. He typed a reply to the person or people sending him the tweets and messages.

Just give me a few more days, please.

He pressed send and had just put the phone back in his pocket when it buzzed. It was them. The tweet said:

Join our amazing cruise and get away from it all. From Alaska to Africa, Kuwait to California, Sydney to Scarborough. It's what you've dreamt of.

Immediately after, a text arrived from them:

Arlo, the window of opportunity is closing, and your chance for redemption is nearly over. All that is left is consequence.

His heart sank. He turned the phone off and looked upstairs towards where Alessia would be lying on their bed. Instead, he turned towards the front door. He needed time to think.

Chapter 17

The latest call from his tormentors left Attwell feeling angry, as well as increasingly vulnerable. He had done everything they had asked, and yet now they had increased his debt?

"What the hell is going on? Why are you doing this?" he pleaded. He knew he mustn't aggravate them as that might make things worse, but he was also struggling to contain his frustration.

"Because we can," came the calm, matter-of-fact reply.

"But you promised! I did everything you asked me to, and yet you've now re-spent the £3,000 available credit on the card that was only paid off a few days ago?"

"I changed my mind. Shit happens, Stephen. Deal with it."

As soon as the call had ended, Attwell stomped around the house, swearing and shouting. The seemingly crazy idea he'd had when this first started, of selling up and restarting life elsewhere debt-free, suddenly felt quite attractive.

"If I get £600,000 for the house, pay the mortgage off and split the remaining £360,000 with my ex, I might be able to clear the remaining debts they've created. That means I'll have £25,000 for rent and to live off, until I get a new job," he reasoned to himself.

After 45 minutes of pacing up and down, talking himself through the pros and cons of his proposal, he decided to run the idea past a trusted friend. He sent her a text to make sure she was available to talk before he dialled.

"Hi, Amanda," he said. Amanda Fox had known Attwell for over 20 years: they'd even dated a few times, but had sensibly decided to just remain friends.

"Hi. What's up?" she asked.

"Nothing's up. Just fancied giving you a call." The initial silence on the other end of the phone meant she had seen through his lie.

"You sent me a text to see if I had time for a chat? You've only done that three times before. First time was when you were arrested for being drunk and abusive at a football match, and you needed someone to come and get you, so your then fiancée didn't find out. Second time was when you said you didn't know what to do because you'd accidentally flushed her tropical fish down the loo while drunk, and..." but before she could remind him of the third time, he interrupted her.

"I'm in some deep shit. I mean *really* deep." Fox thought she heard a tremble in his voice. The third time he'd sent a text before calling was when he'd found out his wife was leaving him, and his voice had trembled on that call, too.

"What's up?" she asked in a softer, more caring tone. Twenty minutes later, including several breaks for him to regain his composure, he'd explained everything.

"No! Why should you have to sell your home when the banks need to sort this out? No, Stephen, absolutely not."

"But I can't see any other way out. The banks and the credit card companies say all the applications seem to be legitimate, and that perhaps I'm just over-extending my credit. They're adamant that I must have signed up for the loans and the credit cards, and they've closed the fraud cases."

"What about talking to the police? Maybe record one of the calls?" suggested Fox.

"I can't. They've threatened to harm Emma if I don't comply," he replied in a submissive tone. This time, Fox remained silent. She knew that despite the strained relationship Attwell had with his young daughter, Emma, she still meant the world to him.

Chapter 18

Reflective doubt was an emotion The Broker couldn't afford in his line of work, so he rarely dwelled on what could have been, or what might have happened 'if only', but today he was annoyed with himself.

He was reflecting on his decision to go through with the murder of Dr Pickett, and could barely suppress his anger. He'd been pre-paid for the job and, in turn, he'd pre-paid the assassin, but there had been no need to complete the kill. The person who had requested the hit was dead, so there would be no-one demanding their money back if he didn't kill Pickett, and yet he still went through with the hit.

"That's what having ethics does to you," he mumbled. He'd been raised to honour his commitments, even if no one was there to judge him, but the consequence of delivering on his promise had been a surprisingly high level of police activity. He couldn't recall the last time they had entered his place of work, but just a week after Pickett's death, DI Steve Denton and two police officers arrived unannounced.

"Just doing the rounds. Good visible policing. Mind if we come in, Matthew?" Denton had said.

"Got a warrant, Mr Denton?" His tone prickled with barely suppressed anger.

"Not yet, but I wondered if we might ask you and your employees a few questions? You know, supporting the fight against crime?"

"I'm afraid we're all a bit tied up at the moment. It's our busiest time of the year, you see," The Broker had replied. "We'd love to help, but perhaps you can make an appointment next time?"

As he spoke, one of his thugs smirked: message received. The reference to being 'a bit tied up' was about a man downstairs in the visitors' room, being interviewed by Tom and Jerry. As old as the building was and as thick as the walls were, if the office was quiet, then very occasionally a victim's wails could be heard during a severe, sustained beating. It was very faint, but it was recognisable and he didn't want to give the police any reason to search his place of work under their right to rescue, because that wouldn't be all they found. The thug pretended to dial externally, when in fact it was a direct line to the basement.

"Hello. I'm calling on behalf of Mr Berry... Yes, that's right. He has a lunchtime reservation with you, but he's asked if you could hold the tenderised steak, because he's unexpectedly delayed... Oh, I imagine about half an hour... That's much appreciated, goodbye." It was actually Tom who had answered the phone and knew the message meant he and Jerry had to stop pulverising the victim until he got a subsequent call to confirm the coast was clear.

"You have time for lunch, Matthew?" Denton quizzed. "Can't be that busy if you can afford to take a lunch break."

"Got to eat, Mr Denton, and because I work so hard, I can enjoy the good things in life."

The two of them looked at each other in silence for several seconds, aware of the growing tension in the room, but Denton then simply nodded a couple of times and said, "Maybe we'll come back at a more convenient time, and with a warrant."

The Broker smiled broadly. "You do that, Mr Denton."

That wasn't the only time he and his thugs had felt under increased scrutiny, though. Denton was convinced The Broker had been involved in the Lottery Ticket Murder campaign, but he had no proof, so he hoped one of The Broker's thugs might make a mistake and trigger a legal search of the property. Stop and search activity also increased, as did the visibility of police in and around The Broker's territory. Informants were repeatedly questioned, and while it didn't stop his day-to-day operation, it slowed everything down, including his cash flow.

"What do you want us to do?" asked Jerry, one morning. "Yesterday, I didn't collect a penny because everywhere I went, there seemed to be a copper nearby. It's as if they're following us."

Eventually, The Broker felt enough was enough. The heightened activity was disrupting his cash flow, which meant his £64m investment with Kendrick was at risk. That therefore meant the £20bn prize was also at risk, and that was simply unacceptable.

"I need to get the spotlight off me, off us. Just keep doing what you do, act normal. I'll distract Denton and his bunch of clowns." Tom and Jerry nodded, then walked out, because there was money to collect and heads to bash. They loved acting 'normal'.

Once they had left, The Broker called a contact to brief her on two things he needed her to do.

"Really?" was all she could say. The idea seemed a little desperate, but she wasn't paid to challenge his thinking if the rationale seemed sound.

Chapter 19

Whenever they went shopping for fresh fruit and vegetables in the nearby town of Crossgates, Arlo was happy to carry the bags and said "Yes, dear" quite a lot, but that wasn't how today had started.

"Arlo!" his wife said, once again struggling to maintain her composure.

"Yes?" he replied, having been lost in his own thoughts. She stopped walking and exhaled in exasperation.

"I said, if you're going to walk any slower, we'll need to go to different shops rather than dawdle our way around together."

"Yes, dear. Sorry. I just feel a little foggy-headed this morning," he lied. He knew he still wasn't being his usual attentive self because he was absorbed thinking about 'them'.

"Please go get some bananas and plums from Anesco's. I'll sort out something for our tea from the fishmonger and meet you by the benches outside the newsagents, okay? Got that?"

"Yes, of course. Bananas and plums, then benches; right."

They headed in slightly different directions, with Alessia soon pausing to look in the window of a dress shop. Mike had told his parents they would be invited over to dinner once he and Tania had settled into their new home. Alessia thought a new dress might be a nice treat. There was a subtle floral one in the window which really caught her eye, and the price seemed reasonable. Arlo often told her not to overthink things; otherwise, items she eventually decided she wanted had been sold by the time she decided to return to the shop to buy them.

"I deserve it," she told herself, and turned to walk into the entrance vestibule. As she turned, a man strolling past bumped into her. It was a gentle collision, rather than something that could cause her to overbalance.

"Oh, I'm so sorry," the man said, apologising profusely as he instinctively grabbed her upper arms to ensure she didn't fall over.

"It's alright; no harm done," she said, looking up at him.

"Sorry again, I..." But as the man glanced up from her arms to her face, he stopped talking. It only took a couple of seconds for his expression to turn from apologetic concern into one of vaguely recognising her, and then into a look of disgust. His nostrils flared a little. "It's you!" he growled. "How can you show your face in public after what he did?"

Alessia was stunned and blinked repeatedly. "P-p-pardon?" she said out of instinct, rather than wanting him to repeat what he'd said.

"You should be ashamed after what he did. How can you sleep at night? I wouldn't be able to," he said and then lowered his face to within inches of hers. "You disgust me!"

After staring into her eyes for a few more seconds, he stomped off, muttering to himself. A couple of passers-by who had overheard some of the exchange whispered as they walked past her, even though they had no idea why the man was apparently disgusted by her. Alessia stood, transfixed and unable to process what had just happened. Panic started to rise as she struggled to comprehend the man's outburst.

What did he mean? she thought, followed by *What is it I've done that upset him?*

"Bananas and plums," proclaimed Arlo, as he stopped next to her. "You've not got very far," he chuckled, before realising she seemed wholly preoccupied and possibly hadn't even heard him. He reached out and gently touched her arm.

"*No!*" she shouted, recoiling slightly before looking up and seeing it was Arlo. Her scream attracted the attention of other shoppers who wondered what was happening, but as soon as she saw it was her husband, she grabbed his hand and squeezed it.

"Your hand is shaking. Are you alright?" Arlo asked. She smiled weakly as he took the shopping bag from her hand and led her to a nearby bench. She didn't protest, which worried him. Normally, she would tell him not to be such a 'worry-pants' and that she was made of sterner stuff, but not this time. They both sat down.

"Alessia, what's wrong?" he asked.

Still processing her thoughts, she replied but didn't look up at her husband. "I... I don't know. A man just told me I disgusted him."

"What?" queried Arlo, as mystified as she was.

"He... he said I should be ashamed."

"Of what?"

"I... I... I'm not sure. He said something about 'what he did', but I... I don't know who 'he' is or what someone has done."

"Did you recognise him?" Arlo asked. He looked around the street to see if there was a man looking over at them, or in case he could see whoever she might be about to describe.

"No. No, I've never seen him before in my life," she mumbled. She then looked up at her husband, as if seeking answers. He looked back, helpless.

"Do you think he mistook you for someone else?" Arlo asked hopefully, but she simply shrugged her shoulders, as tears welled in her eyes.

"I don't know. Maybe?" she answered. She felt helpless, confused, and stunned. She leant into her husband's body, grateful that she was protectively wrapped in his arms. While he held her, Arlo gave a silent prayer for help.

Chapter 20

Mother and son stood at the school gate. She knelt and straightened his jacket and tie, murmuring, "Now remember, Jack, if the boy tells you to give him your lunch money today, what should you do?"

The boy thought for a moment, clear on what his mother had told him, but wondering if his father would also approve. Without looking at his mother's face, he replied, "Say no and, if he won't leave me alone, I punch him in the goolies and tell a teacher it was self-defence?"

"That's right, and punch him like you mean it, otherwise he'll not stop, and you won't have time to run to find a teacher. Punch them..." and she privately mimicked what she wanted him to do "... as if you're trying to push them back up into his tummy." She smiled in encouragement, but her son kept looking down at the floor. She lifted his chin with her forefinger and looked him in the eye. "Got it?"

"Yes, Mummy. It's just that Mrs Bridges says..." But his mother moved her forefinger from his chin to his lips, to stop him talking.

"Mrs Bridges isn't going hungry every day, or asking her friends if they have a sandwich she can have, is she?" The boy shrugged his shoulders in an attempt to end the conversation, and she knew it wouldn't be wise to keep talking about it. "Okay, sweetheart, have a good day, and your father will be here to collect you and your sister at 3:30. OK?"

The boy nodded but resisted a hug from her. *Come on, Mum, I'm 11 now,* he thought to himself as he looked around to ensure none of the other first years at high school had seen the embarrassing attempt to embrace him.

Jenni Cellier was a mother of two: Jack, aged 11 and Alice, aged 14. Alice was like her mother, a no-nonsense type of person who didn't have the time or patience for people who were disingenuous, selfish, and definitely not for anyone who thought they were better than her. Alice had been in a few scrapes at school, and Cellier had been called to the headmaster's office several times, but she rarely berated her daughter for her actions. In fact, most of the time, she approved of them in front of the headmaster.

"It's not my daughter's fault you can't run a well-disciplined school, is it?" she'd snap. Her defence of her daughter's actions was well-known, to such an extent that the headmaster and the deputy-head would often flip a coin to see who would have to talk to her. Jack, on the other hand, was very much like his father: considerate to others, a mediator and a bookworm rather than a street fighter. Alice wasn't a bully and certainly didn't want trouble at school, but she always stood up for what she thought was right. Once, she'd stepped in when some boys, who were several years older than Jack, were pushing him around in the corridor, for fun.

"Hey, that's my brother," she said, just before she grabbed the shoulder of the main bully, spun him around, and then pushed him to the floor. "What's wrong, Dawkins? Struggling to hold your own against a girl?" she'd taunted. "Mind you, I assume to hold your own, even you'd need tweezers, rubber gloves, and a magnifying glass," she added, embarrassing the boy about his sexual immaturity. Alice Cellier wasn't shy about any of that. "Leave my brother alone, understood?"

"Get lost, ya lesbo," he taunted, smirking to his friends as he began to stand up. Alice showed no signs of or inclination for lesbianism, but was offended that some people still thought a woman's or a girl's sexuality could be used as an insult. She walked forwards, teeth clenched, and as Dawkins turned to face her, she threw a powerful straight right at his nose. People gasped as he staggered backwards and cried out, but then some started to snigger as blood began to trickle into the palm of his hand. The deputy-head lost the toss that day and had to face Cellier's wrath.

Having dropped the children at school, she went about her daily routine: picking up some fresh fruit and vegetables from the local greengrocer, tidying the house after the morning rush, and finally sitting down for a well-earned coffee as she logged on to her emails.

"Not interested in that, that one's spam, as is that one. That's the dreadful newsletter from the school, delete, and that's a reminder to renew the car tax," she mumbled as she worked her way through 10 new emails. The sixth one caught her attention, though. The subject line was always the same:

If it ain't broke, don't fix it.

There was never any content in the body of those emails, but then that wasn't their purpose. It was the agreed message The Broker would send when he needed her to log on to her secure device. She deleted the email and then went into the 'trash' folder and deleted it from there, before walking to the bedroom and opening one of the drawers. She moved all the pants and sanitary products to one side before she clicked the rear of the drawer and retrieved the secure device from inside the false back. After turning it on and logging into the device, she read the single email that had arrived.

Open the flood gates. Beloved to get closer. Cue remaining cast.

Cellier nodded. The coded requests were all part of The Broker's responsibilities in Kendrick's carefully coordinated plan, and it was time for her to fulfil her role.

Chapter 21

As Mike sat in the arrivals area at Manchester Airport, he reflected on the meeting at the bank with his father, to try to sort out the problem regarding access to his parents' savings.

"So far, my father has been accused of not remembering he's changed the PIN code or his account password numerous times. He's also been asked to check the computer at home for a virus, and now you're telling me there might be a compatibility issue with the version of coding in the bank's latest security updates, which is delaying the resolution of my parents' problem. What's going on?" Mike had demanded, but the bank manager remained vague, despite promising that resolution to the problem remained his top priority. He had at least offered Mike's parents access to an interest-free emergency loan, should it be necessary.

"You and I don't realise the sort of pressures they'll be facing," Tania had rationalised on a Zoom call that evening, before she headed to the airport. "Any issue with the bank's technology is bound to worry them, and not being able to get to their own money is going to feel pretty scary." Mike knew she was right. Even he had been distracted by irrelevant and confusing information from the branch manager, and he worked in tech.

He looked at the arrivals board again, which showed that her flight from Toronto had just landed. Once she'd cleared Customs, and after a warm embrace and a kiss, they headed for the waiting executive car. The drive from the airport to their new home in Kellington took a little over two hours.

"Thank goodness for that," exclaimed Mike as they finally flopped onto one of the settees in the large lounge. They were surrounded by boxes that had been shipped from their respective homes in Canada, as well as several pieces of furniture they'd purchased online. A pile of mail sat on a small table next to the settee. Mike hadn't had time to deal with it, but most of it appeared to be junk.

"What do you want to do first, unpack or make out?" teased Tania. "The bed is already made." Mike smiled, put his arm around her shoulder and pulled her close.

"Maybe later," he said with a smirk. "But right now, I'm going to have a cup of Yorkshire Tea and a biscuit. Then let's see if we're both still awake."

"I'll be waiting," she said, winking before she theatrically and provocatively walked out of the lounge, undoing her blouse as she headed to the stairs. He sighed as he tried to decide whether he was hungry and thirsty, or whether that could wait. As usual, though, logic won the argument, and he headed into the kitchen. The company he'd paid to get everything into the house had also ensured the oil-fired AGA was on. He grabbed a kettle to fill before placing it on one of the oven's hot plates. His phone had been off for almost four hours, so as he waited for the kettle to boil, he checked for emails and messages. He was hoping for something from his parents, confirming that everything was back to normal after the extraordinary outburst from his father a week ago. He then sat down at the kitchen table with a mug of tea and a cheese and pickle sandwich he'd just made.

He turned his phone on, and there was a series of pings as emails, texts, and a couple of WhatsApp messages arrived. In among the emails was an apologetic but still frustrating email from the bank manager, who had written to confirm the conversation they had had and to explain that he had now updated the IT team in their head office. Mike knew there wouldn't be anything seriously wrong with the bank's IT infrastructure or security coding; otherwise, there would have been some national media coverage. He wrote a curtly worded reply, promising an appeal would be made to the Financial Ombudsman Service in due course, if his complaint wasn't resolved. He also had a text from a friend in the banking tech industry who said he'd be happy to make some of his own enquiries on Mike's behalf.

"Back-channel contacts, gotta love 'em," chuckled Mike.

The text messages were mainly from friends congratulating Mike on returning to England and on his appointment to Kintaro, although a recent one was from the head of human resources at Kintaro. It just asked Mike to call him as soon as possible.

"Hi, it's Mike McCleary. Just got your message. What's up?" he asked, before taking a bite out of his sandwich. Mid-chew, he stopped. "What? When?"

"Two days ago. The police are still investigating, but their first assessment is that it was probably just a tragic accident at home," replied the man.

"Oh... oh my god! Er, thanks... thanks for letting me know," he replied slowly, as his brain continued to process the news.

"Before you go, Mike, we have an emergency board meeting in the morning. I know you've probably only just arrived home, but can you possibly make it into the office?"

"What? Er, yeah, sure. I'll... I'll just need to unpack a few things, but I'll... I'll see you tomorrow." He pressed 'end' on the screen, but remained on the kitchen stool, staring at his phone as the news slowly sank in.

"Hey, a girl can only wait so long," came a voice. Tania stood in the kitchen doorway, leaning against the doorframe. Her bathrobe was slightly open, so Mike could see she was only wearing panties underneath, but she quickly realised that his mind was elsewhere. She pulled the robe closed and tied the belt as she stepped towards him. "What's wrong? Who was on the phone?" Mike looked up, his expression still one of shock.

"It was the head of human resources at Kintaro. He called to say that Harry's dead, and they want me to attend an emergency board meeting first thing in the morning."

Tania softly wrapped her arms around him. "Oh, that's awful. Are you okay? Do you need to call anyone?"

"No. I just need to get some clothes ready and then try to get some rest. I have no idea if I've even got a job from tomorrow."

Chapter 22

Attwell didn't recognise the number that had sent the text, but assumed it was someone he'd mentioned his flight plans to. It simply said:

Enjoy your new life. Portugal is lovely.

There was a knock at the door.

"Morning. Moving day?" asked the postman.

"Yes, yes, it is," Attwell replied.

"I've seen the redirection instruction on the mail-sorting pigeonhole. Going anywhere nice?"

"I, er, I haven't quite decided yet. A few last-minute things to resolve," Attwell lied. The redirection was to a mailbox company, who would hold the mail until he paid for it to be forwarded.

"Well, good luck wherever you end up. It's got to be better than this place: country's going to the bloody dogs," then he smiled and handed Attwell several items of mail. Attwell smiled back before closing the door. As he drifted back towards the kitchen, he flicked through the pile. It was mainly junk from companies who must have bought his details from a database mailing list, as they were either about house moving or new house needs, but one official-looking envelope caught his attention. He ripped it open and pulled out the contents.

Your new loan agreement was printed in large black letters at the top of the paperwork.

"Nooooo!" he growled. With the paperwork still in his hand, he stomped into the kitchen and picked up his phone. Beads of cold sweat were starting to form on his forehead and neck.

"Stephen, what is it?" Fox asked, racing downstairs after hearing him shout out. She had stayed the previous night to help him with the final bits of packing. He slammed the paperwork onto the breakfast bar and, without explaining anything, started to type a text. Then he froze.

"It's got to be a problem with my phone," he suddenly mumbled, as a possibility dawned on him. He'd messaged a few friends to say he was moving, but he'd not actually told any of them where he was going, or when. Only the travel company whose app he had used knew the details.

"Here, you can use mine if there's a problem with yours," offered Fox, assuming he meant his phone wasn't working.

"It's got to be my phone," he repeated, gently rubbing his neck to relieve a growing pain.

"Okay, if it's got to be yours, fine, but mine's here if you need it," Fox called out as she turned to head back up the stairs.

"It's the only common denominator," he continued. He'd used it for everything, including enquiring about the new bank account they told him to open, to surf the net for possible destinations, to swap messages with friends, and emails between him and his solicitor. He also used the credit card apps to check the balance and repayments. His eyes suddenly grew wide. "And my bank!" he exclaimed loudly. He leant against the doorframe as his chest began to feel tight and his breathing became a little laboured.

"What?" Fox asked, hearing him mumbling to himself. She walked back into the kitchen and saw him tapping the screen, then waiting for the face recognition software on his banking app to allow him to access his account.

"Account details, PIN, transaction security codes, everything," he continued to mumble as the screen showed that he was successfully through the facial recognition security. "Please, god, no," he said as he closed his eyes and prayed, waiting for the balance screen to load. He slowly opened his eyes and read the content. He was expecting to see £183,000 credited from his half of the proceeds from the sale of his house, but there was only a few thousand pounds left. A single payment of £180,000 had been sent to a company called Crypto Gateway Inc. Another text then appeared on screen:

We appreciate the final donation, but we left you some money for your air fares, as well as enough to start to pay off your new loan. Farewell, Stephen. It's been fun.

Attwell couldn't move or speak. He felt paralysed.

"Stephen, are you alright?" Fox asked, leaning forwards to look at his face. "Stephen? Stephen, talk to me," she repeated, increasingly worried at the lack of any response. Attwell slowly lifted his head and looked at her, dropping the phone like a hot coal before gasping for breath and clutching his chest.

Chapter 23

The knocking at the front door was persistent but polite.

"Coming," shouted Arlo, who had been upstairs in the study, cataloguing the latest in his collection of first edition books. After walking down the stairs as quickly as he dared, he got to the door and pulled it open. To his surprise, a man with a microphone in his hand stood under an umbrella, and a cameraman stood behind him.

"Yes?" questioned Arlo, a little bemused at the scene in front of him.

"Mr McCleary?" asked the man.

"I am. Who are you?"

"Clive Nugent from BBC North." The man pulled his BBC ID out from under his coat. "We understand that you've been having some problems recently, and wondered if we could talk to you about it? We're always looking for local stories that have national implications." Arlo recalled Mike mentioning the idea of contacting one of his friends in the media about the problem at the bank.

"Oh, hello. Erm, yes, we have." He glanced at the man's ID and then offered them the chance to come in from the rain. The visitors took off their rain-soaked coats and shoes before following Arlo into the conservatory and setting up for the interview.

"Is Mrs McCleary in?" asked the reporter.

"No, she's out shopping for a dress. Our son flew home recently, and she wants to look nice when we go to see him and his new girlfriend."

"Ah, that's nice," replied the reporter, nodding his head before looking around at his colleague, who also smiled and nodded that he'd finished setting up the recording equipment. "Are we nearly ready, Jack?" Nugent asked the cameraman.

"Yep, go for it," Jack replied, looking through the viewfinder to make sure it was focused on Arlo.

"We'll top and tail the interview back at the studio, Mr McCleary, so if we could get straight into the questions?"

"Of course." Arlo smiled, sweeping a few stray hairs away from his face. The reporter cleared his throat, and his smile disappeared.

"How long have you had this problem, Mr McCleary?"

"Oh, a few months now. It really is quite frustrating, although my wife seems very calm about it. I've also discussed it with my son, and he's trying to help me."

"I see: your wife is quite relaxed and forgiving, but your son saw the need for an intervention?"

"Yeeees," said Arlo in a slow, prolonged manner. He found it odd that the man had used the term 'intervention'. "My son's a little worried about it, but we're coping. We get what we need every month from..." but the reporter furrowed his brow and interrupted him.

"So, you don't deny any of the allegations?" Arlo opened his mouth in readiness to respond, but the interruption wasn't what he was expecting. He replayed the question in his head, but before he could clarify anything, the reporter continued. "I also believe your wife has been recognised in the street, and became aggressive when a member of the public expressed his dismay about your conduct?"

"Wh...What?" blurted a confused Arlo. "What's this got to do with the bank?" he asked.

"Do you possibly have a long history of this problem, or will you claim it was a one-off aberration?"

"What?"

"And, finally, why did you decide to ignore the chance to redeem yourself? Do you think you were mad not to, Arlo?"

"Redeem myself? What are you talking abou..." but then Arlo finally realised this interview had nothing to do with the problem at the bank. As his expression reflected this growing realisation, the face of the interviewer turned into a sneer, and the cameraman sat back, smiling in satisfaction.

"We assume you've broken the hidden code in the messages by now, so you know what this is all about if you don't do as we say." Arlo's face crumpled as he wondered if these two were 'them'. "The man in the street who spoke to your wife was an actor, but now you don't need to just imagine what would happen if we spread rumours. I'm sure you don't want your wife to go through that for real." He turned and passed the microphone to the cameraman before looking back at Arlo. "We'll be in touch about what you need to do, and when."

"No, no you won't," replied Arlo. "Your lies won't work, and my wife will believe me. I'm going to call the police. You're sick, all of you."

"Call the police? And say what? You freely invited us into your home, and I'm sure you don't want them to receive information about what the tweets and messages are really about, do you?" The man pulled his phone out and tapped on the screen to send a short text. He then put the phone away and stood, towering over Arlo. "Now do as we say or this just gets worse!"

With that, the man smiled as he and the cameraman walked to the front door and put their shoes and coats back on. They then left without another word being said. Arlo followed them to the door and saw them climb into a Land Rover. He took a faltering step outside as he watched them drive down the lane and towards Barwick. The heavy rain was drenching his cardigan and face, but he continued to watch the car lights until they were out of sight. He then slowly pulled his mobile phone out and cried out in anguish as he glared at it. He threw it onto the concrete path, and the casing fractured, but the screen was still glowing, so Arlo stepped off the garden path and grabbed a large stone from the rockery. With anger exploding in his gut, he dropped to his knees and, even though his clothes were now stuck to his skin from the rain, he repeatedly hammered the rock onto the phone until there was nothing left to smash.

Chapter 24

"What have you got?" asked Jones as she entered a deserted and derelict warehouse.

"Deceased with a noose around his neck, but he'd been shot in the head," replied the lead SOCO, before adding, "And when I say shot in the head, what I really mean is he had most of his head blasted off with what was probably a 12-gauge shotgun from about two feet away."

"Have you been able to identify the deceased?" she asked, flipping the notebook open.

"We haven't, and in addition to the shotgun destroying his face, teeth, and most of his jaw and cheekbones, someone has cut off his hands." Jones knew this sort of gangland murder was usually reserved for those who were grossly disloyal and deserved to die in anonymity.

"I don't suppose you found any ID on him?" she asked, knowing no one that thorough in killing someone would be stupid enough to leave the man's wallet or phone behind, but she had to ask.

"Afraid not, but the coroner will examine the body for any distinguishing marks or tattoos."

"Okay," sighed Jones. "It would be useful if they could prioritise the autopsy. I know they're busy, but..."

"Oh, they're busy alright. Staff cuts mean they're already pulling double-shifts as it is... but I'll see what I can do to help move the request up the list," he replied. Jones thanked him and returned to her car to head to the next crime scene, and then it would be onto the next and the next one after that. She had some leave coming up soon, and could hardly wait. Work took its toll at the best of times, but Denton's mood and the lack of a detective sergeant to take some of his flak were draining even her self-motivation.

Nine hours later, she finally reached the front door of her third-floor flat in a slightly run-down housing development. Sat outside was a cat that often appeared from nowhere, usually miaowing loudly and brushing against her legs. She unlocked the door and glanced down at the hopeful cat, smiling wearily at it. The cat cocked its head slightly, as if waiting to hear the news it was hoping for. It looked at Jones, then at the unlocked but unopened door, and then back up at Jones.

"Come on, then. The milk might be a bit off, but you don't care, do you," she said as she pushed the door open, and the cat raced into the flat. Jones went to the fridge, took out a carton of three-day-old milk and sniffed.

"Pfff, rather you than me," she said screwing up her nose at the slightly pungent smell, but the cat appeared unfazed. She opened the cupboard door and got a chipped bowl out. "Semi-rancid milk in a beggar's bowl," she chuckled as she began to pour the milk, but before she could place the bowl on the floor, her mobile rang.

"This is Jones," she said, shrugging her shoulders at the expectant cat.

"Hello, DC Jones. This is the Coroner's Office. One of the SOCO team said you wanted a murder victim report as soon as possible?"

"The man without a face or hands?" she checked.

"That's the one."

"Have you been able to identify the victim?"

"We have. He had some very expensive metal plates put in his right leg. They're not the usual hardware used by the NHS, but we've managed to trace them to a private clinic overseas. We got in touch with an out-of-hours contact for the practice, and they identified the victim from the serial numbers on the plates."

"So, who is our victim?"

"A solicitor called Adrian Huxley."

Chapter 25

Amanda Fox was sitting at home, feeling numb and broken. Stephen Attwell had died from a heart attack, despite the best endeavours of a rapid response paramedic. She had knelt by Attwell's side throughout attempts to revive him, holding his hand while every effort was made to save his life, but by the time the ambulance had arrived to take him to hospital, it was too late. She'd tried to be strong, hoping perhaps he could hear her encouraging words and that everything would be alright, but today she was alone with the curtains closed. She kept replaying everything that had happened once he was pronounced dead.

"Is there anything I can do? Anyone I can contact for you?" a local police community support officer had offered. She'd been on patrol nearby when the ambulance arrived and held Fox's hand in comfort before walking over to one of the paramedics.

"Heart attack?"

"Yes," replied the paramedic. "Seems something pushed him over the edge. The woman…" and he had gestured towards Fox with his head "… said something about him shouting at his phone."

"Shouting into the phone, like he was having an argument?" The paramedic started to nod his head absent-mindedly, but then paused.

"Actually, it sounded more like she was saying he was shouting at the phone. The way she described it, it didn't sound like he was having a conversation." He then shrugged his shoulders, admitting he didn't really know and had other things to attend to. The PCSO wandered back over to Fox, who was sitting on the settee in the conservatory.

"Hi. I've just spoken to the paramedic. Your friend, was he upset about something?" she asked, as she got her notebook out. It was drilled into them that they had to make notes of what they did every day, who they'd spoken to and about what. Fox just sat with her head in her hands, unsure what to say, if anything, about Attwell's illegal debt issues.

"Had he had an upsetting call or a message?" added the PCSO.

"No, he seemed... he seemed upset *about* the phone," Fox said, slowly raising her face from her hands as she realised that he was angry 'about' the phone. Without saying another word, she stood and walked to the kitchen, scanning all the worktops and then the floor. She saw the phone and bent to scoop it up. As the PCSO entered the kitchen, Fox was twirling the device in her hands, examining it. She saw the PCSO and said, "He kept saying *'it must be the phone'* as if it was faulty or something. It doesn't make sense."

"Did he say anything else?" asked the PCSO as she scribbled notes in her pad.

"He was mumbling about how *'it was the common denominator'*, then said something about his bank, passwords and stuff. Then he stared at the screen and just keeled over."

"He mentioned his bank? Do you know who he banked with?"

"I... I think he had a couple of accounts in different places. Maybe one was for bills and the other was to put money away for his daughter," and then Fox slumped. "Oh no, someone's got to tell Emma."

"That's his daughter, is it? What about his wife?"

Fox shook her head in response. "Divorced," she replied, and she then made the decision to share the illegal debt issues with the PCSO, who immediately called her neighbourhood policing team sergeant. As she made the call, Fox searched the rest of the house for the folder Attwell said he kept all the credit card bills and loan agreements in.

"Sarge, I think we might need to investigate this death." She explained how she had come across the paramedic team, and how a friend of the deceased had just told her about a series of what the deceased man had been adamant were fraudulent activities.

"And he was blaming the phone?" clarified the sergeant. "Is the friend sure he wasn't just unstable?"

"It's a possibility, but his friend has just given me a small notebook in which the deceased wrote that he was forced to act as a money-launderer. We have transactions, with dates and account numbers listed," she said. "I know that could be made-up too, but if CID maybe called one of the banks he used, they could ask if these transactions are genuine."

Chapter 26

Arlo poured some fresh coffee into the cups before carrying them into the dining room, setting one down in front of Mike and handing another to Tania.

"What did the board say?" he asked, popping another paracetamol in the hope it would fight off the cold he had caught from his rain-soaked clothes the other night. Mike shrugged his shoulders as he continued to process everything. Where to start?

"They, er... they confirmed that Harry was dead, and that the police say it appears to be just a tragic accident in the home."

"So where does that leave you? Do you still have a job?" a worried Arlo asked. Mike looked up, his expression one of confusion, and his tone was one of disbelief.

"They asked me if I'd take over as temporary CEO."

"You?" exclaimed Arlo, accidentally expressing his shock. Mike was actually grateful that he had, because he, too, was finding it difficult to follow the board's rationale.

"I know, right? I mean, what experience do I have of being a CEO? I said I thought Bob Hall should temporarily take the helm." His father didn't know who that was, and Tania noticed.

"He's their head of operations," she explained. Arlo mouthed a silent 'oh' of understanding as Mike continued.

"He seems a more logical choice, but for some reason, Bob said no; he thought it should be me."

"And what about the money side of things? Did you say the company is in financial trouble?" Arlo enquired.

"Not so much 'in trouble' as *desperately* in need of some immediate cash."

"I thought you said their focus was on longer-term capital investment?" Tania checked.

"Ultimately, yes, but they, we, need immediate access to some cash just to survive. Without it, there is no Kintaro to invest in," clarified Mike.

"How much do you need?" Arlo asked.

"An immediate injection of £1m, just to keep production going until some of our outstanding invoices get paid. After that, pick a number: depends how much we want to grow."

"And do you believe in the company?" queried Tania. Mike pondered the question, thinking back to the five years' worth of balance sheets and profit-and-loss statements he'd been studying into the early hours of the morning.

"Yes... Yes, I think so. I can see a great future in what Harry was planning, but..."

"But what?" queried Arlo.

"But I can't see past the immediate funding challenge right now."

"Then it's settled," Tania announced as she pulled her phone out.

"What's settled?" Mike and Arlo asked in unison.

"We're going to talk to Uncle Yann," she replied, typing a couple of texts.

"Who is Uncle Yann?" Arlo whispered to Mike. In an equally hushed tone, Mike replied.

"He's Tania's uncle. I mentioned him when we talked on the phone a few weeks ago: he's big in the venture capital world," he reminded his father, who vaguely remembered a reference to him, albeit his most abiding memory of that call was of him asking if Tania was pregnant. Mike stepped towards Tania, who was staring at her phone as she waited for a possible response.

"Do you think he'll do it for you?"

"Oh, he won't invest money just because I ask him to. He'll only invest in something if he thinks it will make him richer." It didn't take long before there was a ping from her phone.

"And?" asked Mike, assuming it was a reply. As she was about to answer, the doorbell rang.

"Oh, bloody hell!" said Arlo, annoyed at the interruption. He was as excited as Mike to hear the news. "Don't tell him until I'm back," he shouted to Tania as he headed into the hall. He reached the door just as the doorbell rang again. "I'm coming," he said loudly, irritated at someone's impatience. He pulled it open, and a motorbike courier stood on his doorstep. "Yes?" Arlo enquired.

"Mr Arlo McCleary?" came the slightly muffled voice from inside the helmet.

"Yes," Arlo replied.

"Package for you, sir. If you could just hold it while I take a photo?" Arlo knew it was common practice with many of the delivery companies nowadays. The man took a photo with his device and thanked Arlo, who nodded back to the man and then closed the door. After placing the package on the kitchen worktop,he quickly made his way back into the dining room to find out what the answer was from Tania's uncle. As he walked back in, Mike and Tania were hugging.

"Guess it was a yes, then?" Arlo checked, a little despondent at missing out on the big reveal.

"It's a maybe," replied Tania. "He wants to meet Mike as soon as possible, as it's almost time for his quarterly investment round." Mike was beaming, although Arlo knew his son would soon want some peace and quiet to gather his thoughts and plan for the meeting. Arlo was relieved there seemed to be a way forward and had confidence that Mike could not only persuade the man to invest, but that he might also revel in the interim role of CEO. As he had predicted, Mike said he needed access to the financial statements he'd been looking at last night. Five minutes later, and after hugs and the promise that his father would tell his mother everything, he and Tania were gone.

Arlo made his way back into the kitchen and saw the package. After emptying the remnants of coffee from the cups and placing them in the dishwasher, he took some scissors from the kitchen drawer and sliced through the tape that sealed the box. Inside, on top of some shredded paper that was packing and protection, was an envelope with his name handwritten on it. He took it out and opened it. The note inside was typed and said:

Thought you might need this

Puzzled, Arlo put the note and envelope down. He pulled the shredded paper out of the box and peered in, before taking an instinctive half-step backwards. Inside the box was a mobile phone with a message on a note. It read:

We wanted to make sure you could stay in touch with us. You'd be mad not to.

Chapter 27

Denton pulled a chair out from under the conference room table. As he sat, Jones passed him a file.

"Adrian Huxley, best known as a legal advisor for hire by anyone willing to pay for unethical advice or support on a dodgy deal. Found yesterday morning with his entire face missing from what forensics confirm was probably a couple of close-up blasts from a 12-gauge shotgun, and whoever killed him also chopped off his hands." Denton flinched at the description.

"How the hell did they identify him?"

"They managed to trace the serial number from a couple of titanium plates in his right leg, back to a private and very exclusive medical practice in Turkey. We're trying to contact them now."

"Motive?"

"Nothing obvious so far, but the list of people he dealt with probably reads like a who's who of the undesirables in and around London."

"So, it could be anything: revenge, a warning to others, punishment for breaching the criminal code by sharing someone's secret?" he mused out loud.

"Rumour on the street is the plate in his leg was needed after someone dished out punishment the last time that he allegedly shared someone's secret."

"And who does that rumour say was responsible for the beating?"

"We don't know yet. No one seems prepared to give that much detail," said Jones.

"Hmm, okay. Let me know if you hear anything from your network, but I'll be honest, Huxley isn't that high a priority. It's as if London's gone murder-crazy all of a sudden. Knife attacks, drive-by shootings, turf wars between gangs, so he falls somewhere near the bottom of the pile."

Ten hours later, as Denton was finally logging off, Jones stuck her head around his door.

"Got a minute, sir?"

He nodded that she should come in, although he continued to put files away and lock drawers and cabinets. "What have you got?" he asked as he put his jacket on and pushed his chair under his desk.

"One of the team talked to a snitch about the beating that led to Adrian Huxley needing those plates in his leg. Word is Matthew Berry ordered that, and his recent execution."

"What? Why?" he checked.

"Something about Huxley trying to blackmail him, apparently." Denton stopped what he was doing to reflect on the news. It didn't make sense.

"First of all, I've never known Berry leave a corpse to be found. It's not the way he works. No body, no trace is his modus operandi," he explained, taking his jacket back off and pulling the chair out to sit down. "Secondly, removing all your recognisable features is a way some gangs show that you've dishonoured or insulted them. It's mainly the Georgians, Azerbaijanis, the Armenians, some of the Eastern Turkish gangs, too, but not Berry. Something doesn't add up."

Chapter 28

Jenni Cellier had been a criminal for nearly 20 years. Her husband and children knew nothing of her past or present job.

Originally, she had been based in Dubai and had accumulated over £1m of savings in less than five years. Some of it was because of her willingness to undertake high-risk assignments, but she also invested her money wisely. As her wealth grew and she reached her 30th birthday, she decided to step up from operative to recruiter. There were plenty of beautiful young women in Dubai, keen to make their fortune in whatever way they could, so she established her own escort company. As her team steadily grew, she offered their services to The Broker. He had used her several times in the past and trusted her, but this assignment felt different from the beginning. Months ago, at the very start of their planning, they had discussed who would be part of her team.

"No, no, no; absolutely not," Cellier had said when he proposed a specific person that he wanted her to take onboard.

"What makes you think this is a request?" The Broker had replied calmly.

"She's arrogant, brash, and reckless. I've never let you down and never will, if you just let me..." but he had heard enough.

"She's in. Discussion over." The person in question was a teenager who had a bit of a reputation for going rogue, although she was usually very good at the roles she played.

"Then I decide how she's used, agreed?" asked Cellier.

"Agreed," he'd replied. "What's your plan?"

"As you know, I've already got one of the team getting close and personal with our target. I've used her many times and she's good. The rest will have very specific roles to play, as will a number of male actors I've recruited."

"And the girl? My choice for your team?" he asked, smirking, knowing that Cellier would be grinding her teeth in frustration.

"She has a special role to play. We'll use 'Insert' as her codename, and her pseudonym will be Jane," confirmed Cellier through gritted teeth and a fake smile. She knew he was enjoying making her work with this woman. It was a power play on his part because although he trusted Cellier, he sometimes felt she needed to be reminded who was in charge. Cellier, on the other hand, had a specific use in mind for Jane, and she didn't care whether The Broker liked it or not.

"He never told me she was indispensable," she muttered to herself after the meeting, but she knew she had to play her hand very carefully.

Chapter 29

A jazz pianist and a singer performed on a small corner stage, but they were almost drowned out by the incessant chatter of the club's members and the clinking of beer or champagne glasses. After handing in their coats to the attendant, Mike and Tania walked down the stairs. She looked around the room and then waved when she saw her uncle. He was talking to a small group who seemed enthralled with his tales, but when he looked up and waved back, he excused himself and made his way across the room to greet them.

"Hello, Uncle Yann," said Tania, placing an affectionate kiss on his cheek.

"Ah, there's my beautiful niece. And who do we have here?" he asked with his soft Scottish lilt.

"Good evening. Pleasure to meet you, Mr Machendrie. I'm Mike McCleary," he said.

"Oh, Mikey, he's just playing with you. He knows who you are. Don't be naughty, Uncle, I might want to marry this man. Play nice," she teased. Her uncle looked suitably embarrassed.

"Please, call me Yann. Tania has told me so much about you, and I've been looking forward to this meeting, Mike," said Machendrie. "I hear you have a wee problem to solve, but I'm always looking for opportunities. Tell me what you can, but I know we've only just met, so feel free to leave out anything commercially sensitive you don't feel comfortable talking about," and Machendrie gave him a reassuring smile.

"Tania trusts you, so I'm happy to do the same, Yann, but perhaps we can discuss this somewhere a little more private?" Mike asked.

"And a little quieter," added Tania. Machendrie nodded in understanding and gestured for them to head towards an unmarked door, next to which stood two of the largest men Mike had ever seen. He involuntarily paused, but Machendrie placed a reassuring hand on his shoulder.

"Privacy is important to me, Mike. Please don't be concerned about the presence of security. They are trusted associates of a friend who lets me borrow them from time to time." Mike gave a weak smile as an informal acknowledgement to the two men. They gave no such gesture in return.

Inside the room was a hostess, who offered them a choice of alcohol, a soft beverage or coffee, before they sat down.

"You're quite young for a CEO, but I believe the company has a promising future if you can resolve your immediate cash flow issue," Machendrie said. Mike was a little taken aback that Tania had shared quite so much information, but Machendrie saw his quizzical look and added, "I didn't and don't need to ask my niece for any inside information, if that's your concern. I'm a very successful venture capitalist: I like to do my own homework."

Mike took a moment to reflect on the statement, but it made sense as, according to Tania, her uncle had access to more than £4bn of venture capital, as well as several million pounds of his own he could invest.

"Of course," he said, looking at Machendrie as he squeezed Tania's hand apologetically. "Perhaps it would save time if you asked questions, rather than me telling you things you might already know?"

"No, Mike. What I have is 2D knowledge, whereas listening to you talk about Kintaro brings 3D colour and life to the facts. Don't get me wrong, I have no intention of ever investing in bad ideas, but even good ideas can have bad pitches. No passion, no drive, no logic, no flus."

"You speak Maltese?" asked Mike, recognising 'flus' as the Maltese word for money.

"No, I just did a little extra research before you arrived."

Mike smiled warmly. "My mother named me Michael Marcus McCleary, but my Cypriot friends used to nickname me Tripplam: that's Maltese for 'triple M'."

"Cute, isn't it? My little Tripplam," Tania said, scrunching up her nose as she playfully pinched Mike's cheek. Mike blushed and chuckled in embarrassment.

"You liked your nickname?" enquired Machendrie.

"I didn't mind it, but as my mum always used to tell me, love or hate your name; it doesn't matter. What matters is what comes after your name that makes a difference in the world. It was a saying from the village she grew up in, apparently. '*What will your name mean beyond just being a lot of letters?*' she used to ask me," and he smiled softly at the memory.

"Family is important, as is making your life count," replied Machendrie, smiling softly at Tania, who smiled back.

"Don't listen to him. He acts like a softie to me, but he's a hard-nosed bastard underneath it all," she hissed, in jest. Machendrie and Mike laughed, although they both knew it was true.

"Yann, I've been asked to lead what could be a fantastic business, and I believe we're on the verge of some breakthrough tech. I'd love to show you around the operation, if you're interested?"

"Interested, yes, but what's the bottom line here, Mike?"

"I'm looking for £50m in total. £1m immediately to address our short-term cashflow issues, as a number of clients are delaying payments to us, and then the rest is for our proposed investment in the new tech, if you're happy it's worth the risk."

"And how risky is it?"

"In the world of ground-breaking tech? Relatively low risk. Compared to buying gold? Very high risk," Mike admitted.

"And if I did decide to invest, how happy are you that I'd want to choose a couple of people to represent me in the firm?"

"What sort of level?" asked Mike, nervously.

"Well, that really depends on how much of my money you might get," replied Machendrie. "The bigger the investment, the higher the level. Board-level, probably, although if you'd only wanted a couple of thousand, I'd just ask for a say in who you hire as the cleaner." Mike laughed at the humorously made point.

"In principle, I agree, but let me show you the production facility and, once you've signed a non-disclosure agreement, we'll talk more about the tech and see if my board also agree, in principle," replied a now smiling, but serious Mike. Machendrie stood and held out his hand to shake on the 'in principle' agreement.

"Let me know when's convenient to tour your operation," he said.

The men swapped contact details, and Mike promised to call him as soon as he'd cleared the idea with the board. Tania gave her uncle a hug, and then she and Mike left the room. Machendrie sat back down, signalling to the hostess that he'd like another cognac. Once she had delivered his drink and left the room, he pulled out his phone and made the call.

"Did he buy it?" asked The Broker.

"Hook, line, and sinker," replied Robert Kendrick, dropping his fake Scottish accent as he peeled off his equally fake hairpiece and moustache.

"And how did she do?"

"'*Beloved*' plays her part well," said Kendrick. "And the name 'Tania' really suits her."

Chapter 30

Professor Gary Hibberd rose at 4am, as always, to complete his exercise and meditation regime before logging on and seeing what was on the dark web.

His most recent case was with Interpol, supporting their investigation into the now-convicted cyber-criminal, Dennis Ruiz. The high-profile case appealed to the showman in Hibberd, as well as fulfilling his passion to find and dismantle the cybersecurity frameworks and cryptic coding used by the seemingly ever-increasing number of digital criminals.

To do his job effectively, he would frequently embed himself in the culture of the dark web or, as its users prefer to call it, 'the onion'. He was sadly familiar with some of the stomach-churning or illegal trading sites: everything from animal cruelty, child abuse, drugs and weapons for sale, through to 'red rooms' where people are allegedly murdered 'live' for a paying audience. His online name was Zugai Katana, and he had several regular contacts who helped him understand what the current conversations and topical threads in the chat rooms were.

"Okay, so let's surf," he mumbled to himself. Today, he was looking for any conversations that might be about Dennis Ruiz and his cybercrime operation, BOrg. The rumour was that someone had shared evidence with the authorities about the BOrg operation because they wanted to take over from Ruiz. As he scoured several online chatrooms, he reviewed the topics and comments from the latest contributors, searching for any new BOrg-related conversations. If he found any, he'd then see if there was a link to a private chat forum. If there was one, he knew someone wanted him to dig a little deeper.

"It's like the *White Rabbit* in Alice in Wonderland. He wanted Alice to follow him down the hole," he had explained in a university lecture.

Scanning the conversations, it didn't take long to find what he was looking for. To the inexperienced, the post entitled '*Destruction of Federation Enemies*' looked like any other sci-fi nerd ranting about *Star Trek*, the Vulcans, and who would win in a fight against the Romulans, but in the midst of the conversation was a reference to what *Star Trek* geeks knew was another well-known enemy of the Star Fleet Federation: the Borg. The post rambled aimlessly about various episodes of the show and explained how the Borg were superior in every way to the Federation, but just as Hibberd began to wonder if he was scrutinising the wrong conversation, the content changed:

Anon: For the Borg to be taken down, the Federation need to stop their infighting and work together. The power of the Borg is that they are a collective, and to take it out requires clear leadership and direction. As the meme goes: 'Borg needs changing. Change my mind' LOL. If you want to discuss more, come see me at AbleOnion Chat. Follow the link and ask for Senyor Fosc at the door.

He recognised the online name of 'Senyor Fosc' from other conversations on AbleOnion Chat, a site that allowed direct messages between individuals, as well as invitations to private groups. Hibberd followed the link to the chat and waited. It didn't take long until his screen lit up again.

SF: Hey ZK. Long time, no type.

ZK: Hey. Yeah. So, are we talking about a Romulan take-down?

SF: LMAO. You know me better than that.

ZK: Think the Federation will bring down the Borg?

SF: No. Picard is facing mutiny problems, and the cyber king is dying. Long live the traitor king.

The conversation link then dropped, but Hibberd had all the information he required. It would need some more investigative work, but he now knew what he needed to focus his attention on before an upcoming meeting at the Home Office.

Chapter 31

"Yes, hello. I'd like to report a crime," said a female voice.

"Alright," replied the Crimestoppers operator. "Firstly, what's happened and when?"

"A woman is going to be murdered, possibly tomorrow or the day after."

"I see, so this murder hasn't happened yet? Where do you think this will happen?"

"At her home, probably. She's almost entirely housebound, so it's the only logical location." The operator began typing on the keyboard, quietly mouthing the answers as she typed.

"Do you have a name and address of the person you believe is at risk?"

"Katie Cross, Fiddlesticks, Seagull Close, Portsmouth. That's all I know, I'm afraid."

"Have you shared your concerns with Ms Cross?"

"No. I don't know her and didn't want to scare her. I'm sorry, but that's all I've heard. I have to go," and the call ended. The operator reviewed the on-screen notes and then clicked 'complete'. In the background, an electronic file was compiled, and the Crimestoppers system transferred details of the anonymous tip to the Hampshire & Isle of Wight Police. Later that afternoon, a despatch control room team member at the police headquarters had a lull between emergencies and priority one calls, so he looked at the enquiry, running it through the THRIVE assessment: Threat, Harm, Risk, Investigation, Vulnerability and Engagement. This helped him decide if the 'standard' rating the force's intel unit had given it was appropriate, rather than it really being an emergency or priority one call.

"Threat to life and within the next two days; better make it a 'high standard'," he mumbled to himself, but he also flagged it to the hub inspector. She had access to information the despatch control room team didn't, such as was Katie Cross an ex-judge that someone might have a grudge against. She reviewed the enquiry and agreed with the 'high standard' rating, so two local uniformed police officers were despatched to visit Ms Cross.

She was in her seventies and confined to a wheelchair for most of her waking hours, with home help four times a day. Sometimes, a night nurse stayed if she was suffering from flu or a viral infection of some sort. When they went to interview her, she was having an afternoon nap.

"Oh no," said her home helper. "Miss Cross, she's never hurt no one. She doesn't even like me killing ants or flies that have gotten in the house," she chuckled.

"And what about people who might have a grudge against her, for something she's done in the past?" questioned one of the police officers.

"Only thing she done is refuse to listen to them religious people who come knocking at the door with their children, preaching to her how Jesus will save her soul."

"And Miss Cross hasn't been involved in any high-profile court cases as a witness or on a jury that you're aware of?" asked the other police officer.

"Not that I know of. Only case I know about was the one for the crash that put her in a wheelchair, when she was in her thirties. Drunk driver hit her on his way back from a Christmas party. She worked in the local supermarket before that, apparently."

"Are you aware of any threats she's received, or has her behaviour changed recently?"

"Not that I've noticed. She's always happy to talk about anything and everything to me. I can look in the log we keep if you like. Whenever I start my shift, I always read the last couple of entries; you know, in case there's anything out of the ordinary happened, or something that's upset her."

"If you could have a quick look through the previous couple of weeks, that would be helpful," asked one of the officers.

"And would you know if there was any mail she might have received that was offensive or distressing?" asked the other.

"She opens all her own post, but we usually take it and either file it or chuck it in the bin, depending on what she says and what we think," replied the home help.

"Depending on what you think?" checked one of the officers.

"Yes. We have strict instructions to ensure she doesn't throw anything away that, even if she thinks it's not important, we think is. There's a file where we keep all that, too."

Ten minutes later, and after Katie Cross had woken up and answered a few simple questions, the uniformed officers left. They told her they were just doing some social calls to ensure nobody had any problems. She had assured them that everything was alright, and they filed their report to suggest the call might have just been a mischief call or a case of mistaken identity.

"Not unknown, sadly," the duty sergeant told them.

Chapter 32

Jones put the phone down, having just talked to the fraud team at the online bank Stephen Attwell had used recently. The bank's anti-money laundering manager explained:

"Yes, it raised a flag, so one of the team ran the usual checks, but everything came back clear. When we asked him some routine questions during his application, he'd said it was for a group of 'penny investors' who had small windows of opportunity to get into the property market. The transactions appeared to be genuine, and the firm he was passing the money to appears legitimate. The value and frequency of payments weren't dissimilar to other things we've seen like this: you know, Christmas clubs, holiday savings clubs, lottery syndicates. That's when we decided not to invite the police to interview Mr Attwell."

Jones tossed her pen onto the desk as she contemplated both the significance and the insignificance of the facts.

"You alright?" queried one of her colleagues.

"You know what, I'm not really sure."

"What's up?" asked the man, pulling his chair across to her desk and picking up the case file to browse through it.

"It's this case. I've just finished with the bank he had two accounts with and, while they said they viewed the transactions as legitimate, something just doesn't feel quite right."

"In what way?"

"If you look through the notes, most of the small transactions were completed using his phone, but the really large ones were done via a computer that had no visible IP address. Then, he'd close one account and open another about a month later."

"Okay," he replied, unclear on why she felt that was an issue. "So, he was a busy guy who used his phone a lot, and he was a finance manager who knew how to keep his online identity safe. If he had campaigns to run, it seems unnecessarily complicated, but maybe separate accounts was his way of coping? On top of that, the bank did all the usual checks and gave him the all-clear. Case closed; move on," he suggested, dropping the file back into the wire basket on his desk. Something was clearly still bothering her, though, so he remained seated. "What?" he asked, sighing. Everyone knew Jones could be like a dog with a bone, sometimes.

"I don't know. You know the feeling, when things just don't seem to add up but you quite can't put your finger on it?" she explained.

"Alright, let's go through the options. Option 1, it's all legit, but you're trying to look for something out of the ordinary because you feel there's something to find," he said. "Option 2, it's fraud, but there's not enough evidence to confirm it from the banks or the techies. Option 3..." but Jones cut across him.

"Hold on, let me re-read the tech report on his phone and laptop. The friend who was with the victim when he collapsed said he was shouting at the phone; something about how '*it was the common denominator*'. Then he said something about his bank, passwords, and stuff." She pulled the case file out from a wire basket, opened it, and flicked through to the tech report again. Her finger traced the words as she read them at pace, but she finally exhaled in defeat.

"Well?" asked her colleague.

"No, nothing. Phone is clean, no unusual apps, and the SIM is from a legitimate supplier called Kintaro. His laptop is clean too and has the usual security software on it."

"Hey, not every case we get is a criminal case, right?" suggested the man, patting her on the shoulder in both sympathy and encouragement as he stood and walked back to his desk.

"Guess so," Jones replied, closing the file and tossing it back in his filing pile, but she wasn't entirely convinced that all her instinctive doubts had been adequately allayed.

Chapter 33

A few days ago, The Broker had sent Cellier a text demanding an update, but with both children off school for the weekend, she needed to create the time and space to make her calls.

"Alice, I need sugar for some baking I'm going to do with Jack today. Can you two go to the shop and get some?" she called downstairs.

"Why can't he go by himself? I'm busy," came the disgruntled reply. Cellier took in a calming breath before responding. She just needed them out of the house for 10 minutes.

"Take some extra money and get yourself some chocolate, or something," she suggested.

"What about some nail varnish?" came an opportunistic response. Alice was clearly in a negotiating mood, and Cellier didn't have the time or the inclination to have a lengthy debate.

"Only the purple one, not the black. You're not a goth!" she shouted back to her. There was no reply, but she heard clomping footsteps, which suggested her clearly inconvenienced teenage daughter was preparing to go out. "Take £20, and no more," she added. Alice was downstairs, but Cellier was sure she heard her daughter sigh. A minute later, the front door slammed closed, and through the bedroom window, she could see the children heading down the street. She retrieved the encrypted phone from the back of her underwear drawer and dialled the first number.

"Hello?" came a hushed female voice.

"Beloved? It's the conductor. I need an update on the musical score," said Cellier.

"All going according to plan. Movement one was finished after a meeting with the composer, and he's starting to play movement two, now," replied Tania.

"Melodic so far?" Cellier asked, checking Mike and his family didn't suspect anything.

"A couple of off-keys, but nothing the audience seemed to notice."

The call ended, and Cellier dialled her second contact.

"It's the director," she said, switching codenames: standard practice for a woman the police had yet to identify, let alone ever arrest and question. "The musical score is progressing well. How is the play coming along?"

"Acts One and Two are complete. We're just awaiting production cues to start Act Three, once Insert confirms she's ready to make a dramatic entrance," the man replied.

"Don't lift the curtains yet. I'll be in touch," confirmed Cellier. It was imperative that no one move early.

"Understood," the man said and then ended that call.

Her final update was with the woman codenamed 'Insert'. Cellier nearly always chose the team for her operations, but this time The Broker had insisted she include this specific teenager. She rarely disliked people she was told to work with, but she viewed 'Insert' as overly self-confident, to the point of arrogance.

"Insert, it's the stage manager," Cellier announced. "Update?"

"I'm ready to make my dramatic entrance, stage left. It will be my finest performance," replied the teenager.

"I'll tell the rest of the cast we're about to start Act Three. No showboating, and stick to the script," she instructed, her jaw lightly clenched. She heard the teenager snort in derision before she ended the call. The girl disliked Cellier's attempt to impose her authority, but there'd be time to make sure Cellier understood the new pecking order, once this assignment was complete.

Chapter 34

"You waiting to hear about a lottery win, or the results of a cancer test?" Alessia asked.

"What?" queried Arlo.

"You keep staring at that phone as if you expect it to ring or something," she explained. "Or is it a mystery girlfriend?" she joked. Arlo gave a feeble chuckle. "Is it new?" she added, looking a little closer at the phone.

"Not really. I accidentally broke the one Mike got me, so I got this one second-hand. It arrived in the post a few days ago. Didn't cost much," he said, trying to hide his anxiety.

The phone stayed silent that day, but several days later, a text message arrived from a phone number he didn't recognise. It wasn't from the usual number 'they' used. He was in the garden, and although Alessia had gone inside to watch one of her favourite films, he checked she wasn't looking out of the window before tapping on the text message icon:

Meet me at HIT Coffee in Crossgates in 2 hours. All will be revealed

Arlo had no idea who 'me' was, and he felt his heart begin to race. The coffee shop was a popular spot for many of the locals with its simple but value-priced food, as well as offering space for community events from time to time. Arlo had been in a few times, although not often enough that he'd be recognised by the owners or the regulars. He got there a few minutes early, paid for a coffee and a toasted teacake, and then went to sit at a small table tucked in the corner in an attempt to be unobtrusive. The bell on the door rang when it was opened, and he looked up every time, but the people who came in all went straight to the counter, ordered, and then either took seats at one of the tables or took their order away.

"Top-up?" asked the owner as she approached Arlo's table.

"Yes, please," he replied. She tipped the percolator jug and filled his near-empty mug with steaming hot coffee before turning to another table. As Arlo picked up the drink, the door opened and the bell rang. He nearly dropped the mug in shock as the new arrival stopped, looked around the small interior, and then locked eyes with him. She walked up to his table, pulled out a chair and sat down, with a diabolical grin on her young face.

"You?" he gasped, almost silently.

"Hello, my knight in shining armour. Fancy meeting you here."

Chapter 35

The Kintaro board always sat at a large, round meeting table: a deliberate statement that no one sat at the head. Today, a vacant chair was left in memory of Haruhisa Sakamoto, with space made for an additional seat, for Mike. He was there to present the investment proposal from Machendrie.

"We know we need cash. Without it, the financial projections say we could be forced into administration within weeks," he stated. The finance director nodded her head to support the statement.

"What about reducing your operating hours to slow expenditure?" suggested the new non-executive who had joined the meeting at Machendrie's request. He needed someone he trusted to assess the quality of the Kintaro board, not just the financial status and opportunity of the company.

"We can't," replied Bob Hall. "Production needs to be at full capacity to meet current demand. If we go on reduced hours, we'll fall further behind and lose orders." Mike nodded in agreement.

"Bob's right. This isn't about slowing expenditure, it's about surviving until we receive payment for some of the bigger, overdue invoices. We know that two-thirds of medium-sized businesses are reporting cashflow issues, and we're not immune from those market pressures," he stated.

"What's the proposal from Mr Machendrie, and how much of the crown jewels are we giving up?" asked the risk director.

"If we agree to the proposal, Mr Machendrie will inject £1m immediately, to ease the pressure on the cash flow. He's also interested in committing a further £49m to our medium-term growth and expansion."

"Is factoring the debt a possibility?" asked the non-exec.

"We've looked at it, but we could be losing five percent in fees, plus it sends the wrong message out to the market," replied the finance director.

"It's a small price to pay compared to going into administration," replied the non-exec.

"It's an option, but it's not our preferred option," interjected Mike. "If we could just get some of the customers to pay their invoices, I wouldn't even consider venture capital, but we need to keep our options open."

A phone buzzed: it belonged to the finance director. She took it out of her pocket and read the message. "Shit," she said. Everyone looked over. "DigiDOS has gone under."

"What?" said a shocked Hall, as gasps came from those around the table.

"Who are they?" asked the non-exec.

"Our biggest debtor," said the finance director. "They owe us almost £850,000." The room fell silent as the news and the implications sank in.

"Then it sounds like you're going to need that £1 million ASAP," the non-exec said. "Maybe £2m."

"Wait a minute," demanded Bob Hall. "We can all see the benefits of an immediate cash injection, and a possible £49m follow-on investment, but let's look beyond the immediate future, shall we? The proposal states that if we accept the £50 million, we sign up to some challenging targets. If we meet those targets, we can decide whether we trigger a further £50 million investment, but if we fail to meet those targets, we must hand over all our shares in Kintaro to this venture capitalist who, by the way, holds his interests through a company based in Panama." Hall had done his homework and continued: "That company is partially owned by seven other companies, all based overseas. Don't we want to know a little more about that ownership before we sign up with the devil, by mistake?"

The non-executive shuffled uncomfortably in his chair at the outburst, and the rest of the board looked at each other, signalling their discomfort at the tone and implications of what Hall was suggesting.

"I propose we accept the offer from Mr Machendrie in principle, taking the £1m for 1% of the company, but assess the rest of the offer after some more due diligence," said the risk director.

"Seconded," added the finance director.

"Wait," said Mike. "I'm happy to be involved in this provisional debate if you want me to be, but I don't think I should have any say in the outcome. It feels like a conflict of interest."

"Mike," said Bob Hall, "Harry trusted you to lead this company into the future, with an expanded R&D team. You know I have reservations about you taking the interim CEO role, given your lack of experience, but the future of Kintaro is as much a part of your future as it is ours. I say your vote counts as much as anyone else's." Mike saw everyone nodding.

"Thank you, Bob, that means a great deal to me. I know we all have reservations, including myself, and that's good because I need people who'll challenge my strategy. My vote is to accept the initial £1m investment, but then to run some due diligence on the additional £49m, as well as on the proposed second £50 million investment, even though I believe we'd hit the targets in the proposal."

Everyone around the table smiled and nodded, except the non-exec.

"I'm sorry, but Mr Machendrie has never offered an 'initial £1m' option. You either sign up to the first £50 million as a whole and the associated targets, or you get nothing. By all means, take your time with some due diligence, but the offer closes in five days. He has investment commitments to meet, and if he's not investing in you, he has plenty of other people eager to take it. You're not the only opportunity he has, and you're probably not the most attractive, but I know family matters to him," he said, referencing that Tania introduced them.

"Give us 48 hours," said Mike. He didn't want to discuss the situation with the non-exec in the room, but the team had to face reality. With the collapse of DigiDOS, the financial situation they faced had escalated, from severe to critical.

An hour later, he swung the car onto the gravel driveway of the farmhouse and looked forward to a hot, refreshing shower. Tania had heard the car and met him at the door.

"How did it go?" she asked.

"Could have been better, could have been worse," he replied wearily.

"Did you make a decision about Uncle Yann's offer?"

"Not yet. I know it's important, but I want to have the rest of the day to consider my stance, as it's not just a business deal: we have over two hundred people's families and livelihoods to consider."

Chapter 36

Arlo and the teenager sat looking at each other. She had no need to speak and was enjoying the tortured look in his eyes. He simply couldn't speak, albeit his mouth moved several times as if he was about to say something. After what seemed like an eternity, the words finally stumbled out of his mouth.

"Wh… what are *you* doing here?" he asked, feebly. The first time and only time they had previously met was on that foggy night, when he had let her into his car to escape from three thugs who were chasing her.

"I've come to say hello and to say thank you, again," she replied, pausing before adding, "Oh, and to give you a message." She smiled and scrunched up her nose, cheekily, as if this was a fun reunion.

"What happened was a mistake," he said, looking down as he nervously played with his fingers.

"You certainly didn't act like it was a mistake," she whispered, winking at him. That evening, after previously placing a transmitter on his car that forced his satnav to send him on the desired route home, she was pretending to run from the three men she was actually working with. It had been hugely traumatic for Arlo and, back at her apartment, she'd offered him a drink to steady his nerves. He assumed that his subsequent fatigue and dizziness were a result of the huge burst of adrenaline he'd experienced in helping her escape, and most of the rest of that evening had become hazy. Now, she was eager to tell him the truth. "The drink I gave you had a little something in it, to make you a little less inhibited, and more willing to and able to... you know."

"*Stop it,*" he said in a low growl, his jaw and fists clenched. His voice wasn't quite low enough, though, as customers at nearby tables glanced over. She turned to them and smiled, before turning back to Arlo and feigning a momentary look of fear. "You drugged me!" he hissed.

She leant forwards and whispered, "I doubt the police will believe you, so don't make a scene. You know there'll only be one winner if you do," and she put her hand gently on his, as a child might to indicate affection towards an aged relative. "In a few weeks, we'll be in touch if we need you to do something," she explained.

"To do something? Like what?" Arlo mumbled nervously.

"If and when the time is right, we'll let you know. For now, try to remain calm because someone's life might depend on it. Make the right decision for your son's sake, Arlo, and be someone else's hero." She then stood, leant forwards and kissed his cheek, before whispering into his ear, "We don't want our naughty little secret to get out, do we?" and she mockingly crossed herself, before turning and walking out. As he watched the door swing closed, it felt as if the rest of the customers were staring at him, so, without looking up or looking at anyone, he grabbed his coat from the back of the chair and stormed out into the street.

As he stood in the middle of the pavement, with people bustling to get past him, the phone buzzed in his pocket. He pulled it out and read the message on the screen.

See you again soon, maybe. Jane xx

No sooner had he put it back in his pocket than it buzzed again. This time it wasn't a text, though; it was two photos of them sitting at the table in the café. One showed her kissing him on the cheek, and the other one was of him looking furious, fists and jaw clenched, with her looking afraid. He glanced back at the coffee shop, where someone must have been taking photos. He took a half-step back, reeling at the thought that they were everywhere, watching.

"Oh, sorry," said a passer-by as they bumped into Arlo, and then another bumped into him, holding his hand up apologetically. Arlo turned left and right, staring wide-eyed. Were they both accidental collisions or were they in collusion with 'them'? Were all the passers-by in on this twisted scheme? As his paranoia grew, he started to feel dizzy, and his vision began to blur just before he collapsed.

The teenager stood further up the street, but she had a good vantage point from which to watch the drama unfold. She waited until a bystander checked that Arlo was still breathing and, when she was sure he wasn't dead, she sent a text to Cellier.

This is Insert. Message delivered. End of Act Three.

Chapter 37

The Broker loved the new aquarium in his office. It held over a hundred fish, with several colourful varieties mixed together. If he'd had a particularly taxing day, he'd tell his thugs he didn't want to be disturbed and would spend an hour watching them flit hither and thither. It was both peaceful and absorbing, but it also reminded him that life was really just a brutal façade, given some of the bigger fish often ate the smaller fish.

Today, he was reflecting on last weeks' meeting with the now deceased solicitor, Ade Huxley.

"You're sweating. Are you alright?" he had asked Huxley, worried the man might have something contagious.

"Had to park the car a few streets away, Mr Berry. It's a nightmare trying to find somewhere to park, what with all these bloody new builds."

Feeling assured by the response, The Broker asked, "What's so important you absolutely had to talk to me?" given Huxley had demanded to see him, albeit he'd emphasised that he had The Broker's best interests at heart.

"This is why," Huxley said, pulling a piece of paper out of his pocket and passing it to him. As The Broker began to read it, Huxley provided some context. "An ex-client of mine shared some information about a plan he and his girlfriend were executing," and then he chuckled.

"What's so funny?"

"My apologies, but the word 'executed' works on multiple levels in this story."

"Why did he send you this?"

"He said he was increasingly worried his girlfriend was going to turn on him, so he thought he'd send me some notes in a sealed envelope, to keep in case he needed them. He told me never to open the envelopes, but, unfortunately, he died, so I thought he wouldn't mind me having a look."

"Is that it, Adrian, a photocopied piece of paper? As much as I've enjoyed your visit, I do have other things to do," he said, slightly exasperated as he tossed the sheet of paper back onto his desk, but Huxley hadn't finished. In the top corner of the photocopied sheet was a small, almost invisible '2'. The quality of the photocopying was very poor, so The Broker hadn't noticed it.

"Not exactly, Mr Berry." Huxley tried to suppress his smug, weasely smile. "You see, my client actually sent me four separate sheets, in total. This is just one of them. I didn't bring the others with me in case I got mugged or something, and they fell into the wrong hands. They contain additional and very specific pieces of information related to you, which might be considered circumstantial by most people, but some of the accusations he makes, if true, *could* be proven if someone had the motivation and resources."

The Broker shuffled uneasily in his chair at the implication.

"Go on."

"I don't understand," replied an increasingly smug Huxley, feigning confusion.

"There must be a reason you're telling me this."

"This isn't a shakedown, Mr Berry; please don't think that. That would be incredibly stupid of me, but I know there are some ne'er-do-wells out there who might want to use this sort of information against you. I wanted to let you know that the sheets exist, but I'm happy to destroy the originals and this photocopy to protect you." It was clear there was an unspoken proposal at the end of the sentence, but Huxley knew not to play his hand too soon. After all, he wasn't threatening The Broker as that would be beyond stupid, but he did want to garner favour with him.

"Where are the originals?"

"Locked away in a safe."

"What about digital copies?" The Broker checked, but Huxley shook his head.

"I don't like computer drives, memory sticks, and all this cloud stuff. I don't feel safe storing it where I can't see it, touch it, burn it."

"And this is the only photocopy you've made?"

"It is," lied Huxley. He actually had a photocopy of one of the other sheets in a briefcase he'd left in his car, in case he needed to tease any potential bidders with some titbits, should The Broker not consider his generous and supportive request. The information was pure gold, so although he knew he was playing a very dangerous game, the rewards could be astronomical.

"Who else has seen the sheets?"

"As far as I know, only my ex-client, me, and now you've seen one of them," said Huxley, which was true to the best of his knowledge.

"And what would you expect in return?" He knew there would be some quid pro quo associated with the offer.

"Nothing; well, not immediately, of course, but, over time, maybe there could be some business dealings you'd like me to help with."

The Broker settled back in his chair, steepling his fingers and resting them against his chin as he debated his options. It was an unconscious mannerism, but his thugs knew it meant he was deep in thought whenever he did it. The conundrum he faced was he despised blood-sucking leeches like Huxley, who were usually unwilling to put in the hard yards and spill their own blood to make it to the top, but were happy to reap reward on the back of people who had earned theirs. However, could he really have some incriminating information that he hadn't shared yet?

"Thank you for talking to me. I'll keep this copy, if that's alright with you?" The Broker finally said, and they both knew the question wasn't really a question. "Let me sleep on your generous offer, and I appreciate your loyalty, Adrian."

Huxley knew this man was a cool-headed thug who would neither kill impulsively nor give favours without due thought and consideration.

"Of course. No rush, Mr Berry."

The two gave each other a cursory nod before Huxley was shown out of the building.

Once outside, he knew there was the risk that he would be followed back to his car, so he decided not to walk back. He would hail a passing black cab to go to his next appointment, and then take another cab back to his car.

As The Broker watched him walk across the street and disappear around the corner, he reflected on what the other three sheets of paper might contain. It would be an incredibly bold or unbelievably stupid lie to tell someone like The Broker if the additional sheets didn't exist, or if they didn't actually contain incriminating information. If they did exist, though, Huxley would probably keep them in his own safe, ensuring he always knew where they were and that no one else could access or read the content. The question was how best to extract the information from him.

Five hours later, Tom and Jerry returned from the assignment he'd given them.

"We traced the cabbie and found out where he'd taken Huxley," said Tom.

"Where did he go from here?"

"Ardzoun Marutyan's lunch spot." Marutyan was the leader of a somewhat reckless Armenian gang in East London. They mainly specialised in drugs and trafficking, but the man had openly expressed his aspiration to expand his operation, and that meant he was a threat.

"Did you see him with Marutyan?"

"Not face to face, boss," replied Jerry. "But he went in the front of the restaurant, and two of Marutyan's thugs led him through to the back."

"The private dining area," concluded The Broker, in dismay.

"What do you want us to do, boss?"

The Broker began to smile to himself, as this risk could become an opportunity. He turned to his two loyal thugs and explained what they needed to do to Ade Huxley. Both were a little surprised at part of his request, but loyalty meant never questioning the boss.

Chapter 38

The tour of the Kintaro production facility took place just two days after Mike had suggested the idea to Machendrie. It was far quicker than he had anticipated, but he took it as an indication that the man was very interested in investing. He had only expected Machendrie to attend, though.

"Good morning, Mike. I've brought along a couple of my team to help assess the opportunity, given I'd want them in the day-to-day operation if I invest. This is Athena Miklianos, who I'd expect to oversee the supply chain, and this is Martin Williams, who would oversee quality."

"Welcome," Mike said as he held his hand out to each of them.

"Morning," replied Miklianos, but Williams didn't respond or react in any way. Mike noticed a Liverpool Football Club lapel pin on his jacket.

"Never Walk Alone; what a great footballing anthem," he said in an attempt to engage Williams in some dialogue, but the man looked at Machendrie.

"Are we going to look around the facility, Yann, or am I wasting my time?" he asked wearily, already tired of Mike's attempt at small talk.

"I was going to show you around the production facility myself, but once we've talked through the proposal in a little more detail, perhaps Miss Miklianos would like to spend some time with Bob Hall, my head of operations, and Mr Williams with our lead QA, Penny Büggs?" suggested Mike.

"That sounds sensible," replied Machendrie, nodding at the other two.

"Great. We'll start in the conference room, where I'm keen to show you our development and expansion plans in a little more detail. I'll need Miss Miklianos and Mr Williams to both sign a non-disclosure agreement first, though," but Machendrie held up his hand to indicate that wouldn't be happening.

"They're covered by the agreement I've already signed on behalf of my investment company. My written agreement with them contractually ties them to the non-disclosure agreement," he explained. Neither had signed any such agreement, but Machendrie's goal wasn't to leverage any technology secrets: he simply wanted to buy Kintaro so he could grab billions of pieces of data from its end users.

"Okay, then please follow me." Mike led them into the conference room where the rest of the board were waiting. Both Miklianos and Williams knew there were some specific assumptions in Kendrick's overall plan that had to be validated or altered, so for the next three hours, they asked lots of questions. After the presentation, Mike introduced two of them to Hall and Büggs, respectively, but he and Machendrie continued with their investment discussion.

"Any initial overall thoughts, Yann?" Mike asked.

"The tech design seems solid enough, but the real winner is the extra security we can embed into the design. Privacy and security are important to users nowadays. What gave you the idea to implement it?"

"It came from the research I did for my university thesis, on fighting data security in an increasingly digital world."

"And is the security solution patented, or are you at risk of fast followers?"

"The patent is going through its final assessment, as we speak. I should be hearing about it in the next week or so." Machendrie nodded and smiled, delighted by what he'd seen and heard.

"Good. I think we're close to bringing your hard work to a successful conclusion, subject to final validation by my team, of course," announced Machendrie. Mike immediately brightened, eyes as wide as his smile.

"Really?" he yelped in unbridled enthusiasm.

"Absolutely. You've done an impressive job today. In fact, you've done an impressive job as the CEO in a very short space of time, so I'd like to make my offer official. The draft contract is ready, and you'll need your lawyers to go through it, but in principle, I'm in. I do have a couple of additional conditions your board will need to sign off, though." Mike's enthusiasm visibly waned, and he narrowed his eyes, inviting Machendrie to explain what he meant. "Don't worry, they're nothing earth-shattering," he responded.

"What are they? It would help to know in case I think there is going to be a problem with the rest of the board."

"The first one is that I want you as CEO. Not interim; permanent. You've done a great job, and my investment is conditional on this being agreed."

"And the second one?" asked Mike, trying not to look too pleased at the first one.

"Family is important to me, and I've always found people with their name above the door work that little bit harder. I know Kintaro was Mr Sakamoto's creation, and I'm sure the board remain loyal to his vision, dedication and creativity, and to his memory, but this is the start of a new era, Mike. If we sign the deal, I propose we rename the company. Let's call it TripplaM."

Mike's jaw unconsciously dropped. He was stunned and tears of joy began to well as he realised how Machendrie had used the Cypriot term.

"Triple M; Michael Marcus McCleary," Mike replied.

"I thought you might like it, and I think your mum will too, don't you?" Machendrie said, breaking into a warm smile, before raising one of his eyebrows. "But it's just a name, Mike. It's what comes after the 'Triple M' that counts," he reminded him. "The hard work starts now."

Chapter 39

As Alessia entered their bedroom, she realised Arlo was trying to get out of bed. "Where do you think you're going?" she asked.

"I feel a fraud just lying here," he replied. After losing consciousness outside the coffee shop, he'd been taken to a local hospital, where a doctor had prescribed some anti-anxiety pills as well as several days of complete rest. Alessia had insisted he comply, and she had suppressed her natural desire to ask him exactly what had happened, because that might add to his anxiety. She checked his temperature and his pulse before sighing.

"Okay, you're fine. Just don't go digging up the garden and put yourself back in bed."

"Thank you, doctor," he joked, pulling the blanket off his legs before slowly standing, then sweeping his fingers through his ruffled hair. "What's for lunch, oh, and where's my phone?" he tried to ask nonchalantly. Alessia took the blanket and began folding it.

"There's some roast chicken left from yesterday. I thought we might have it with some freshly baked bread and coleslaw. It's quite mild out, so we could sit on the patio."

"Sounds lovely. I'm starving," he replied, feigning enthusiasm. He knew she had heard both of his questions, and he'd expected a frosty response to the one about his phone, so he decided not to push for an answer. As she placed the blanket in the blanket box at the foot of their bed, she turned to face him. He smiled weakly, but didn't want to ask her what was wrong. It didn't take long to find out.

"I can't do this. I feel I'm about to explode, Arlo. What happened outside the coffee shop?"

"I think perhaps I had too much coffee, stood too quickly, and then whoops; over-balanced and banged my head." He shrugged his shoulders to indicate he didn't really know, but that seemed as good an explanation as any. Alessia wasn't falling for it, though.

"The doctor said he thought you'd probably had a stressful or emotional trigger. What's going on, and why was your phone one of the first things you asked about?"

"I... I wanted to see if Mike had sent a message about how the board meeting had gone." He stood, but then held his head pretending to feel a little dizzy, again. He took a faltering step back so he could sit down on the edge of the bed. He remained seated, head bowed, but gesturing with his hand that he just needed a moment, and then he would be fine.

"Arlo, you're clearly not well. Please stay in bed." She eased him back onto the pillows: her anger temporarily replaced by concern. As he lay there, he knew he had to come up with a more plausible response about his obsession with the phone, so 30 minutes later, he walked slowly into the kitchen.

"Please don't give me my phone," he said, even though he had already found it in a jacket pocket. "I think I've just been a little obsessed about the problem with the bank. I keep checking for updates. I suppose

I'm hoping to see some sort of resolution. It's been on my mind for weeks now, and I've been losing sleep. I'm sorry. A watched pot never boils, eh?" he lied.

Alessia had her back to him as she sliced the baguette, but as she listened to his explanation, she stopped slicing and put the knife down. He took that as a cue to step closer and put his arms around her, which is when he felt her body gently heaving. Tears were running down her cheeks, partially in relief and partially in guilt that she had doubted her husband. Arlo held her close as he slowly turned her around, so she could bury her head into his chest.

After a minute, she sniffed back her final tears and mumbled, "Thank you, and I'm sorry for being so angry. It's just..."

He squeezed her a little tighter and said, "Shh, it's alright. I'm sorry, I should have told you about this earlier." As he held his wife, his mind wandered back to the tweet he had read a few minutes before he came downstairs.

Have you been offended by something on Twitter? You're not alone, according to a study from cyber guru Scot McDougal. Instead of bringing us together, social media is apparently tearing us apart.

c46% of responders admitted to interacting in a negative manner online!

We can help each other. Don't ignore us, Arlo!

He had made a mental note of the key letter within the message – the letter 'c' – before he then opened a direct message from 'them', which explained exactly what they expected him to do. It also included a very different photograph of Arlo and Jane. This time, it showed her kneeling on the floor by the side of a settee, topless, but smiling broadly at the camera. Arlo was lying on that settee, his eyes closed, perhaps asleep, but seemingly naked from the waist down.

Chapter 40

The back door burst open, with loud laughter and chatter from Eugenia Maffioni's two sons filling the kitchen of the family farmhouse, just outside Treviso. They were apparently sharing a joke, but as the aroma of the freshly cooked food hit their nostrils, they immediately fell quiet.

"Mamma, sei un angelo con un mestolo," said the oldest, Emilio, kissing his fingers in approval.

"No, today we speak in English. Today we celebrate," she replied, stirring the contents of the large pot as she gestured towards the table with her head. The men looked over to the table.

"Perché quattro, Mamma?" asked the youngest, Paulo, unclear on why there were four places set for lunch.

"English!" demanded Eugenia, in an unusually stern tone. This only happened when she was either angry with one of them or expected trouble of some sort.

"It's okay, Mamma, let them speak Italian," said a female voice. The two men looked over to the stairs that led down from the first-floor bedrooms, and their broad smiles dissolved immediately when they saw who was walking down them.

"What the hell is she doing here?" asked Emilio.

"This is her home, as well as yours," replied their mother.

"And 'she' needed somewhere to stay for a while; to relax and rest," replied Daniella Maddox. She knew her brothers would hardly lay out the red carpet if she ever returned home, but even with Dennis Ruiz in a high-security prison, she'd felt she had to get out of England. After travelling around America for a couple of months, she decided to return to the family home. Earlier, she had explained the situation to her mother, it was agreed that her brothers didn't need to know why she was there.

Eugenia indicated that the food was ready and that everyone should sit down. As they ate, the men kept their heads down and maintained total silence. Maddox smiled occasionally at her mother, but preferred to look around the room rather than try to engage in any conversation with her brothers. After several minutes, their mother slapped her hand on the table in disappointment and anger.

"Your sister comes to see us, after nearly 15 years, and neither of you have the courage or respect to welcome her home? You make me ashamed," she said, rather over-dramatically. The men kept their heads low, but glanced up at each other, deciding if one of them dare talk.

"It's okay, Mamma. I didn't expect a warm welcome from them," admitted Maddox.

"Why would we?" muttered Emilio. "You left your family and your home to become a rich solicitor in England. What was wrong with making your future here?" he asked.

"And do what? Serve in a shop in Treviso, or work for one of the vineyards in these hills, perhaps?" she replied.

"Why not? What's wrong with any of those?" he replied with a touch of anger in his voice.

"Because I'm not you. You would want me to stay when I have bigger dreams?"

"You leave here, you change your surname, shaming your family. Where is the honour in that?"

"You think being a solicitor with an Italian surname of Maffioni would work? Everyone would think it was Italian slang for mafia! Perhaps you don't understand, or perhaps you'll never understand because too much of your brain was knocked out of your head when you crashed that tractor?" she spat back; anger rising in her tone too. Her younger brother spluttered as he tried to hold in his laughter, but he only succeeded in spraying some of the sauce back over his food.

"What the hell are you laughing at?" snapped Emilio.

"She's right, that tractor crash was funny and explains so much about you," said Paulo, and he twirled his finger by the side of his head, to indicate perhaps his older brother was a little crazy since the accident, before howling with laughter. Even Eugenia smiled. The ice was finally broken.

Twenty minutes later, as they all drank some wine to toast her return, Eugenia said, "Maybe it's time, Daniella."

The two of them looked over at their sister, quizzically. She swallowed the sip of wine she had just taken, gathered her composure, and sighed. Tears formed in her eyes as she looked at her brothers.

"A man, a very powerful man, threatened my life and, although he is now in jail, I needed to come home to feel safe."

"But if he's in jail, surely you are safe?"

Daniella smiled at her brother's innocence. "He ran a global crime operation worth billions of euros and, even in jail, he can get messages out to people who work for him, his hired killers. I just need to disappear and, as no one in England knows my real surname or where you live, I hope to stay here a while, until perhaps..." but she didn't know what she was waiting for: for Ruiz to die? He would certainly never forgive her.

"Until perhaps what?" asked Paulo.

"Until she decides if she wants to leave," interjected Eugenia.

"Are you going to get a job, to help pay for the food you eat?" asked her still irritated elder brother.

"Enough!" growled Eugenia.

"Well, if she's planning to stay here a while, it's important she pays her dues," he stated indignantly, but his mother sighed and her shoulders slumped. Maddox held up her hand to ask her mother to stay silent, but her mother smiled softly as she shook her head, before turning to look at her sons.

"What, you think when your father died, he left us a sack of gold? Who do you think has been paying the bills for the farmhouse for the past 10 years?" she said in a gentle tone. Before anyone could answer, she continued, "Do you think we earn enough money to eat so well every day? Do you think the money you earn working in the vineyards in summer allows us to stay warm in the coldest of winters? Who do you think paid Senor Albasini to repair the tractor? Do you think he did it out of the kindness of his heart? You are both able to go to the local birrerie and enjoy a drink, because the *whole* family pulls together," and she emphasised the word 'whole' as she looked across at Daniella: the absent daughter who'd sent thousands of euros to her mother every month for the last 10 years. In unison, the brothers turned their heads to look at their sister, who was gently weeping. Paulo instinctively went to embrace her, but Emilio remained seated as he felt no such affection towards her.

Chapter 41

"The PM has asked me to pass on his sincere thanks for bringing Dennis Ruiz to justice. He'll be announcing the success of the joint venture between our National Cyber Security Centre and Europol in the House later today," said the parliamentary minister of state for cyber security. He sat at the head of a large conference table in the Home Office. Also sat around the table were a trio of senior private secretaries, two senior police officers, and the management team from the joint task force. At the corner furthest away from him, sat Professor Gary Hibberd.

"Thank you, minister," replied Howard Pritchard, director of GCHQ, who was responsible for the work of the National Cyber Security Centre. "Our team, including our Europol colleagues and our cyber specialist, Professor Hibberd, were delighted to hear that Ruiz had been found guilty and could be spending up to 30 years in jail." The minister smiled and nodded at Pritchard, but there was no such gesture towards Hibberd.

Ten minutes later, as they filed out of the meeting room, Pritchard spoke quietly to Hibberd.

"Sorry," he said.

"Don't worry. I didn't expect anything else from the pompous prick," replied a slightly irritated Hibberd. "Whenever I'm in the room, the only reference he ever makes is about how highly paid he thinks independent consultants are. No reference at all to value."

"Hey, you and I both know that with the evidence we found and your testimony in court, Ruiz never stood a chance. We all worked together to bring him down," Pritchard replied, as he patted Hibberd on the shoulder in gratitude. Hibberd smiled back, but it was forced. Although they had both worked on the Ruiz investigation, it was Hibberd who had turned the information Pritchard passed him into the explosive case.

Their professional friendship went back a long way, although there had always been a competitive streak throughout their formative careers. They first met at an Oxbridge event. Hibberd was an Oxford graduate; Pritchard was a Cambridge alumnus. When Hibberd went to Europe and America to teach, he had been to École Polytechnique Fédérale de Lausanne, MIT, and Harvard. Pritchard did something similar, but at LMU Munich, Caltech, and Yale. When it finally came time to return to the UK, even though they moved in slightly different career directions, they continued to swap interesting reports and insights.

"You got time for a coffee and a private discussion?" asked Hibberd, keen to move on from the parliamentary meeting. Pritchard furrowed his brow at the request, but as Hibberd had already started walking away, he decided to follow him. "It will only take a couple of minutes, as I have other clients to meet and flights to book," explained Hibberd as he hailed a passing black cab.

"Ah yes, the jet-set life of the private sector," Pritchard teased, as the cab pulled up next to them. When they were in and had asked the driver to turn off the internal microphone and speakers all London black cabs have, Pritchard asked, "What do you think is happening inside BOrg, now Ruiz is in jail?"

"You know as well as I do that the concept of '*cut the snake's head off and the body will die*' is utter nonsense in today's criminal operations. Although he's in jail, Ruiz is still in charge. He's still running his operation, for now."

"What do you mean '*for now*'?"

"There's some chatter on 'the onion'. I'm not certain, but I think someone is making a play for Ruiz's empire, and I'm worried someone on our wider team might be colluding."

Twenty minutes later, the taxi pulled up outside a plain, unbranded building. They walked up three flights of stairs to the Cyber Samurai office, where Hibberd entered a six-digit code, then placed his thumb on a scanner to release the electronic lock. He walked to his desk and logged onto his secure drive. Pritchard grabbed a chair and sat down next to him, staring at the three screens Hibberd used to navigate his business.

"Why three screens?" he asked.

"Three screens, two separate processors linked to two separate VPNs, anonymised IP addresses, twin power supplies from the mains grid with back-up UPS, and both GCHQ and Homeland Security levels of software security. It's great for productivity, as I can run separate investigations and comms strings simultaneously without anyone tracing me."

"Impressive." Pritchard himself had authorised the software security from GCHQ, but he didn't realise just how sophisticated Hibberd's set-up was. On one of the three screens was the transcript of a conversation, and Hibberd had highlighted a particular entry.

SF: No. Picard is facing mutiny problems, and the cyber king is dying. Long live the traitor king.

"Who is Picard, and who is the traitor?" Pritchard asked. "And I wonder if the '*king*' knows he's dying?"

"I don't know who the first two are yet, but I'm fairly sure they're referring to Ruiz as the dying king."

"Do you think your friend knows more?"

"Possibly, but I'm pretty sure he won't share anything else. He'll feel he's led me to the rabbit hole and it's my choice as to whether I dive in, or not," explained Hibberd.

"And?" asked Pritchard, fearing he already knew the answer.

Hibberd raised his eyebrows in submission. "Just call me Alice."

Chapter 42

The latest spreadsheet forecast, based on the interim results of the pilot, showed the return-on-investment model that Kendrick had designed was beginning to unravel.

"Robert, I'm not going to cover this up any longer. I gave you two versions of the spreadsheet last time, as instructed, but this is getting beyond simple interpretation. Another one has died, and a trend is emerging. I'd need to be smoking something illegal to miss it, and I'm not telling your investor a lie," the accountant blurted out before Kendrick could even say a cordial 'hello'.

"You're fired!" Kendrick snarled down the phone before abruptly ending the call and sweeping his paperwork onto the floor. The size of the group that had been targeted for the trial of the new software wasn't statistically robust, but Kendrick had persuaded everyone involved that it was at least representative. He leant forwards, arms ram-rod straight, and his clenched fists resting against the desk. His chest was heaving with his deep breaths, and his heart pounded as he tried desperately not to spiral into panic. It didn't help that The Broker had recently texted him:

Wherever you are in the world and whatever plans you think you might have, be back in London in two days' time. We need to meet. Do not disappoint me. I will invoke the cancellation

A subsequent text had confirmed he would send two of his men and a car to collect Kendrick from anywhere in the country, if necessary. It was obvious that if he avoided the meeting, The Broker's men would no longer be collecting him; they would be hunting him. He'd been in difficult situations before, so he told himself that he just needed to gather his composure and work a way through the next two days. As he began to feel his pulse slowing and self-confidence returning, his phone rang. It was the third man in their scheme.

"How's things?" said the man.

"Alright. Just looking at the latest numbers, and they're looking good," Kendrick lied.

"That's great news," replied the man, knowing they were not looking good as he'd just had a final call from the accountant who had briefed him on the real interim results. "I was a little worried."

"Why?" asked Kendrick, forcing a smile and light-hearted tone.

"Because I got a text about being picked up by two of The Broker's men yesterday. I think he was worried we're avoiding him."

"Thanks for the information. He's not someone we want panicking or questioning his investment," chuckled Kendrick. He could feel his pulse beginning to race again. The Broker had made the terms of any cancellation very clear: his money back or he'd kill them himself, and it wasn't that long ago that he had put a bullet in the office wall next to Kendrick's head.

"Absolutely," agreed the man. "He's not the sort of person who'd forgive and forget."

"Well, it won't come to that. I'll make sure. See you in a couple of days," Kendrick said before ending the call without another word. He needed something to go right, and quickly. Everything was now in place if the Kintaro board agreed to sign the investment contract that would save their company and, at least for the time being, his life.

Chapter 43

The battered and bloodied bodies of Ms Katie Cross and one of the overnight home-help team were discovered by a nurse who was there to take on the morning shift. Jones was on a call with the lead detective at Hampshire CID, getting the latest update.

"SOCO estimate the time of death anywhere between midnight and 4am," said the detective.

"Any signs of forced entry?" asked Jones.

"They found a patio door open at the back, but the nurse who found them said the care team used to go into the back garden for a smoke. Maybe it was already unlocked, rather than jimmied."

"What else have you got?"

"SOCO says they both died from strangulation, and that they pulled a copy of a lottery ticket out of Miss Cross's mouth."

"What are the numbers on the ticket?" Jones checked.

"Er... 3, 17, 22, 32, 37, 47, and 1."

"Shit," Jones whispered. The numbers on the ticket were different to the ones on the lottery ticket at the murder scene of Dr Pickett. The detective politely cleared his throat: he had more information to share, and she didn't appear to be listening. "Sorry," Jones apologised.

"The nurse said that the carer's logbook showed Miss Cross had a visit from some local uniforms earlier this week."

"Why?" queried Jones.

"Someone made a call to Crimestoppers. Call info was passed to our intel unit, who had it down as a *'high standard'*. Two of our blues went, checked, and found nothing of concern."

Jones thanked the detective and asked for any further updates as soon as they became available, whatever time day or night. She then sent a text to Denton:

Got 5 minutes to talk? It's urgent!

Less than two minutes later, her phone rang. It was Denton.

"I've got 30 seconds. Just come out of court, but they'll be calling me back in shortly. What's up?"

"We've just found another body with a copy of a lottery ticket in her mouth, sir."

Someone in the background started calling Denton's name, because he was needed back in the courtroom.

"Fuck," was all she heard him say, before he ended the call.

Chapter 44

Mike had called a meeting at Kintaro, even though it was the weekend. The decision couldn't wait any longer, with employees starting to ask questions and a handful of rising stars in the company debating whether to resign.

"I need to get a secure job, Mike. I'm sorry, but Melissa and I have another baby on the way, and the rumours are we're going under," said one.

"Advoc8 don't offer as much as I earn here, Mr McCleary, but I need to know I've got some regular income," explained another. Mike understood and had persuaded both to wait just a few more days before making any final decisions. The invitation for the board meeting was also extended to key members of the senior management team, including Bob Hall. They didn't all have voting rights, but Mike thought they should hear direct from him, too.

"Okay, so we know our cash flow needs to improve and Machendrie wants to see improvements in our management of working capital," said Mike.

"We can improve our cash flow by chasing payment of invoices," said the finance director.

"We can't just alter an existing contract with our clients," replied the head of legal and compliance. People nodded and mumbled their agreement. "Can we work on our stock levels?" he asked. Bob Hall quickly quashed that idea.

"We're already running a Just-In-Time approach. If we work our stock levels any harder, we'll increase the risk of stock shortages, our output slowing down, and face financial penalties for late delivery."

"What if we postponed our payments to suppliers?" suggested the finance director. She had run some numbers, and it would make their cash flow positive, albeit she knew that a simple spreadsheet exercise was far easier than the reality.

"I'm... I'm still not convinced that we should take his offer," said Bob Hall.

"What other choices do we have: take the offer or go under, leaving over two hundred people without a job?" asked the head of human resources.

"I know, I know," replied an agitated Hall. "But something just isn't sitting comfortably, that's all."

"Like what?" challenged the head of HR.

"I don't know... just something. Call it intuition, but I don't trust this guy. Why would he invest in us?"

"I understand that you may have some inexplicable concerns, Bob. You've committed so much to Kintaro over the years," assured Mike. "Let me talk to him and try to find out a little more about the supply chain angle. We'll reconvene tomorrow."

Once the meeting had ended, everyone had filed out except Mike. He stayed behind and felt quite isolated in the position of CEO. Was this how it was going to feel whenever they had key decisions to make? Was he supposed to broker an agreement between the team, or lead them even if some of them opposed his decision? He grabbed the remote control for the screen in the boardroom and turned the television mode on, in an attempt to distract himself from the psychological vortex raging in his head. It was tuned into one of the 24-hour news channels, which was closing one feature on Donald Trump being the first sitting US president in history to step into North Korea, before turning to a follow-up story on the aftermath of the Dennis Ruiz case, in which he briefly caught sight of his interim lecturer at MIT, Professor Hibberd. He and several others were gathering at an Interpol meeting in Bucharest to support a global campaign on cyber defence.

"Hmm, I wondered what had happened to you," muttered Mike, smiling at the memory of how simple studying seemed compared to his new role. As he turned the screen off, he wondered what was going through Machendrie's mind. He was unlikely to sit on his investment options much longer, and he probably had several other attractive opportunities. Maybe he was only giving the Kintaro team this extended period because of Tania's involvement?

"Even if that's the case, I'm just glad you *are* investing in us," he mumbled to himself.

Chapter 45

Rather than continue with her studies at the Instituto Politécnico de Castelo Branco in Portugal, Lucia Vergara had decided to take a gap year and travel around Europe. Even as a child, when her mother went to the hairdressers, she would spend the whole afternoon sitting in any spare chair she could find, looking through old copies of *National Geographic* magazine. Today, many years after she last looked at those magazines, she was living her dream and currently in Bucharest.

Throughout her travels, she took hundreds of photos, and despite the limitations on some social media sites, she loved to upload as many as possible and as frequently as possible. Sometimes, as often as four times a day. She had friends from university, a few extended family members who could afford smartphones or iPads, and a lecturer who had encouraged her to put her education as a journalist to good use. She would therefore post a lengthy blog entry every day, with links to it on her social media pages. Each blog entry would feature three or four of her favourite photographs and some interesting facts about the locations she had been to, or the things she had done. When her friends logged on for a fourth day in a row and found there was still no new blog entry, let alone a collection of photographs on her Facebook and Instagram accounts, they became curious.

How is everything? Have you run out of words, or has Facebook finally decided you need your own cloud server for all the photographs you're sharing ha ha? one of them had typed, trying to hide his growing concerns for her safety. Little did he and the others know that the Romanian police had just pulled her body from the Dâmbovita River.

"What do we have?" asked the investigating officer.

"Young woman, possibly early 20s, but she's been in the water for a couple of days so difficult to say for sure," replied a constable. "She's not carrying a passport, so we'll need to wait for the forensics team to try to identify her."

"How did she die?"

"Broken neck, and her feet were tied to some iron weights, like the ones people lift in a gym." The constable mimicked someone lifting dumbbells. "Feels like a gangland execution," he said before glancing at his notes and adding, "There's no indication that the attack was sexually motivated, and she had €200 in her pocket, so theft doesn't appear to be a motive either."

"No indication of drugs, or any missing person report by a wealthy family?"

"No obvious link to drugs and, as far as we can tell, this isn't the result of an unpaid ransom."

Nearly 1400 miles away, at the GCHQ offices in Scarborough, a data analyst was monitoring a system that scanned all the popular social media networks. It was a primarily automated process, with facial recognition software scanning recently uploaded photos and videos. It never failed to surprise the authorities how many criminals voluntarily put something on platforms such as TikTok, YouTube, or Facebook. There was an automated ping on his screen.

"Got a match!" he shouted triumphantly. The unit manager walked over to look at the screen. "It might actually be a double match, but I'm a bit confused," explained the analyst. They peered at a photo of the front of a local coffee shop that had been uploaded onto Facebook a week ago by a woman called Lucia Vergara. The photo was primarily of the ornate front of a coffee shop, with its spectacular awning, but through the window, three figures could be seen as they approached the door, although only two were sufficiently clear for facial recognition. The software calculated a 98% match for one of the men and a 67% match for the second man. As the analyst clicked his mouse, a second and third screen brought up the files on both men.

"Well, well," said the unit manager. "One is Simion Apostu, but according to official records, the other man has been dead for over a year. Why is a known thug leaving a Bucharest coffee shop with a walking corpse?"

Chapter 46

DC Rachael Jones joined the Met as a graduate entrant and had often been teased about her lack of experience on the beat, which led to a few confrontations during her short but stellar career. She had, however, proven her value to the force several times in the last few years.

"Jonesy," mumbled a clearly grumpy Denton, as she entered his office. He closed his desk drawer and pushed a pile of files to one side. How he hated the administration that came with the role.

"Sir," she replied. After the murder of Dr Mark Pickett a couple of weeks ago, there had been no further lottery-ticket-related deaths, and everyone assumed that his death was a one-off. Denton was even planning to reassure the DCI that the original suspect he'd named really was the brains behind the murders, if not the actual killer. He also still believed that The Broker was involved in planning the murders, but as he'd found over many years, finding sufficient evidence against the man for anything other than a parking ticket remained elusive.

"I've been talking to Hampshire CID this morning. They're still compiling information, but they've confirmed that a Ms Katie Cross, 74, and one of her carers, Mrs Evelyn Buchannan, 46, were found dead. Both had been strangled, and they've found a lottery ticket in Ms Cross's mouth. They're still waiting for the final forensics report, but..." and then Jones stopped.

Denton's head had dropped. It was perhaps the worst news he could have had. It took several painful seconds of silence before he lifted his head in resignation and said, "Don't tell me, no immediate sign of trace material and no obvious motive."

"Actually, no. The lead SOCO described it as quite a clumsy murder scene, and they've got some prints. Our suspect is a known gang member with an arrest record as long as your arm."

Although Denton was pleasantly surprised at the news, he then furrowed his brow. Every previous lottery ticket murder scene had been meticulously clean, so why was this one different?

"Best clear some space on the wall and write up what you have," he instructed. Jones did as she was requested. As with the original Lottery Ticket Murders, she wrote up the alphabetical sequence of the postcodes, and the numbers on the third lottery ticket.

Postcode:	OX	PO	R(3*)	S(15*)	T(8*)	UB	W(9*)
# on ticket:	4	~~19~~ 17	27	32	35	44	6

* = number of different postcode cities/areas that start with the primary letter.

She stood back once she'd completed the information, ready for the usual discussion and debate, but he looked at it, nodded, and said, "Okay, thanks. Keep me updated on any arrest, please," and then started typing. She was unsure how he might have reacted to the news, but this wasn't one of the scenarios she'd imagined. She'd expected him to explode, perhaps bury his head in his hands, or even thump the desk. After a few seconds, he looked up.

"Was there anything else?" he asked, almost casually.

"Er, no, sir, nothing."

"Okay," he replied, and returned to his computer screen, fingers poised over the keyboard. Jones stood and walked out of the office, slightly bewildered.

Once she was out of the office, Denton sank back into his chair and turned to stare out of the window. He had been listening to her, but the clumsy murder scene she had described wasn't the sort of hit The Broker would accept, so who was murdering people now and leaving a ticket? Add to that, the rumour about him ordering the hit on Adrian Huxley and then leaving the body to be found. No, something just didn't feel right, but he couldn't quite pinpoint what, and it worried him.

His anxiety rose again, three hours later, when Jones informed him that they had already found the body of the suspect.

"And?"

"Local blues were called to the scene after a man found a body in a disused garage. His face had been blown off, and his fingers and thumbs severed. SOCO are there now."

"So, like the Huxley scene?"

"Seems so, sir. He's a member of a local Armenian gang, and he had several copies of the same lottery ticket we found at the Portsmouth scene in his pocket, and the name 'Matthew Berry' scribbled on the back of a note that was wrapped around them."

Now, Denton was sure that someone was trying to point the finger at The Broker, but why?

"A local rival, trying to take him out of the picture if they can get him arrested, maybe?" Jones offered, once he had shared his thoughts.

"I don't think so. Even if we arrested him, we don't have enough evidence to charge him with anything, and it would be a blood bath if anyone tried to lay claim to his territory. It's almost as if someone is teasing us," said Denton, cogitating the implications and scenarios.

Chapter 47

Alessia had insisted that she and Arlo help clear out the various outbuildings and tidy the garden at Mike and Tania's house, but Arlo was again preoccupied with another two tweets that had arrived.

"Why don't you want to go?" she asked him when he protested.

"I'm... I'm just not feeling quite myself. I'll be fine after a bit of a snooze and some paracetamol."

"Well, you're going to see the doctor if this continues. We need to make sure there's no underlying health issue," Alessia stated as she logged on and booked a train ticket to Selby. She called Tania to ask if she could collect her from the local station, which she agreed to do.

After Arlo had dropped his wife at Garforth train station, he drove home. As he swung off the main road, he saw a police van parked up the hill, towards their cottage. A uniformed officer stood in the middle of the road and held his hand up, indicating Arlo should stop. As he slowed, he lowered the window.

"Morning, sir. Sorry, but there's a group of demonstrators up ahead, blocking access to some of the cottages and the farm. Where are you going?"

"I live up at Rose Cottage, officer," Arlo replied.

"Oh," said the policeman, screwing his face up. "You're going to have to be careful because they're blocking access after the first few properties on that street. If you slowdown 10 or so metres from the brow of the hill, one of my colleagues will escort you through."

"Okay. Thank you. Is it a protest about the farmer raising laboratory rabbits?"

"No, sir, but best not get involved, eh?"

"I'll take extra care."

The policeman nodded and stepped back, speaking into his radio as he did so, as Arlo slowly drove up the hill. As suggested, he came to a stop a safe distance from the small crowd. He estimated there were perhaps six or seven people, with most holding what looked like homemade banners, and one man had a megaphone. He was facing away from Arlo, so with his windows closed and the radio on in the car, the man's voice was thankfully muffled. Arlo waited for a second police officer to notice him, and he then gestured that he wanted to turn left, onto the track that led to the cottage's driveway. The officer indicated he could move forwards slowly, as he spoke to one of the protesters to explain a car was coming through. The protester glanced over at Arlo and then alerted her fellow protesters, gesturing they should move aside. Most did so, but one remained in the centre of the road. As the second policeman encouraged the final protester to move to one side, his colleague walked over to Arlo, who again lowered his window.

"Sorry, sir, but it's taking a little bit more persuasion than we expected to get this one to move. Won't be long," he explained.

"Not a problem, Officer. What are they protesting about, anyway?"

"Apparently, leaflets have been pushed through letterboxes telling residents there's someone on the sex offender's register living nearby. We've told them there isn't, but they don't believe us." Arlo furrowed his brow, hoping the police really were telling the truth. He'd read reports of people like that living near schools, despite denials from the authorities. He could now see some of the placards:

Sex offenders out, for the safety of our children

No to paedophiles in our neighbourhood

Safety first, sex offender's privacy second

'Could there really be someone from the sex offenders register living near here?' he wondered. He was glad Alessia hadn't seen the protest, as she'd more than likely join in and probably get arrested. As he reflected on the question, the policeman finally waved him on, now the final protester had moved aside.

"Thank you, Officer," Arlo said as he slowly moved forward. With his window down, and given he was much closer, he could now hear the man with the megaphone:

"Justice for us. Justice for Jane," he was shouting, as he waved a placard in the air with a photo of a young woman on it. Arlo unconsciously slowed to a stop as he recognised the face in the photo.

"Justice for us. Justice for Jane," the man repeated loudly, before turning towards Arlo. "Justice for us. Justice for Ja—" but he stopped before he had finished her name. He looked straight at Arlo and sneered. Before the police officers could react, the man lunged forwards. His eyes were as wide as his sneer, and he was next to the open car window in seconds. He leaned forward and whispered:

"Justice for us. No secrets about Jane. You were mad not to, Arlo."

"Oi, back *away* from the car!" shouted an officer who had seen the man lunge forwards and was now trying to get between him and Arlo. "Come on, let's keep this peaceful," he instructed. The protester held his hands up in mock surrender, but maintained eye contact with Arlo for a few more seconds before turning back to the crowd and restarting the chant with renewed vigour:

"Justice for us. Justice for Jane!"

The policeman leaned towards the window. "You alright, sir?" Arlo jumped. "Sorry, didn't mean to startle you," the officer apologised.

"It's... It's alright. I'm just a little shocked, that's all. I'll... I'll be fine. Just need to get home and sit down with a cup of tea, I think," replied a clearly shaken Arlo, trying to maintain his composure.

"Of course, sir. Well, hopefully there'll be no more unpleasantness, and they'll disperse soon, now you've got the message." It took a moment for Arlo to process what the officer had said, but he slowly turned his head to look at the policeman, who was also now sneering at Arlo.

"Good job your wife isn't here. Not sure how you'd explain this little incident, are you?" asked the officer as he passed Arlo a folded copy of the local morning newspaper. Arlo looked down at the newspaper and slowly unfolded it, while the policeman waved at his fellow actors to indicate that their performance was over. A photo took up almost half the front page. It showed the smiling face of the girl he thought he had saved from the three knife-wielding thugs a few months ago. The same girl he had met at the local coffee shop a few days ago. Next to her photo was the headline:

SUBURBAN MURDER OR SUICIDE?

Social media posts she wrote suggest local man involved.

"It's not real," said the policeman. "But it would be such a shame if it ever happened, so make sure Mike and the board make the right decision and accept the offer from Mr Machendrie, or the police will receive compelling information about who the local man might be."

Arlo looked up, wide-eyed. *"Me?* I didn't do anything. I wasn't involved!" he implored.

"That's not what they'll think when we send them the photographs and some carefully crafted witness statements from the coffee shop. You looked quite angry in the photos, and the least said the better about some other photographs we have."

Chapter 48

Hibberd logged off the office computers around 4am and didn't bother to go home or try to sleep. The chatter on the dark web had changed, and although the subject of BOrg remained active, the tone of the conversation was different. He'd sent Pritchard a text message and knew the man would want to know more as soon as he woke up. Given UK and foreign security services probably tried to monitor the traffic from their phones, they'd previously agreed a series of seemingly innocent texts for urgent and important situations. The one Hibberd had used earlier that morning was:

Just been watching paint dry in an attempt to beat this ruddy insomnia

It meant he had pulled an all-nighter and needed to urgently talk about something he'd found or heard. Two hours later, there was a rap on the office door. Hibberd wearily rose and opened it.

"You look absolutely shocking," said Pritchard as he walked in.

"It was an early one... or a late one, depending on your perspective," Hibberd mumbled wearily, as he sipped what was already his third coffee since he'd finished in the chat rooms.

"What's so important?" Pritchard asked.

"I've mainly been talking in East European and Muscovite chat rooms, but my contact on Able Onion, Senyor Fosc, sent me another link for a private chat. I took a screen grab of it to show you," he explained to Pritchard, pointing to one of his three computer screens.

SF: Seems like Picard has problems.

ZK: Yes, you said he was facing mutiny problems.

"Who is ZK?" asked Pritchard.

"Me. It's my online tag," Hibberd reminded him, before Pritchard re-looked at the screen.

SF: He is, but he needs to look up, not down.

"Is he saying my boss is a problem?"

"Difficult to say without digging a lot deeper," Hibberd sighed.

"What do we do next?" questioned a still confused Pritchard.

"There's only one thing to do. I have to go even deeper down the proverbial rabbit hole, but I might not come out."

"Let me know where you keep all your notes, just in case what you find aren't the winning numbers for the lottery," replied Pritchard. It was gallows humour, but it was also operationally prudent as it wouldn't be the first time an operative looking into something on the dark web had disappeared or died.

"Everything is already on the secure closed network," Hibberd said, referencing the electronic filing system they'd set up that was only accessible via direct connection, thus avoiding the internet and the threat of hackers. "By the way, what was that new folder called 'Yann' all about?" he asked. He had noticed it last night.

"Robert Ian Kendrick, alias Yann Machendrie, the former mule manager for Ruiz. Despite being reported as dead over a year ago, he was spotted in Bucharest, accompanied by Simion Apostu."

"Apostu? Whoa, that's a heavy-duty link-up. What's that all about?"

"Once we know, I'll let you know," replied Pritchard. "Keep it to yourself, though." Hibberd furrowed his brow. It was an unusual statement from Pritchard.

"Who else would I tell?" he asked innocently. Pritchard realised his error and tried to make light of the comment.

"Your ex told me you used to talk in your sleep, and I've got no idea who you're seeing nowadays," he chuckled. Hibberd laughed lightly in response, accepting the possibility, which eased Pritchard's concern that he might have slipped up. He had his own contacts on the dark web, and a trusted source called DoxDoll had advised him that perhaps Hibberd might have an ulterior interest in BOrg.

DoxDoll: After all, who else knows as much detail about how BOrg works, what might still work, and is well-placed to misdirect any further scrutiny from your investigation? Mucho moolah for a trusted gamekeeper turned poacher.

Chapter 49

As spring arrived and the trees and flowers sprouted new growth, Daniella Maddox spent most of her days outside. There were newly born chicks to care for, goats to tend, and she had expanded the family's vegetable patch into what her mother now described as a small industry.

"I'm going to the market," her mother shouted as she closed the back door of the house.

"Okay, Mamma. Ciao," Maddox shouted back. A warm glow swept through her body, and she smiled to herself. "This is the life," she whispered as she put new tomato vines in the freshly prepared soil. After wiping her brow, she took off her outdoor gloves and picked up a flask she had. As she sipped the cooling water, she saw her younger brother, Paulo, walking towards her. He waved in a casual, friendly manner. She raised her hand in acknowledgement.

"Ciao, Dani," he said as he reached her, using her informal family name. He embraced her.

"Ciao, Paulo."

"Mamma asked me to prepare dinner tonight. Do you... want to help?" he asked, looking a little sheepish.

"You mean you *need* my help because you're not as good a cook as I am?" she teased.

"Hey!" exclaimed Paulo, pretending to be hurt by such a statement, but he couldn't stop a broad smile of admission spreading across his face. "Maybe," he added.

"Sure, it will be fun," said Maddox as she placed her gloves inside a pocket of her gardening overalls. They walked back to the house, with Maddox making some more humorous jibes at her younger brother, before wrapping her arm around his shoulder. She and Paulo had become quite close over the last few days, and often teased each other or could be found laughing at something together. This irritated their older brother, Emilio, who continued to disapprove of her returning to the family house.

Inside the kitchen, their mother had laid out all the ingredients on the large table, as well as some pots and pans. Maddox looked at the handwritten note from her and glanced up at Paulo. Even though it was a mild spring day, Eugenia often made this winter meal, given evenings could still be quite cold.

"Seriously? You need my help to make some fresh bread and an Ossobuco alla Milanese?" and she shook her head, albeit she was smirking.

"I just thought... you know... it might be fun to cook together," replied a bashful Paulo.

"Then let's get one thing straight: you're the sous chef, and I give the orders," she said. He spent several seconds reflecting on the implications if he agreed, but when Maddox looked up at the clock on the wall and tapped her wrist, implying time was going quickly, he nodded eagerly. They busied themselves around the kitchen, chopping vegetables and preparing the ingredients for the bread. In his haste, Paulo knocked over some flour. Maddox sighed and shook her head as he dropped to his knees and tried to scoop up the flour from the floor.

"You'll be doing that for ages," she said. "Where does Mamma keep the dustpan and brush?"

"Over in that tall cupboard," he replied, slightly embarrassed at his attempt to clean up. Maddox smirked at him and shook her head, chuckling to herself as she walked over to the cupboard. She opened it and then took a half-step back.

"What's wrong?" asked Paulo. On opening the door, Maddox was surprised to find two shotguns standing alongside the brush.

"I... I'm just surprised about the guns, that's all. Why are they in the house?"

"Why wouldn't they be?" a bemused Paulo replied. "This is the Italian countryside, not London or Leeds. Italy has rats as big as cats, lynx, brown bears, snakes, wolves. You expect us to go out to the barn if we need to frighten off a bear that's roaming outside the back door?" he chuckled.

"Sorry, you're right. It's just a shock to a city dweller like me."

After cleaning up the mess, they continued preparing the meal. Paulo kept glancing up at his sister, a question on his lips that he dared not ask, but he eventually plucked up enough courage.

"What's it like living abroad, having a career, a new name, not being..."

"Not being what?" Maddox asked. Paulo hesitated before he continued.

"Not being treated like the baby of the family."

Maddox stopped kneading the dough and stared at him, quizzically. "What do you mean?"

He looked up sheepishly and shook his head slightly. "It's okay, it doesn't matter."

"Paulo?" she asked again, as something was clearly bothering him. He drew a deep breath but kept slowly carving the raw meat so as not to have to look at her.

"Not being treated like the baby of the family, treated as if your views and dreams are the least important." He glanced up at her to see if she was mocking him, but she wasn't. Maddox put the dough down, wiped her hands, and walked around the table to talk to him.

"What makes you feel you're not important?"

"Mamma makes the big decisions for us. Sometimes she asks Emilio, as the eldest male in the house, but they usually agree. Even if they do ask my opinion, it feels as if they're doing it out of pity, whereas you don't need to ask them to consider your opinion. You're the successful lawyer, living abroad in your own big-city apartment, who's been supporting this family without Emilio and me even knowing about it." He felt a little embarrassed admitting his opinions, but Maddox gently took his hand.

"Paulo, you mean everything to Mamma. If she takes decisions, it's not because your opinion and dreams are not important, but she will feel that if things don't work out, she should be the one to shoulder the responsibility and let you live and be young. There will be plenty of time for you to take on such responsibilities when you have a family of your own and, believe me, it's not as much fun as you might think. Okay?"

He nodded; grateful she had not mocked him. She kissed her younger brother on the cheek and squeezed his upper arms in support.

"Okay?" she checked, and he nodded silently again.

As she returned to her work and he to his, he felt emboldened, so he said, "I have plans to make my own life, you know?"

"Plans," she replied, concentrating more on the dough than Emilio.

"Yes, big plans," he added with a touch of confidence, but Maddox didn't press him for details. She was just happy that her little brother had shared his fears with her. There would be time to ask him more, but they were in danger of running out of time to make the family meal.

Later, as the bread was baking in the oven and the veal shanks were slowly cooking, they started singing together, quietly but happily as they tidied. When the door opened and Emilio walked in, the singing stopped immediately, and the positive mood disappeared.

"Where is Mamma?" he asked curtly, as he looked around the kitchen for her.

"She's gone to the market. She should be back soon," replied Maddox. "What's wrong?"

"I need to talk to her. It's local business; you wouldn't understand," he snapped dismissively.

"Hey, why are you still being so nasty to her?" asked Paulo.

"Shut up and get back to your woman's work," Emilio scoffed. Paulo took a half-step towards his brother to confront him, but Maddox gently placed her hand across his chest to encourage him to stay calm. When Eugenia returned, she could tell there was tension in the air.

"Who is bringing malumore into my house?"

"It's nothing, Mamma," said Maddox. "Just a little misunderstanding, that's all." Eugenia gave the two brothers an accusatory glare before deciding not to intervene.

"Mamma, abbiamo bisogno di parlare," said Emilio. Eugenia sighed and glowered at him.

"How many times do I have to tell you: speak English! We have no secrets in this family. What do we need to talk about?"

Emilio, feeling suitably chastened, begrudgingly replied in English:

"It's about Mrs Valorio. The bank is going to take her house."

"*What?*" snarled Eugenia. "That poor woman, she loses her husband, and now those bastards from the bank in Venice want to take away her beautiful home?"

"They say they have the right," he replied.

"No. This will not do. I will not allow it," she stated. "Why? Why do they think they have the right to take her house?"

"I... I don't know. Mrs Valorio's granddaughter says they want to force her to sell, so they can build a large villa for someone. Something about a clause in the original contract for the land. I don't know any more than that, but I agree, Mamma, we must fight this together," he said, trying to take the moral high ground. He had always been the one she turned to with family matters, until his sister had turned up.

"A clause in a contract?" queried Maddox. It was an instinctive question, but she immediately knew the error she'd made.

"Ah, my bambina, of course! You are an angel!" Eugenia said, almost in holy celebration. "You, you can look at this contract and, and.." she was stuttering with excitement.

"Mamma, wait," Maddox protested. "I haven't studied Italian law and regulations for years, let alone the Civil Code on ownership," she tried to explain, but her mother was having none of it.

"You do this because you can save a proud and wonderful widow from heartbreak. You do it because, one day, maybe I will need help, and you would be angry if someone could have helped me but didn't. Am I right?"

Maddox bowed her head. Her mother still knew how to make her children feel humble. Emilio's gaze flitted from his mother to his sister, and back. He scowled and tried to hide his anger that his little sister had taken the spotlight away from him, again.

Chapter 50

"This is Crimestoppers," the man said.

"I need to report a murder," the woman replied.

"Okay, can you give me some details?"

"I... I don't know if I can without the murderer knowing it must have been me who told you."

"I can assure you this is completely anonymous. If you can tell me..." but the woman blurted over the top of him.

"You don't understand. He'll just know it's me."

"If you're in any danger, we can ask the police to..." but she interjected again.

"*No!* No, I don't want them involved." The operator was starting to run out of options, but he tried a different tack.

"Is there any way you can go into hiding for a while? Stay with some friends abroad, or at least stay off the digital network?" It went quiet, as if the woman was contemplating the idea.

"It's... It's possible, but I need to think where I can go that he can't find me, and how to get there. If I go via the airport, he'll be able to track me."

"Do... do you want to tell me who you're in danger with?" Again, there was a short silence as the woman contemplated the implications of telling him. Saying who he was would be an enormous risk.

"Voch," she finally gasped.

"Is that his surname or…"

"I mean 'no', I don't want to tell you. Sorry, when I'm stressed, I automatically speak my native language. I'm Armenian, and voch means no."

"It's alright, you don't need to tell me his name. Is there anything you feel comfortable telling me? Anything at all?" For a third time, there was an uncomfortable silence, but the operator was trained not to make a caller feel pressured. Although there were potentially calls waiting, he mustn't rush this caller for fear a serious crime could go unreported.

Eventually, hesitantly, the woman said, "There is a body at 27 Adamson Grove, Redhill. She is linked to another death. That's all I can say," and the call ended abruptly.

As the operator logged the details onto the system and prepared to take their next call, Cellier smiled.

"Job done," she said, and she turned to see The Broker smiling too.

Chapter 51

It was already late into the night, but Mike still had a decision to make on his recommendation for the board. Over the last few weeks, he'd gone from being offered an exciting new role as head of research and development at Kintaro by Harry Sakamoto, to now being on the verge of leading the company away from a financial cliff-edge. Two days ago, the decision was simple because there was only one offer on the table, the one from Yann Machendrie, Tania's wealthy venture capitalist uncle. That changed less than 24 hours ago, though, when a start-up in Silicon Valley contacted Mike.

"We've already raised $4bn, Mike, and we think adding your vision and the operational capability of Kintaro to the mix would give us the competitive edge we're looking for before we launch," their young Californian CEO had said. He was three years younger than Mike, but had vision and energy that made Mike feel amateurish in comparison. The offer had two fundamental differences to the one Machendrie had proposed. Firstly, Mike's role would be head of UK operations, which would reduce the pressure he was feeling at being thrust front and centre by Machendrie's offer of CEO. Secondly, the indicative targets he discussed with the start-up were far less aggressive than Machendrie's, and there was no associated 'perform or sell-up' threat. If he accepted the offer from the start-up, there would be regular travel to California, but Mike assumed he and Tania could also incorporate a weekend trip back to Toronto. The only problem was their offer would expire in a few days, and Mike wasn't the only person they were talking to, albeit Kintaro was their preferred choice.

He had driven over to his parents' house for some familiarity and to avoid Tania regularly asking him why he was reconsidering her uncle's offer. Arlo had stayed up after offering to be a sounding board for a now grateful Mike, and brought in another cup of tea.

"Thanks," said Mike as he took the cup. "No more, though, Dad, or I'll be drowning from the inside," he chuckled.

"So?" asked Arlo, sitting down next to him and glancing at the almost indecipherable notes his son had scribbled on a pad. Mike sat back, stretched his arms in the air and puffed his cheeks out.

"I don't know. Everything about the start-up offer screams 'take it'. The pressure will be less, and the future of the company, as part of a larger organisation, is pretty tempting."

"What about the longevity of the start-up, though? Those things can burn through billions in months, with the risk that the bubble bursts. At least with Tania's uncle's offer, there's a degree of family loyalty to see it through," proffered Arlo.

"Come on, Dad. He's a businessman and, even with Tania involved, she's already said he'll only continue to invest his money if it's making a return."

"Have you discussed the decision with Tania?" queried Arlo.

"I have," Mike replied, although he quietly admitted to himself that Tania had appeared a little withdrawn since Mike mentioned this second offer. "I get it that she wants to feel she helped save Kintaro and give me a wonderful opportunity, but our relationship is strong. Once she sees we have time to spend together and enough money without all of the stress that goes with the CEO job, she'll be fine."

Although that might be true, Arlo shook his head.

"I thought you had more hunger, more thirst for success than this, Michael. Don't turn into me."

The statement took Mike by surprise.

"Wh... what do you mean, Dad?" he asked, hesitation in his voice. His father had never suggested that he been anything other than happy with his own life and career.

"Don't get me wrong, your mother and I are very happy together, but I do look back and wonder whether I didn't take some opportunities because I felt comfortable. Maybe I settled for 'easy' rather than 'promising'. Perhaps if I'd looked further ahead than the end of my nose, we'd be living in a bigger house and not struggling with money, sometimes."

"Dad, if you need..." but Arlo held up his hand to indicate Mike should stop.

"We're fine, son. Don't worry. I just mean that perhaps life could have been different. Maybe you wouldn't have had to rely on a scholarship to MIT if I'd been brave enough to take one or two chances. You get that brave, adventurous streak from your mother, and weren't you always telling me you wanted to look beyond the obvious, to avoid taking the paths others readily follow?"

189

Mike smiled softly at his own words being used in a debate to convince him there was an option to consider, after all. He took a piece of paper and scribbled something on it before gently tossing the pen he was using onto the pad, and slumping back in the chair in a mood of relaxed submission.

"Thanks, Dad. I'll sleep on it, but maybe you're right."

"No, maybe *you're* right," smirked Arlo, reminding Mike he was simply submitting to his own philosophy.

"I'll give you a hand to tidy up, and then I'll be heading home."

"Don't worry, I'll tidy up. You get yourself off and have a good night's sleep," suggested Arlo. Mike nodded wearily in submission and then stood. As he turned to walk out of the dining room, he placed his hand on Arlo's shoulder and gently squeezed it, as a silent gesture of thanks.

When Arlo had waved goodbye, he closed the front door and went to tidy the tea cups away. He saw the piece of paper Mike had scribbled on. It was a drawing of a star and, underneath it, he'd written *My dad rocks!* He stared at the words for a few seconds, and then simply couldn't hold back the tears. His body quivered with the sadness and guilt.

"I'm so sorry for what I've probably made you do, Mike," he whimpered, but hopefully it meant the pressure would be off Arlo and the tweets and messages would finally stop. After all, he had done what 'they' had told him to do, and Mike was probably now going to take Machendrie's offer. He heard footsteps on the floorboards above the dining room and Alessia unexpectedly calling down.

"Was that Michael leaving?" she asked. Arlo wiped his tears and cleared his throat as quietly as he could before calling back up.

"It was. I'll be up soon. Just clearing up the mess."

"Well, don't be too long. We need our sleep."

Arlo wondered whether he really could sleep more easily tonight, or would his manipulation of Mike give him nightmares.

Chapter 52

It was only 11am, and Denton had been in three budget-related meetings, four case meetings, and was about to start reviewing yet another stack of files. Jones thought he looked physically and mentally drained.

"Jonesy," he said, implicitly inviting her to come in.

"Sir, got some updates for you, but thought you might need something to keep you going." She knew he'd had an intense start to the day and, given the frequent shadows under his eyes and evidence that he was either trying to grow a beard or had simply given up shaving, she assumed a fresh coffee and a hot panini from the coffee shop over the road would be welcomed. He nodded his head in gratitude before unwrapping the panini and taking a huge bite.

"Mm," he said in satisfaction, as the brie and bacon filling danced on his taste buds. "What have you got?" he mumbled through his mouthful of panini. "I have to go see the DCI later today, so some good news would be nice."

"Not a lot more to tell you on the Pickett case. Forensics confirmed the paper stapled to the folder was part of a cheque, but we don't know if it was a cheque for him or from him. There's no record of any cheque being banked or drawn against his account, although it would bounce if anyone tried, given nearly all the money in the account was transferred to the cryptocurrency company in Dubai."

"What have you found out about the offshore company?"

"Not much," replied Jones. "We asked the Dubai police to visit the address, but all they found was a temp sat behind a desk, updating her Instagram account on her phone. When they asked who'd hired her, she said a well-spoken Arabic woman approached her and explained that while it was her job, she urgently needed to return home to Riyadh for a while to care for her sick mother. She only planned to be away for a few days and just needed someone to cover the desk, short term. The temp also said that in her time there, no one ever came into the office, the phone on the desk never rang, and the computer didn't even work. She'd been paid cash in advance and would be moving on in a few days, because the real receptionist was due back. When they went back to the office a week later, in the hope of finding the woman who'd hired the temp, they found another temp sat behind the desk who described her offer of employment in exactly the same way the previous one had."

Denton sipped his coffee and was starting to look far more alert and engaged in the conversation.

"Okay, keep digging on the offshore piece. What about the Portsmouth murders; found anything on the employee checks at the care company?" he asked.

"Everyone checks out. Couple of unpaid parking tickets, but that's it."

"What about the suspect's body we found?"

"Prints found at the double murder in Portsmouth match a severed finger found in the dead man's jacket pocket, and DNA tests show the severed finger belonged to the dead man. His name is Paylag Mesropian;

Armenian, but had moved to West Ham a few years ago. Other than that, it's a dead end at the moment, but we're still asking."

"And Huxley?"

"No one's talking beyond what we've already heard about the beating he once had."

"Did anyone question Matthew Berry about it?"

"I did, but he said he hadn't seen Huxley in months, maybe even years, and he denied ever punishing him, although he'd say that whether it was true or not, I suppose."

Denton sighed. It wasn't that the team weren't making progress on the other cases they were dealing with, but there was something particularly vexing about these ones. Maybe it was that they all somehow seemed to be linked back to Matthew Berry, as tenuous as some of the links might be, or maybe he was just fixated on Berry, given the uncertainty about the previous conclusion to the Lottery Ticket Murders.

Jones was unsure whether his sigh was because there was still no breakthrough, or because he had to go back to his stack of files now that he'd finished the panini and coffee. Whatever it was, she knew she'd given him nothing of value to tell the DCI.

Chapter 53

The meeting between Maddox and the bank finally took place in a bright, grandiose room on the second floor of the bank's Venice headquarters. She sat next to Mrs Valorio, whose house was under threat of repossession, and across the table from two of the bank's lawyers.

"Clause 42 is quite specific and conclusive, Signorina Maffioni. I understand that perhaps you have been away from your home for quite a while and, well, it is easy to become unfamiliar with how things might have changed since you last studied any Italian law," one of the patronising lawyers suggested. Maddox looked at him over the rim of her glasses before she removed them, sat upright, and pushed a copy of the contract back across the table.

"Or perhaps you haven't been away enough, Signor Alberti? This contract might have stood up in court in the 1950s, but the rest of the world has moved on considerably. If the bank tries to enforce this repossession, it will not only fail, but the bank will be liable for all costs and a considerable amount in damages, not to mention the unwanted media interest. Do you still wish to proceed?"

Twenty minutes later, Maddox and Mrs Valorio walked out of the bank. The latter had tears of happiness still damp on her cheeks, even though she had stopped crying several minutes earlier. Holding back sniffles of joy, she called home to share the news as Maddox hailed a taxi.

"Bellissima, bellissima," Mrs Valorio kept saying as she stroked Maddox's cheek and hair before re-reading the letter of apology from the bank that included the promise of a compensatory payment of €15,000 for her inconvenience. It was really hush money, but the woman didn't care.

"Devi prendere questi soldi per salvare la mia casa," she said, but Maddox shook her head. She wanted none of the money Mrs Valorio had just offered her, as payment for saving her house. She told the woman that her family deserved all the money, along with the freedom it would facilitate.

By the time the taxi pulled up in the small village square, 40 minutes later, a crowd of 30 or so people had congregated to greet them and celebrate their success. As the car slowed, Maddox saw the crowd, and although she managed a weak smile at an uncontrollably joyous Mrs Valorio, any thought of a quiet return to the family's farmhouse vanished when she saw her family were among the crowd. The car doors were opened for them by the welcoming throng, and Mrs Valorio's tears of joy were renewed as her family and friends threw their arms around her, shouting and cheering. Although she enjoyed the celebration, Mrs Valorio quickly broke the embraces and searched for Maddox.

"Tutti, tutti. Questa donna è la mia eroina. Grazie, Daniella. Tu sei un santo. Hai salvato la mia famiglia," she shouted, making sure everyone knew that Maddox was, in her opinion, a heroine and a saint who had saved her family. The crowd looked over to Maddox and, for a second, it was as if everyone collectively held their breath, before suddenly surging forwards en masse, cheering and eager to now embrace Maddox. The local press was there and requested a photo of Mrs Valorio and Maddox.

"No grazie," Maddox politely protested, thrusting Mrs Valorio and her children forwards. The last thing Maddox wanted was any sort of exposure. Thankfully, the reporter and his photographer were more than happy with a photo of the happy Valorio family surrounded by the throng of supporters. It made a great front page, and the photograph was so much better than the one a local boy had taken a little earlier with his mobile phone, and subsequently uploaded onto his Facebook page.

Chapter 54

Alessia had heard a helicopter buzzing overhead earlier in the day, but assumed it was someone flying in and out of a local event. One of the nearby landowners often had friends and celebrities attend their posh do's, but today's activity was different. As she stood in the kitchen, washing some pots, she looked out over the fields behind their house and saw several police officers walking slowly through waist-high wheat. Alessia wiped her hands dry and was about to pick up the phone to call her neighbours when there was a knock at the door. She wondered if one of the neighbours had decided to come around to see if Alessia knew what was happening, but it was a female police officer.

"Good morning, madam. I'm sorry to bother you, but we have an ongoing operation in the area and are going from door to door to ask a few questions. Do you have a few minutes?"

"Yes, of course. What's going on?"

"We're looking for a missing person." The officer took a leaflet from a binder she was carrying, handing the leaflet to Alessia. It was something that would probably be in most of the shop windows in the village by now, asking people to call the police if they'd seen the young woman featured in a photograph. "This young woman."

"Oh no, how terrible. What do you want to know?"

"We're trying to find out if anyone has seen her in or around the village recently? There were reports of her being in Crossgates a few days ago. She might be lost or a little disoriented, as she's been reported as a previous victim of sexual abuse. We're worried about her mental state, as well as her physical wellbeing, so it's crucial we find her quickly." Alessia thought for a moment, but didn't recall seeing anyone like the person in the photo.

"No, no, I'm afraid not. Oh dear, how terrible, and she looks so young."

"Is there anyone else in the house we can talk to?"

"There's my husband, but he's popped out to do some errands. I can ask him to get in touch when he gets back, if that helps?"

"That would be very useful, thank you. If you can ask him to call this number..." she reached into her jacket pocket again to take out a card "... and ask for PC Brackenberry, that would be..." but a crackle on her comms unit interrupted her. She held up an apologetic hand to indicate she needed to listen to the information, as she unclipped the unit and held it closer to her ear. At first, she nodded but then furrowed her brow and shook her head slightly, pursing her lips in contemplation.

"This is 1-7-0-4. Instruction understood," she said into the comms unit. Slowly, she clipped it back onto her jacket and gave Alessia a soft but sad smile. "We appear to have found the missing person, but any information from your husband would still be very much appreciated," she said, passing the card to Alessia. From her tone and facial expression, Alessia knew it probably wasn't good news.

When Arlo returned, he called out to her: "There's a lot of police wandering around out there. I wonder what's going on?"

"In here," Alessia called from the kitchen. Arlo found her staring out of the window, towards the fields behind their house.

"I said..." he started to say, but without looking around, Alessia replied, "I know. They've set up a tent in one of the fields."

"What?" he said, in surprise and shock as he stood beside her. That's when he saw a dozen police officers and some technicians in the field behind their house. Some of the officers were keeping watch, while others scurried to and from various official vehicles. In the centre of all this activity was a large tent; the sort they'd seen on television, when a crime was being examined. It was a morbid scene, and yet unnervingly addictive to watch it all unfold.

"Doesn't look good," he said, shaking his head and placing his arms around Alessia. "I wonder who it is?"

"Probably the young woman they were looking for. A police officer came by earlier and was asking questions. She left a leaflet; it's on the dining room table," she said, pointing over her shoulder as a tear trickled down her cheek. "Someone's world is about to be turned upside down." Arlo gave her a hug, shook his head in sadness, and then wandered into the dining room to look at the leaflet.

His jaw dropped and his heart pounded when he saw whose face was on it.

Chapter 55

The solicitor walked along the concrete corridor, his heels click-clacking on the floor in time with the footsteps of the two prison officers that accompanied him. After being buzzed through the latest in a series of steel security gates, they eventually stopped outside the door of one of the many private interview rooms.

"Sign here, please," said one of the officers, holding out a clipboard with a disclaimer form on it. It was standard practice in all high-security prisons. The form confirmed that, given the prisoner's right to confidentiality with their legal advisor, officers were not allowed in the room, but they would be stationed outside. Dennis Ruiz was classed as non-violent, so he wouldn't be cuffed or chained, so if things turned unexpectedly violent, they'd protect the solicitor to the best of their ability, but he was signing to confirm he knew they couldn't guarantee his safety. Ruiz, who was already in the room, despised the solicitor, but he was useful as a messenger so he decided to tolerate him for now.

Once they were alone, Ruiz began slowly pacing back and forth and, in a tone that suggested he was already tired of the man's presence, asked, "What is it you want to tell me?"

"A friend heard about an upcoming film he was keen to see. Reviews are in and it's very exciting," his solicitor replied. He knew that the coded message he was delivering today would please Ruiz.

"What is it?" Ruiz enquired as he continued to walk slowly around the small room.

"A local Italian production, starring Monica Bellucci."

Ruiz immediately stopped. He didn't look around at the man but tilted his head slightly to indicate he was now listening intently. The name of the actress, Monica Bellucci, was a codename for Daniella Maddox, given both women were Italian and both were beautiful. He had threatened that if she failed to get his conviction quashed, he would kill her. He knew it was an airtight case against him, but he expected people to perform miracles because he was Dennis Ruiz. When she failed, as he lay on the courtroom floor, restrained after attacking the prosecution barrister, he had hissed to her that she should savour her final breath. Now he had the opportunity to fulfil that promise.

"Are you sure it's her?"

"Positive!" replied his solicitor, hardly able to hide his enthusiasm. "I've checked with a local studio official who told me she's on set right now." That meant that someone in the security services on Ruiz's payroll had confirmed the sighting.

"Where is Monica filming?"

"Last seen in Treviso, four days ago. A local boy took a photograph of some sort of celebration and posted it on Facebook. She was in it. She's using the name Maffioni for her character."

Ruiz sat down on a chair, smiling.

"So, that's where you've been hiding," he mused. She had suddenly disappeared before he was finally sentenced, and despite a £50,000 reward he'd offered, even his extensive criminal network had been unable to find her. It had taken a young boy's photograph to accidentally reveal her whereabouts. His desire to punish her for failing to get him acquitted had never faded.

"Maybe I should send the boy the reward money?" he chuckled, knowing he would never do so, but the idea tickled him.

"Would you like to send Ms Bellucci a gift?" asked the solicitor.

"Oh yes. The biggest one you can find. Get someone local to deliver it, personally."

Chapter 56

So far, everything was going to plan, but Hibberd felt somewhat uneasy. Although it broke their agreed protocol, Hibberd had to check that the plan hadn't been compromised.

"I'm sorry to reach out, but I need to check we're still 'green' for go?" he asked.

"We are. Don't worry; neither Pritchard nor Ruiz know about our plan. I'll deal with any unforeseen distractions," came the reply.

"You say that, but I'm worried that Pritchard is onto us."

"The stakes are incredibly high, and you've done everything we needed you to do, so far. Don't mess this up, we're nearly there and we're talking about billions!" Then the line went dead. It was true, their plan did seem to be progressing as expected, although Hibberd still wanted to double-check. He logged onto his computer and then into the dark web chat rooms under his online persona of 'Zugai Katana'. He sat waiting to see if there were any messages from 'Senyor Fosc', and it didn't take long for someone to initiate contact, but it wasn't who he expected.

A-Jab: If you're looking for SF, he's AWOL.

ZK: Long?

A-Jab: Long enough.

ZK: How?

A-Jab: Hooked by a sock puppet honeypot, so the rumours say.

ZK: Erased?

A-Jab: No one knows. All quiet. Too quiet.

ZK: Thanks.

The dark web rumour was that 'Senyor Fosc' had been caught by the authorities, known as 'sock puppets', in a sting operation.

"So, either Fosc is under arrest or in hiding, but hopefully my relationship with him is as I'd hoped; wholly anonymous," Hibberd muttered to himself, and then he relaxed. Before he had time to log off, though, another persona entered the private chat room.

DoxDoll: Rumour has it you've turned?

ZK: From?

DoxDoll: Gamekeeper turned poacher.

ZK: Tall tale

DoxDoll: No smoke without fire. Watch your back

ZK: Thanks

Hibberd finally logged off and then sat back, mulling over what he had just read. If Pritchard was looking for proof that there was gossip about Hibberd's activities on the dark web, that was it.

Chapter 57

The judge looked dispassionately at the solicitor. "Access denied, Mr Lafferty," he said.

"Your Honour, I politely request you reconsider your initial decision. The police are investigating the horrific murder of Mr Huxley and the apparent suicide of his office manager. If we could just…" the solicitor started to say, trying to convince the judge he had made an error in judgement.

"I have *made* my decision, Mr Lafferty. I'm fully aware of the constraint this puts on the investigation into these dreadful deaths, but if I created a precedent by inexplicably allowing the police the right to search a solicitor's confidential files on an assumption that they *might* find something of value, the legal system would fall into anarchy. Anarchy! Access is *denied*!" he repeated, accentuating the final word. The solicitor looked at Denton and shrugged his shoulders. Denton, who was sitting behind him, nodded, knowing the request was likely to be denied, but he'd hoped the particularly gruesome death of a solicitor might have influenced the judge.

"Where to now for the investigation?" the solicitor asked as they walked down the steps outside the courthouse.

"Difficult to say, but I expect there'll be a few criminals breathing a lot easier knowing we can't access his records."

"Sorry I couldn't be more help," replied the solicitor, holding out his hand. Denton shook the man's hand and thanked him for trying before they headed in separate directions. Although he knew the judge was unlikely to allow the police access, even after the discovery of Huxley's office manager's dead body from an apparent overdose, thanks to an anonymous tip-off call to Crimestoppers, Denton increasingly felt the files would provide them with invaluable insights into the last days of Huxley's life. As he climbed into a taxi, he called Jones.

"How did it go?" she asked.

"As expected, unfortunately. The judge said we need something specific if we want limited access to any of his files. I don't blame him, but it was worth trying."

"Well, I'm still digging, but even our informants don't or won't share anything. I've also put a call out to the taxi companies, in case any of them have any information that might help us piece together his final movements, but that feels like a long shot."

"Nothing wrong with trying. Do we know any more about his appointments that week?"

"When she was alive, I'd asked his office manager if we could have access to Huxley's diary, or at least if she could provide us with some information about it that wouldn't break client confidentiality rules. Her last email said she'd be happy to help, but she wasn't sure how much she was allowed to tell us. She did send me a screenshot of her view of his online diary, but most of it is blank; he apparently didn't trust computers."

"Okay, keep digging, Jonesy. It's still a low priority, but somebody out there must know something more than they're telling us."

Chapter 58

The rickety Fiat could be heard from over half a mile away. With a rattle and a splutter, they turned off the dirt road and slowly trundled to a halt next to a gate. As it did so, the engine chugged one more time and a small cloud of fumes erupted from the exhaust, like a final belch. Emilio Maffioni let out a near-silent exasperated sigh before surreptitiously glancing to his right, where his sister Daniella was sitting: her arms folded and an irate grimace on her face that reminded him she had said taking that car was unwise.

"It's fine," he said, responding to an unstated point. "It will only take a few minutes for the engine to cool, and then I can pour some more water into the radiator." Maddox remained silent, staring straight ahead but breathing quite forcefully through her nostrils. "We can't all afford a new car," he muttered snidely.

"What?" she snapped back, turning her head to glare at him. "I told you we should ask the farmer to bring the produce from the market, but no... No, you wanted to take this... this pile of rust all the way to Cison di Valmarino via the 'scenic' route." She huffed and turned to stare out of the window, muttering "Idiota." Emilio was about to respond, but he could hear his mother's words in his head:

Take your sister with you. Make the problem that only you seem to have, go away.

He yanked the door handle to open the door, but then exhaled in defeat and closed his eyes as the handle came off in his hand. She looked over to see what the hell he was playing at, but her anger quickly dissolved. She fought hard to contain her laughter but failed, with a short snigger escaping her lips. He glared at her, irritated that she found it so funny, and then tossed the handle onto the back seat and wound the window down, so he could reach out to use the external handle. Maddox found this even funnier, but this time she managed to suppress any audible laughter. As he climbed out of the car, she checked her phone, but there was no signal. As Emilio headed to the rear of the car, Maddox gently shook her head and decided enough was enough. She opened her door and climbed out.

"Why do you hate me?" she demanded. He didn't reply as he opened the boot, so he could inspect the engine. "Damn it, Emilio. I've done nothing wrong, but you treat me like this?"

"Just leave it," he answered, trying to appear wholly focused on the engine.

"No," Maddox snarled. "I've kept this family's head above water for years, and yet you're so cold, so angry. Why?" Emilio gritted his teeth: he could restrain himself no more.

"*What about Papa!*" he yelled, standing and glaring at her. His fists were clenched in anger, although he had no intention of striking her.

"What?" she exclaimed in incredulity.

"Where were you when Papa was dying of cancer? When Paulo nearly died from a broken heart? When Mamma needed you most? You think your money buys you the right to feel part of this family, part of the sacrifice and pain we have been through without you? And yet, when you turn up unannounced and uninvited, you expect to be treated like our saviour?"

Maddox was stunned. She had never heard him so angry, so passionate, and his words cut through her. She was suddenly overwhelmed by the realisation that perhaps he was right. Her life was in England, as was her all-consuming career. That had been her life. Yes, she had sent money because her mother had written asking for help, as their father was no longer able to work. She thought that sending them a few thousand euros every month would ease their burden, while she was wholly consumed by a case that had the potential to elevate her within the company. She could have handed the case to a colleague and flown out immediately, but she assumed she had time; that her father had time. When her mother called her to tell her that her father had died, she could hear the tremble in her mother's proud voice. She also heard her brothers' angry voices and tears in the background. Maddox was overcome with guilt. She'd not saved her family; she had let her family down when they perhaps needed her most: when she should have needed them the most, too. Although she had continued to send money to her mother every month, today was the first time in her life she admitted to herself that it was probably as much about relieving her guilt as it was about helping them cope.

"You're right," she finally whispered.

"*What?*" asked a still angry Emilio.

"I said, you're right," she repeated as her tear-filled eyes looked up at her brother. "I'm sorry, Emilio. I... I... I acted selfishly and... and I should have been here to help. I'm so, so sorry." She began to weep. Emilio was caught off guard. He had expected her to argue back, to tell him he was lucky she had put food on their table, which was true; she had. Without her money, the family would probably have lost their home, and who knows what would have happened to them after that. His anger dissipated as quickly as it had exploded. He took a few faltering steps forward and held out his arms, pulling her into them. Once his arms enveloped her, she allowed all the emotion and guilt to pour out. The more she cried, the tighter he held her.

After several minutes, her sobbing subsided, and he whispered to her, "You might not have been here for the family, but you did something I could never do. You provided for us all. Without you, our survival would have been left to me and... and I would have failed my mother and my brother."

Maddox gently broke the embrace and looked up, blinking the tears away. She knew this was painful for her oldest brother to admit. After all, in the Italian countryside at least, men were still expected to be the providers. She smiled softly, kissing him on both cheeks, and Emilio was grateful his sister didn't make more of his guilt and failure.

"Perhaps we make a better team than we knew," she suggested. He smiled at her and gently nodded.

"Maybe this team needs to work together now, to get this pile of rust back on the road?" he said. She laughed lightly, grateful that the tension between them was finally gone.

Ten minutes and several profanities later, they slammed the boot of the car closed. The engine showed no signs of life, and the sun was at its peak. Sweat sparkled on their skin, and they flopped onto the grass, lying down in a shady spot.

"We need help," Maddox said as she pulled her mobile phone from her pocket again. She held it in the air to see if she had any signal, but there was none. She sat upright, slowly waving it around, but there was still no sign of service.

"You won't get anything sat there. The hills mask the signal, but there's a tiny gap over there, looking over to the west." He pointed to a rocky mound. "Perhaps you can get something there?" Maddox looked over to where he was pointing. It was only 10 or 15 feet on the other side of the car, so she wearily stood and, phone still held in the air, wandered over to the rocky mound. No sooner had two bars appeared than a text arrived.

"Got a signal," she shouted over to a prostrate Emilio, who was still enjoying the shade and a cooling breeze that now swept across the fields.

"Okay, coming," he grunted as he got up. Maddox opened the text: it was her other brother, Paulo.

Affrettati a casa. Abbiamo una sorpresa per te.

"What is it?" Emilio enquired.

"A text from Paulo. He wants us to hurry home. Apparently, there's a surprise for me." She turned to look at him. "Did you know about this?" Emilio smiled wryly. Paulo had said he wanted to surprise their sister, and Emilio had begrudgingly agreed to get her out of the house while preparations were underway. He was now glad that he had, because it had led to at least the start of healing the rift between them.

"Come on, get in."

Maddox was confused. She pointed at the car and was going to ask about the overheated engine, but he winked at her, which was when she realised that he'd tricked her.

"The engine is fine. Just a little something I learned to do, so I didn't have to drive Mamma to church every Sunday in summer," he chuckled as he rattled the keys, indicating it was time to go.

"Wait, just let me tell them we're on our way," she said, walking slowly as she typed and then pressed send. "Okay, let's go." Maddox smiled, given the cheeky trick her eldest brother had played as well as grateful he had finally explained why he was so angry with her. She also felt excited as she tried to imagine what sort of surprise could be waiting for her.

Back at their family farmhouse in Treviso, Paulo stared at the message on the screen that confirmed they were heading home, before slowly handing the phone back to his captor. The woman smiled as she checked the text Maddox had sent, before waving her gun to indicate Paulo should move.

"Good. Go sit down next to your mother," she instructed. "And now we wait."

Chapter 59

"Well?" asked Arlo apprehensively as soon as Mike stepped into the conservatory. He and Alessia had driven to Tania and Mike's house, eager to hear the news following the latest board meeting. Mike's expression was solemn, but he couldn't maintain the façade for long. A broad, beaming smile broke out.

"Deal agreed, contract signed, and the first batch of software arrives in the next couple of days!"

After a split-second of collective silence, all four of them exploded into cheers and hugs. Arlo was especially happy as, several days ago, when Mike was leaning towards not accepting the deal, he had stayed up into the early hours, discussing the finer details and ultimately convincing his son to agree to it. 'They' had demanded he do everything to ensure the deal went ahead, so 'they' should now be happy that Arlo had fulfilled his commitment and had promised to stop tweeting and messaging him if he was successful. Tania gave Mike a kiss and then raced into the kitchen, where she had chilled champagne on ice. She, too, was relieved as it meant the immense pressure she had been under recently also eased.

"*Cheers!*" shouted Alessia, once the champagne was poured and glasses clinked in celebration.

"What happens now?" Tania asked, once everyone had taken a good swig and the exuberance had subsided a little.

"Yann has applied for ISO accreditation. We're getting an initial assessment on the production and QA process, as well as on our documentation. We'll also check that the software from the new supplier works on our new chip design. There's no point in us ramping up production volumes of the new chip and sending thousands to the assembly company if they just send them back because the software hasn't loaded properly."

"Why wouldn't it work?" Alessia asked, confused. "Isn't that the software company's problem?"

"Not if our new design is the issue. That then becomes my problem, but if the initial accreditation visit goes well, which Yann thinks it should, we can start full-scale production and despatching to the assembler, Anakart, for them to include our chips in whatever devices they've agreed to supply."

Arlo suddenly felt a huge wave of relief. The deal was signed, and Mike felt the ISO accreditation visit should be positive. Could it all really be over?

"Back in a minute," he said. "Just need to use the little boy's room." No one said anything as they were enthralled by Mike's tales of his success. As Arlo walked through to the toilet, he pulled his mobile phone from his pocket. He'd brought it with him in the hope that everything had gone well and his nightmare would be over. As he closed and locked the door, he sent them a message:

Deal signed, so now please leave me and my family alone. I don't ever want to hear from you again

He waited a few minutes to see if there was a response, but when nothing arrived, he deleted his

Twitter app, breathed a huge sigh of relief, and then flushed the unused toilet. He suddenly felt freer than he had in months. When he walked back into the house, Tania was putting her phone away.

"I sent Uncle Yann a thank-you message, and he's just replied saying he hopes we're all having fun, celebrating," she said, smiling broadly. "Think I'll get some water before I drown in champagne, though," she giggled, asking if anyone else wanted some. Mike, Alessia, and Arlo all shook their heads, but thanked her. When she got to the kitchen and reached for a glass, she heard footsteps. It was Arlo.

"Actually, I think I will have some. I drank that last glass of champagne a little quickly, but don't worry, dear, I'll get it myself," he said, smiling broadly. Tania only had one glass, so he walked towards the cupboard to get himself one.

Tania half-turned towards him, and in a light tone full of relief, asked, "Do you think the pressure is off, now the contract has been signed?"

"Oh, I hope so. I'm so happy he had you to lean on," Arlo replied. "Thank you. Without your idea of talking to your uncle, I'm not sure there would have been such a happy ending."

"I... I didn't mean that. I meant, do you feel the pressure is off you, now?" she explained, clarifying her question.

"Well, I still think the real pressure is on Mike, especially being such a young and inexperienced CEO with such a lot of responsibility," he replied as he pulled a glass from the shelf. "But it's so lovely of you to recognise that his mother and I have felt under some pressure too. I have to admit..." which is when Tania turned to face him.

"Oh, Arlo, you sweet, confused old man," she said in a ridiculing tone, as she sneered at him. Arlo's smile slowly faded. He looked at her quizzically as he walked over to the sink to fill his glass. He felt a little offended at being referred to as old and confused.

"I'm... I'm not sure what you mean?" he said, trying to hide his irritation as he filled the glass with water.

As he was about to take a sip, Tania whispered, "Just because Jane's dead, don't think we've finished with you. Keep your focus. You'd be mad not to, because I'll be the one watching you from now on."

The sound of a glass shattering on the kitchen's stone floor was heard in the conservatory. Mike and Alessia snapped their heads around.

"Is everything alright in there?" Alessia called out.

Chapter 60

Emilio was still smiling as the Fiat pulled up outside the farmhouse. Maddox got out of the car and marched around to his side, opening his door.

"Thought you might need a hand opening your door," she said as she glanced at the door handle that he'd accidentally pulled off and then thrown onto the back seat. She winked, and he smirked back, but as he opened the back door of the house, his smile fell away instantly.

"What?" he exclaimed as his gaze fell upon their mother, bound and gagged. Maddox also stopped abruptly.

"*Mamma?*" she squealed in shock, before running over to her.

"Welcome back," said a woman's voice from behind the door. She slammed it shut and, using the semi-automatic pistol she held in her hand, gestured that Emilio and Maddox should stand still with their hands in the air. Maddox, who had been kneeling by her mother, stood up, quivering with fear. Emilio stood perfectly still to their right, next to one of the tall cupboards. The woman turned to Paulo and smiled.

"Thank you."

"This isn't what we agreed," Paulo whimpered. Maddox looked at the woman and then at her brother. What did she mean? What did he mean?

"Paulo?" questioned Maddox. "What's happening?"

"It wasn't supposed to be like this," he mumbled, before turning to the woman. "You said you were a reporter and wanted to talk to my sister, to get her side of the Ruiz story." He then looked at Maddox, apologetically, adding, "She just said she wanted to talk to you, that was all."

"Be quiet. You'll get your €50,000," the woman said dismissively.

"What €50,000?" asked Maddox.

The woman raised an eyebrow and smirked. "Your brother offered to help me meet you for an exclusive interview, in exchange for €50,000. Actually, an old friend of yours wanted to send you a present," the woman taunted.

"Paulo, is this true?" Even though she asked him the question, she instinctively knew it was. He nodded his head. Maddox then turned to the woman. "Who wanted to send me a message?" she asked warily.

"Mr Ruiz."

Maddox suddenly felt as if her gut had been ripped out. She remembered the conversation she had had with Paulo a few days ago, where he said he had plans to make his own way in life.

"You said you were tired of being the fourth member of the family. Tired of feeling stuck in this village, on this farm, with no prospects. You said you wanted to travel, and to become your own man," she recalled out loud.

"I thought this money would help me do that, but I promise, Daniella, I never thought it would be this," he explained.

"Mr Ruiz has already transferred the finder's fee into a crypto account he set up," the woman added, because

Paulo could no longer talk to nor look his sister in the face. "And Ruiz sends his regards, as well as a message; something about savouring your final breath?" the woman taunted.

Maddox no longer had the time or the energy to be angry with her naive younger brother. All she could do was look around at her mother and Emilio, sadness and regret in her eyes.

"Let them go. They have nothing to do with this," she requested, resigned to her own fate.

"Sorry, but there must be no loose ends," the woman replied as she raised the gun towards her.

"*No,*" shouted Paulo as he lunged at the woman, but he was too slow. She swayed to avoid his outstretched hands, swinging the barrel of the pistol in an upward arc and striking him across the face. He fell to the floor, instantly tasting blood in his mouth.

"*Enough,*" she said as she pointed the gun at him.

"You never said you were going to harm my family," wept Paulo, but the woman simply sneered as she readied herself to squeeze the trigger. The sound of a shotgun barrel being clicked shut jolted her from her smug sneer. She turned to see Emilio pointing it at her. While she, Paulo, and Maddox had been engrossed in their discussion, he had retrieved it from the tall cupboard next to him. He fired the buckshot it was pre-loaded with. The woman instinctively moved to her left just as the pellets tore through a wooden beam next to her, but as she lost her balance, Paulo threw himself onto her, landing an elbow on her cheekbone. The woman cried in agony, and the pistol fell from her hand, skimming across the stone flooring. Emilio lunged back towards the cupboard where he'd retrieved the shotgun from, looking for more buckshot, as Paulo and the woman rolled on the floor, struggling to gain control of their opponent. She managed to pin him to the floor with her knees before pulling a knife from inside her boot and sinking it into his chest. He arched his back as the knife punctured his lung, and he began gasping for air. She raised the knife again, this time plunging it into his neck, but a shot reverberated around the room as she raised the blade a third time. Her throat was ripped open, and most of her face was shredded by buckshot. She fell backwards, choking on her own blood as it pumped unfettered from the wounds. Maddox ran over and retrieved the pistol. Her whole body was shaking with anger and fear. There was muffled crying from behind her, and Emilio ran to untie their mother. Maddox stared at Paulo before flinging the weapon to one side and running over to him, dropping onto her knees in the gathering pool of blood. He stared in her direction, but his eyes couldn't focus, and his voice was a raspy whisper. She took his hand in hers, but she couldn't speak: what was there to say? He had led her into a trap, and yet she didn't hate him for it. He coughed and choked a little as he tried to talk, but she rested one hand on his forehead and gently shushed him.

"Help is coming, Paulo. Please don't go," she whispered, but she knew her words were hopelessly optimistic. He had lost too much blood. Their mother raced over to his side. She hugged herself as she rocked back and forth. She, too, was angry at his betrayal, but he was still her baby, her youngest child, and she knew he was about to die. As Emilio joined them, Paulo coughed one final time and was then still.

"*Noooo,*" shrieked Eugenia, wailing and screaming in both anger and sorrow. Emilio held her in his arms as they watched their sister gently move her hand from Paulo's forehead down to his eyes, closing the lids. She said a silent prayer, but it wasn't for his soul.

I swear on Almighty God that Dennis Ruiz will pay for this. There is no room in my heart for mercy or forgiveness; only for revenge for my beloved family.

Chapter 61

The police were successfully confused by The Broker's plan to distract them with the unusual murder of Adrian Huxley, and by framing members of a rival Armenian gang for the messy lottery ticket murder scenes of Katie Cross and Evelyn Buchannan, and Huxley's office manager. All three victims had actually been murdered by one of The Broker's trusted associates, but only after the gang member had been killed and his severed finger had been used to make prints at the crime scenes. Cellier had made both calls to Crimestoppers, and The Broker ensured the lottery tickets found at the two scenes were different to the one found at Dr Pickett's house; confusing the police even more.

His men had tortured Huxley's office manager to try to get her to share the combination for the safe in his office, but even if she had known it, they were instructed to kill her anyway, so it really didn't matter; she was a loose end either way. They hadn't been able to find Huxley's car, but luck finally appeared to be Denton's side.

"How did we find it?" he asked, as he and Jones drove to the forensics garage.

"A legal temp, hired to assess and dispose of Huxley's case files, found a final demand letter in his mailbox. It was from one of those private car park companies, explaining that if he didn't collect it and pay the fine in the next 48 hours, they were legally entitled to sell the car. She passed it to her manager, who thought we might want to check it in case it was a crime scene."

"Where was it found?"

"According to their records, it was originally at a car park on Brick Lane. After it had been reported as officially left unattended, they put it onto a low-loader and took it to their secure compound. That's where we retrieved it from."

"I don't suppose they treated it carefully, like a crime scene?" Denton said dejectedly, knowing how most of the car parks operate their tow and stow services.

"It's not great, but it's not as bad as it could be. Because Huxley drove one of those electric Jaguars, they handled it with care, given its resale value is probably north of £30,000. I dare say, if it had been a ten-year-old Micra, things would have been different."

"Forensics say anything about what they'd found?"

"There were no blood stains or bodily fluids in the car, and no obvious signs of a struggle, but they found a briefcase hidden in a custom compartment in the boot. They've already checked it for trace, and there's only Huxley's prints on it, but they thought we might want to look at the contents."

Ten minutes later, they pulled into the forensics compound and, on entering the building, suited up to avoid further contaminating the evidence.

"Afternoon, detective," said the lead analyst.

"What have we got?" Denton asked.

"A few binders, an A5-size diary, the usual stationery you'd find in a lot of briefcases, and a bottle of prescribed NSAIDs."

"NSAIDs?"

"Nonsteroidal anti-inflammatory drugs, used primarily to treat arthritis. Quite a sizeable dose, too."

Denton nodded, but it hadn't piqued his interest, whereas the binders and diary did.

"Can we take a look inside them?" he queried. The lead analyst looked over to one of the lab technicians, who nodded back.

"We've checked the contents and taken copies, so feel free."

Over the next 15 minutes, Jones and Denton pored over the contents of the folders, which held little of significance, and even if they related to a crime other than the death of Huxley, they would be classed as inadmissible under the client confidentiality rules. While he continued to look through the final folder, Jones picked up the diary and opened it at a place that had a piece of folded paper inside. As she scanned the piece of paper and then the entries on the day-to-a-page diary itself, she smiled.

"Sir," she said, looking to grab Denton's attention from the folder he was looking at.

"What have you got?" he asked. She held the diary open and pointed to an entry.

"Brick Lane isn't far from there," stated Denton, mildly curious about the entry.

"And then there's this," she said, holding out the now-unfolded piece of paper.

"Looks like a photocopy of some handwritten notes."

"Yeah, and look at the entry highlighted at the bottom."

Denton pulled his glasses from his pocket. He hated wearing them in public, but he had little choice if he wanted to read the faint writing. It wasn't a very good photocopy, but when he read the highlighted sentence, he looked up at Jones as a broad smile appeared on his face.

"Get someone to check the CCTV coverage for the whole area, two hours either side of that time on that day," he said, pointing to the diary entry. "Let's see if we can trace his steps from Brick Lane. It might just give me enough to go to the DCI with."

Chapter 62

"I'm pleased to say that everything seems to be in order," said Steve Morris, the lead assessor for the ISO accreditation visit at Kintaro, as he ticked off everything on his iPad. Penny Büggs and Bob Hall smiled at each other, but while they were relieved that the external audit had initially approved all the production controls and the original test results for the chips, the man's demeanour seemed unusual. He was sweating profusely, even in their air-conditioned offices, and had avoided direct eye contact for most of the day.

"Are you feeling alright?" asked Büggs.

"Yes, I'm fine," he said hurriedly. "Just… just a bit of a fever or maybe I had a bad clam for lunch, yesterday," and he chuckled unconvincingly. "Perhaps some fresh air will help," he said, wiping his brow with a handkerchief and then patting his pockets, as if searching for some pills.

"I can get you a paracetamol from our first aid box, if you like?" Hall offered. "You're not allergic to them, are you?"

"No, I don't think so."

"Nevertheless, I'll need you to sign a waiver, just in case," Hall said apologetically. The man nodded his agreement before Hall went to look for some, and Büggs escorted him through the offices to a side door that led to their secure car park. As she re-entered the building, she bumped into Hall.

"There's something weird going on," he said.

"I know what you mean," replied Büggs. "Do you think whatever he's got is contagious?"

"I don't mean that. Something about his overall behaviour just feels... odd." He paused to reflect on the situation, but she interrupted his thoughts.

"Get that tablet and water to him, and we'll see how he is in a few minutes. Maybe he did eat a bad clam?" and she chuckled at her own joke. As she headed back to the office, Hall stepped outside and found the assessor had vomited. The man was shaking slightly and was breathing deeply.

"Are you sure you're alright?" Hall asked, more than a little concerned.

"What? Yes, yes, I'm fine, thank you. Are those for me?" he replied, looking at the water and tablet.

"Yes, they are. Here, take this. Hopefully, it will help," said Hall sympathetically. He put the glass of water on a windowsill, then reached forward, cupping the man's trembling hand with his own to steady it, as he placed the tablet in his palm. Rather than lifting his finger, though, Hall kept it pressed firmly on top of the tablet. Morris looked up, confused. Hall was glaring at him.

"You're close to fucking this up. Stay calm, confirm the accreditation, and you'll be back with your family tonight, but mess this up and you'll be a grieving widower before the end of the day. You were warned when our men came to visit you, weren't you! You said yes to helping us, so do your job." Morris's eyes grew wide as he recalled how the two thugs had burst into their home and pummelled him into submission. He tried to withdraw his hand from Hall's, but it was held firmly.

"Understand?" Hall repeated. Morris nodded frantically.

"Now, take your tablet and pull yourself together. You've got five minutes, then I'll be back to take you to your car," said Hall, releasing the man's still trembling hand. Hall turned and headed back to the security door. He looked at Morris once more and hissed, "Five minutes... Or do we need our men to revisit you and your family?" before he softened his facial expression and returned to the façade of being the friendly, introverted Bob Hall.

Chapter 63

The letterbox rattled as the postman pushed through several items. As usual, most of them were leaflets or junk mail, but one envelope was addressed to Alessia. It had a card back and a sticker with *Photo: please do not bend* printed on it.

"Nothing for you today," muttered Alessia as she dropped the junk in the bin. Arlo nodded absent-mindedly as he popped some freshly-made toast out of the machine, buttered it, and placed it on a plate. She was sitting on the settee when he carried their toast and morning tea into the lounge.

"Something for you?" he asked as he bent to place the tray on the coffee table.

"Yes. Don't know what it is, though. Maybe Mike and Tania sent it?" she replied innocently. As she turned the envelope over, a name was printed on the back. "Hmm, wonder who Jane is?" The contents of the tray clattered as Arlo accidentally dropped it the last few millimetres.

"Careful," scowled Alessia.

"Sorry... slipped. Must... must have some butter on my... my fingers," he replied, pretending to look at his hand, although he was wholly consumed by anxiety. He had been on tenterhooks ever since Tania had revealed she was part of the twisted scheme, and that he should expect another surprise.

As Alessia tore the tab on the envelope to open it, he tried to appear uninterested.

"So?" he eventually asked after she pulled a photograph out and stared at it, quizzically.

"I'm... er... I'm not sure." She handed it to Arlo. His muscles tensed as he recognised it as one of the photographs of him and Jane, taken at the coffee shop. It was one of the photos he had received on his phone just moments after meeting her, although this one thankfully had him entirely blurred out, so it was impossible to make out any of his facial features or clothing. He relaxed a little and said a silent prayer of thanks. He handed it back to Alessia, who noticed his hand was shaking a little.

"Are you alright?" she checked, concern etched on her face.

"Yes, I'm fine. Why?"

"Your hand is shaking." She took it in hers and stared at his face, checking for any signs of his dizziness returning. He patted her hand and withdrew his.

"I'm fine, Mrs Worry-Pants. You were up a little later than usual this morning: guess I'm just hungry." Arlo smiled assuringly as he took a bite out of a slice of toast. Alessia accepted the rationale and leant forwards to pour the tea, but as she glanced at the photograph again, she put the teapot back down. Arlo paused mid-chew. Should he ask her what the problem is, or should he act uninterested? She picked the photo up and narrowed her eyes as she peered at some of the detail.

"Everything alright?" Arlo eventually asked when he couldn't maintain the silent façade any longer.

"I'm... I'm not sure," and she peered a little closer at something on the photo. "Is that... it looks like that coffee shop you took me to once, in Crossgates."

"Is it? Let me look," he replied, playing along. He found his reading glasses and peered at the photo intently. "Oh yes, it might be. Hmm." Arlo tried to pass it back to Alessia, but she shook her head and indicated he could put it back down on the table. As she picked the teapot up for a second time, she paused, and the teapot was placed back on the tray yet again. Arlo closed his eyes, hoping that she hadn't seen what he had seen: a faint but possibly recognisable reflection of his profile in the window on the photo.

"I think I recognise someone in that photo," Alessia speculated.

"R-really?" Arlo's anxiety was becoming audible as well as visible.

"Yes... Yes, I think that's the young woman they found in the field behind the house a few days ago," she said as she stood.

"Where are you going?" he asked, but she didn't reply as she rose from the chair and walked into the kitchen. She was too lost in her thoughts. Arlo sat, unsure as to whether he should follow her or stay where he was. If he followed her, he must appear intrigued about her observation, but not alarmed. He stood, then started to sit back down, and then stood again, before hesitantly wandering into the kitchen after her. Alessia was looking at a crumpled newspaper she had taken out of the recycling bin and laid out on the breakfast bar. Her gaze flitted from the photo to an article in the paper. She noticed Arlo stood a few feet away.

"It is her," she announced, indicating that Arlo should come and look, too. As he did so, she turned and marched towards the hallway. He glanced at the photograph of the woman in the newspaper, which was the same photo in the leaflet the policewoman had left with Alessia a few days ago, when the protesters had been near their house.

"What are you doing now?" he called after her.

"Do you know where we put the card that police officer gave us? The one who came around asking if we'd seen anyone acting suspiciously or disoriented. They need to know about this. Whoever she's with in that photo might have been the last person to see her alive."

As his wife looked for the card, Arlo began to feel physically sick. An overwhelming feeling of panic began rising from his gut, and it took all his mental strength to stop himself from screaming.

Chapter 64

The Broker studied the spreadsheet and then looked up at Kendrick.

"Four of the pilot group have now died. That wasn't in your original forecast, was it?" he said.

"It's a glitch, that's all: an anomaly. If you look at how well the four of them were performing before they died, take Stephen Attwell, for example. We had access to his personal information and initially used it to successfully apply for £50,000 in credit and loans. We then got another £13,000 of credit using his data and found out he'd sold his house, so we raided his bank account, sending £180,000 to one of our shell companies. With just one of our chips, we're over two hundred grand richer and, if he hadn't died, we'd still be slicing and dicing the data or selling it to someone else!" Kendrick sat back triumphantly. Although the figures he had just quoted about Attwell were true, the other three deceased victims had not been a success, but if he admitted that, he could forget getting the £64m he so desperately needed. He was already close to running out of money because he'd used most of his available assets as seed money until he could get the deal with Kintaro signed.

"Show me the balance in the BOrg bank account," requested The Broker. He appeared calm, but Kendrick noticed his nostrils were slightly flared.

"No," Kendrick replied, politely but assertively. He needed to present an air of authority, but knew there was a very fine line between what this man would see as confidence and what he might perceive as arrogance. The two stared at each other for several seconds before The Broker opened the drawer in his desk and pulled out a revolver. He placed it on the desk in front of him.

"Show me the balance," he repeated.

"I can't and I won't," replied Kendrick in a slightly softer tone. "You have to understand, that money belongs to BOrg and remains in their account, along with other revenue. Until you transfer the initial investment of £64m, their detailed finances are none of your business."

The Broker stroked his chin before gently resting his hand on the revolver. With his head bowed in thought, he started to twirl the gun slowly, around and around, until it eventually came to a stop, facing Kendrick.

"Do you know who I am? What I do?" he asked in a low growl. He wanted to hear if Kendrick's voice cracked a little when he replied.

"I do," Kendrick said, his voice equally low but controlled.

"Do you know how much the world would miss you if I put a bullet through your skull right now?"

Kendrick paused before responding with, "A lot less than how much you'd miss the £20bn you'd be throwing away." It was such a clever response that it momentarily threw The Broker, who was then grateful that there was a gentle knock on his door. He waited a couple of seconds as he stared at Kendrick, before taking his hand off the gun and sitting back.

"Yes?" he called out. The door opened slowly, and one of his thugs put his head around the door. He saw the revolver on the desk, so he knew something serious had happened.

"Sorry to interrupt you, boss, but I've got some news you might want to know."

The Broker narrowed his eyes. The thug knew Kendrick was in the office and had clearly seen the revolver on the desk, so it must be something important if he still wanted to talk. As he signalled for the man to walk into the office, he also looked at Kendrick.

"Leave the spreadsheet, and we'll continue this discussion tomorrow."

"I'm afraid I won't be here, tomorrow. I'm flying to Bucharest to finalise things with Apostu immediately after this, which we both know needs to happen if we want to stick to the plan. I'll be there for a week," replied Kendrick. The thug's eyes grew wide. Had this man just said 'no' to The Broker? He glanced down at his boss, who was frowning, then at the gun on the desk, and then back up at Kendrick.

"A week on Thursday, then?" suggested The Broker. Kendrick nodded in agreement.

"And if you can have your deposit ready by then, otherwise we'll lose the deal I've struck with the company. I can only hold out so long by telling them I'm just waiting for some capital to be repaid," he said, before walking out of the office and closing the door behind him. The Broker took a few deep, calming breaths before turning to the thug.

"What is it?" he said, turning to the thug.

"That gentleman who was just in here," queried Stan.

"What about him?"

"We wanted to wait until he'd gone to tell you, but we've had a call from one of our contacts in the security services. Some girl photographed him coming out of a coffee shop in Bucharest a week ago, with Simion Apostu. She posted it on Facebook, along with a bunch of other photographs from the city. The fact he was in that photo was probably accidental, but she's since been found at the bottom of a river with her neck broken. It's only a matter of time before the authorities might link the two things." The Broker sat back, reflecting on the news. Was Kendrick now a liability, rather than an asset? Even though Kendrick's failing pilot was a concern, the idea of just letting his multi-billion-pound idea fall into someone else's hands felt wrong.

"Maybe you're more of a risk than I'd appreciated, Mr Kendrick," he mused, as a smile spread across his face. He had an idea. He had a copy of the business case and perhaps, just perhaps, Kendrick's secret partner was still willing to be part of it. If he could establish a link into BOrg and ensure the three companies he was supposed to invest in kept operating, perhaps Kendrick wasn't necessary anymore?

"Get me Tom and Jerry," he finally said. Two minutes later, Tom and Jerry knocked on the door.

"Yes, boss?"

"Who do we know in Bucharest? I need someone to take out the trash."

Chapter 65

Today's update with the parliamentary minister had gone as expected. While he was keen to ask questions of Pritchard and had plenty of praise for his team, there wasn't even a cursory glance at Hibberd, let alone any reference to his contribution to the prosecution of Ruiz.

Once the meeting was over, the two friends strode across Lambeth Bridge, in total silence, Pritchard kept glancing at Hibberd to see if there was any softening of his expression or relaxing of his posture, but Hibberd kept staring straight ahead. Eventually, the speed Hibberd was walking at meant Pritchard started to drop back a little, as he drew some deep breaths.

"Hey," he called out, trying to catch Hibberd's attention, but when he didn't respond, Pritchard jogged a few steps and put his hand on his shoulder. He knew Hibberd was furious, and rightly so, but ignoring his requests to slow down wasn't making the situation any better. Hibberd stopped, put his hands into his overcoat pockets and glanced up, but not really wanting to engage in conversation or eye contact.

"Hey, we're not all ninja warriors, you know." Hibberd still didn't respond, but Pritchard had an idea. Ahead on the left, he could see the Riverside Café.

"Why don't we grab a coffee at the café and talk about what happened," he offered. Hibberd looked up at him with an expression of total incredulity. Either Pritchard was nuts, or he must think Hibberd was.

"No, why should we? We both knew how he was going to be, and yet I still went. I stayed quiet in the meeting, but right now I'm bloody furious," Hibberd snapped. "And seriously, you now want to add caffeine to the equation?"

"I... I just thought..."

"No, absolutely not. Enjoy your coffee," Hibberd said, before turning on his heels and striding away. Pritchard held his arms out in mock surrender.

"They do de-caff, you know," he called out, but Hibberd was already weaving his way through the mass of office workers and tourists, on their way to lunch or to take photographs of the Houses of Parliament. He bumped into a few as he impatiently made his way to the end of the bridge, en route to his next appointment. He offered them no apologies, even though a few had offered theirs to him. As he continued to reflect on the meeting, he shook his head and admitted to himself that it wasn't Pritchard's fault, but he had acted as if it was. He'd call him later to apologise.

As he entered a building for his next meeting, a small group of European tourists reached the Westminster side of the bridge, and most began to take photographs. One of them meandered a few metres away from the main group and casually gazed around. A woman wearing a baseball cap, sunglasses, and with her coat collar turned up, drifted towards him, also apparently casually looking around. As she reached him, she slowed, but they made no attempt to acknowledge each other, acting as if they were strangers who were coincidentally at the same place at the same time.

"The package was delivered," the man said in a low, quiet voice. The woman didn't respond or react; she just turned around and crossed the road. Now all she had to do was wait.

Chapter 66

Now that the Kintaro board had agreed to the investment deal and its targets, production of the new chip had finally started, and the ISO assessment was a success. It felt as if a huge weight was lifted from Mike's shoulders. The board had agreed to Mike becoming the permanent CEO and to prepare the legal documentation to rename the company 'TripplaM Limited'. Even the somewhat reluctant Bob Hall had agreed to the deal.

"This is to you," said Machendrie, raising his glass in acknowledgement. "Without your commitment and vision, this would never have been possible."

"And without your money, my commitment and vision would have sunk without trace, so thank you," replied Mike, raising his glass to 'chink' with Machendrie's.

"Money is surprisingly easy to get, Mike, if you have the right connections. Never forget that."

As the men sipped their drinks, Machendrie received a text. It was from his secretive partner:

Great news and a great day, Robert (or should I say, Yann). Bet you can't wait to tell The Broker.

He smiled. The plan had been primarily his idea, his hard work, and ultimately his reward for everything he'd sacrificed, but he had to admit that the third man in the scheme had delivered some key objectives, including getting Dennis Ruiz out of the picture.

"Good news?" asked Mike, seeing his smile.

"Oh, just confirmation that a business I'm investing in seems to be signed and sealed," he lied.

"It must be fantastic being involved in the future of so many organisations. How do you juggle it all?"

"Oh, it's about being involved in the right level of detail, otherwise you could easily be sw..." but his comment was interrupted by Mike's phone buzzing, as several texts arrived at once.

"Sorry, intermittent coverage in here," Mike said, gesturing he'd like to check them. Machendrie smiled and nodded. Most were from grateful employees, but one was from a withheld number:

I'm sorry for what I've made you do.

Mike stared quizzically at the message.

"Everything okay?" checked Machendrie.

"Er, yes. I... I think someone's sent a text to the wrong number: something about... Well, I don't really know what it's about to be honest," Mike admitted with a dismissive shake of his head, before changing the subject. "I promised to give Tania and my parents an update about how today is going, so if you'll excuse me, I'll go make a couple of calls," he said.

"Please pass on my regards to your parents, and say hi to my niece," Machendrie replied, happy to be left alone to celebrate his success. On leaving the board room, Mike headed towards his office, calling Tania on the way there.

"Hey, it's me. Have you just sent me a text?"

"A text? No, why?" she replied.

"I got a text from a number I don't recognise, but I know you said you were looking at moving network providers, so thought maybe you'd got a new phone."

"No. That's strange. What did it say?" she asked, feeling a little apprehensive.

"It said *'I'm sorry for what I've made you do.'* No name, no explanation."

"And you thought I'd made you do something and I needed to apologise for it?" she chuckled, trying to hide her concern. Mike laughed in response.

"Sorry. Maybe it was a wrong number after all." They said their farewells and ended the call. As Mike reached his office, Tania was dialling Cellier. It went to voicemail.

"Is that the director? This is Beloved. I think we might have a problem." She explained about the text Mike had described to her and then ended the call. Back in his office, Mike decided to reply to the anonymous text.

Who is this? I think you might have the wrong number.

He placed the phone back on his desk and logged onto his emails, and whoever had sent the text clearly had got the wrong number, because it didn't buzz again.

Elsewhere, Cellier had picked up the voicemail from Tania and called The Broker.

"I think we might have a problem." She told him about the message from Tania. He then called Machendrie, who promised to deal with it. He knew exactly who the message to Mike was from.

Cellier then made a final call back to Tania. As soon as the call was answered, Cellier said, "Beloved, be prepared to strike the set in case the run comes to an unexpected end. Ensure you are ready to send the extras home, kill the lights, and return to rehearsals."

Chapter 67

Arlo had barely slept since Alessia had given the photograph that arrived in the post to the police, and now he had manipulated his son into accepting a business deal. Today, he felt at breaking point. He sat in his potting shed in the garden and typed a message to 'them'.

Are you there?

> *We are always here, Arlo, watching you.*

I have done everything you asked me to do.

> *Yes, you have. So?*

Then why won't you leave me alone?

> *Who said we've finished asking you to do things?*

My son signed the business deal!'

> *Yes, he did. Thank you for your help.*

What else is there for me to do?

> *We haven't decided yet.*

What is there to decide????

Calm down, Arlo. Don't want you fainting again.

LEAVE MY FAMILY ALONE

Oh dear. Have you forgotten who's in charge?

What do you want from me?

Respect would be a start. We could destroy you.

You ARE destroying me

Things could get a lot worse. Did your wife like the photo we sent her?

You can't keep doing this to me. Please

Stay calm and wait for your next instruction. Oh, and we know about the apology text you sent to Mike. You're ours, now & forever, and even though she is dead, Jane is our witness and winning hand.

I can't take this anymore. Why won't you stop?

Are you still there?

Hello?'

SPEAK TO ME!!

There was no response, and the silence deafened Arlo. He felt he only had one course of action left.

Chapter 68

As he stepped out of the Metropolitan Police HQ, The Broker was simmering. News that the police had interviewed him with his solicitor would spread quicker than herpes at a kissing booth. He also needed some serious damage limitation to avoid it impacting his reputation and his cash flow.

As soon as he heard from one of his corrupt members in CID that their colleagues were on the way to escort him to the police station, he immediately told Tom to delete all of the security CCTV archives for their building, starting two days before Adrian Huxley had been to see him. It was a wise precaution. At least that made him relax a little as he replayed the interview in his mind.

"Matthew, a few days ago you were asked if you'd seen the solicitor, Adrian Huxley, recently. You said, and I quote, that you'd *not seen him for months, maybe even years.*' Do you still stand by that statement?" asked Denton.

"Of course."

"Okay, then let's take a look at a few items that might suggest otherwise," and Denton flicked open a file that lay in front of him. "Adrian Huxley's car was found at a Brick Lane car park." The Broker looked at Denton quizzically.

"So? Lots of people park there, I assume," he replied before turning to his solicitor, shrugging his shoulders and putting his hands out to silently express scorn at the statement by Denton.

"What is your point, Detective Inspector?" asked the solicitor.

"We have CCTV imagery that shows Mr Huxley walking from the car park towards your offices."

"It's a busy area," replied The Broker, again expressing confusion at the apparently general statement and implication. "There's lots of local businesses around there. He could have been going anywhere."

"Do you have any images of Mr Huxley actually entering my client's building?" asked the solicitor, knowing the answer was no because his client had had all the council's CCTV cameras that were close to his building, vandalised.

"We don't, as well you know, but we do have this." Denton slid a photocopy of a page from Huxley's diary that said '*Matthew Berry*' for a time that was only 20 minutes after his car was logged entering the Brick Lane car park.

"I assume there's more than one Matthew Berry in that part of East London, detective," suggested the solicitor. It was Jones who replied.

"There are three within a five-mile radius, actually. There's you," and she indicated The Broker. "There's one who is 87, but he's been in a nursing home for over a month, rather than at his home address, and the other is 12 and his head teacher confirmed he was in school all day. Besides, I'm not sure either of the latter two is typical of Adrian Huxley's usual clientele," she said.

"Maybe he thought he'd try a cold-call visit or something, but I never saw him," replied The Broker, matter-of-factly. Denton paused before slowly sliding another piece of paper across the table towards him. The slow and deliberate way he did so made The Broker feel a little apprehensive, and his solicitor more than a little curious.

"And then there's this. Found this in his briefcase, too," said Denton. Both The Broker and his solicitor leant forwards to see what was on the piece of paper. It was a faint photocopy of what looked like some handwritten notes. The solicitor didn't recognise it, but The Broker did. He also saw a faint '3' scribbled in the top corner and then saw his nickname, 'The Broker', mentioned in an incomplete paragraph at the bottom of the sheet, which someone had unhelpfully highlighted. He realised it was more confessions from Huxley's ex-client, but this time the content fell just short of confirming The Broker was involved in the Lottery Ticket Murders.

"That suggests you were involved in some sort of scheme, Matthew. Sadly, whatever it was must be listed on the subsequent sheet, but we'll find it and let you know what it says," promised Denton.

Although The Broker was a little concerned by the content, the solicitor remained calm and matter-of-fact.

"There's a lot of circumstantial evidence here, detective, and who knows who wrote whatever that is, about my client. It could be the work of a lunatic, an overly imaginative wannabe journalist, a vindictive police officer, or someone who just wants to besmirch my client's spotless reputation. Do you have anything unequivocal and admissible, otherwise I think we're done here?" The Broker nodded in agreement, as if all that seemed sensible and plausible explanations.

"Possibly," replied Denton. "But why would two of your men then follow Mr Huxley out of the area until he got into a taxi, and then turn back towards the direction of your building?" He slid further images across the table, showing this to be true.

"They're lovely blokes, but a bit dim, Mr Denton. Why, only yesterday they set off to get some milk and tea bags for the office, only to return five minutes later because they realised that they'd forgotten to take some petty cash to pay for it," replied The Broker, chuckling at the humorous tale and again holding his hands out to indicate there was a very simple explanation.

As he walked down the steps of the building towards the waiting car, while that lie had made him smile, his mood had soon darkened again. He turned his phone on, and a voice message came through immediately. It was Cellier, and she was furious.

"I don't know where you are, but we need to talk. You are pushing an old man too hard and putting one of my team and my whole operation at risk! If anyone ever fucked with your reputation, you'd be a mad as hell. Well, guess what!"

If The Broker was annoyed at how Denton had tried to intimidate him, he was furious at how Cellier had spoken to him. He accepted that if she knew what he had just been through, she would probably have held her tongue, but she hadn't held back at all. As he climbed into the car, he looked at Jerry.

"Take me back to the office, and then get someone to visit Cellier. She needs teaching a lesson in respect. She needs reminding who's in charge!"

"Yes, boss."

Chapter 69

Arlo was sat on the bed. Gazing around the bedroom, he smiled gently at the mementoes on top of the Welsh dresser and at the photos on the wall. He recalled the day they had chosen the flowered wallpaper that had subsequently adorned the walls.

"Wouldn't you like something different, for a change?" he used to ask Alessia in the ensuing years, but the answer was always the same.

"No. I love this pattern, it's so soothing," so they just kept re-sticking any corners that peeled, and patched any gouges or tears.

He looked down at the rug on her side of the bed. He had selected it and brought it home as a surprise to cover the flooring and make sure her feet were warm in winter, when she sat up to put her slippers on. He looked at the chair in the corner of their bedroom, where he would stack his clothes before bed, and then over at the wooden door to their room, that used to creak so loudly it would wake her up when he brought her a cup of tea and a crumpet in bed, on her days off. All of the memories were now irrelevant, stained by the tidal wave of threats he had received.

He looked at the smartphone they had sent him and started to weep. It reminded him of the people who had destroyed everything. He'd been persuaded to try social media by Mike.

"Once you get used to it, it will change your life, Dad."

Oh, how true that innocent statement had turned out to be. At first, Arlo had been scared about touching anything on the device, for fear of 'breaking the internet'. Over time, though, he'd started to explore the world these devices opened up. Pinterest, some gardening websites, and he'd found out how to follow his favourite authors and sports heroes on Twitter. His head dropped: Twitter. He had been quite happy learning how to 'like' things, but he had never instigated messages or posted anything. When their savings account was inexplicably inaccessible, Arlo had looked for ways to save money. That was when he'd seen their first advert on his feed:

In the month of May, our promotions will be MASSIVE.

A website address was attached that spoke of bargains to die for, so he 'liked' their tweet, because he wanted to try to help; to feel useful until the bank sorted out the technical issue, but now it had come to this. He stood slowly and walked into the hallway, picking up a small bag from under the stairs that he had prepared and hidden late last night. Then he walked out of the house and started the car.

An hour later, a young woman walking her dog found him hanging from a bridge. Her scream shattered the peaceful surroundings, but he couldn't hear it. He was free of 'them' now and hoped Alessia and Mike would be, too.

Chapter 70

A couple of nights ago, when he had arrived back at his apartment, Hibberd decided he wanted a hot shower and then to read before bed. He took his watch off, placing it next to his wallet and mobile phone on a small silver tray that sat on top of a tall drawer unit in his bedroom. As a matter of habit, he checked his trousers and jacket pockets, in case there was a ticket from the Underground or something similar in them. He always paid cash for things like that, so as to minimise his digital footprint. Although computers trawled CCTV coverage every day at various security service agencies, usually the easiest way to monitor and track someone's habits and movements were credit card and debit card transactions. As he checked his jacket pocket, he found a small piece of paper.

"What's this?" he mumbled to himself as he unfolded it. It contained a handwritten message.

It's axle lad diamond

Underneath the message was a mobile phone number. He reached for his bedside notepad, put his glasses on, and then sat down on the edge of the bed. Ten minutes after scribbling the message onto a blank page, he tossed the notepad aside as he reflected on the anagram he'd decrypted. It was from someone he'd not seen in months. He picked his phone up and typed a text, sending it to the number on the piece of paper.

How do I know it's you?

A few minutes later, a response arrived.

You must have a lot to lose if you are willing to gamble everything on nothing

That suggested the sender was who he thought it was, because that's exactly what Hibberd had said the last time they'd spoken in a private meeting. Hibberd knew he needed to arrange a meeting.

f2f, he typed.
Where and when? came the reply.

That text exchange was three days ago. Today, Hibberd was sitting in a plush private cinema owned by a business acquaintance, several miles west of the city. As the opening credits rolled on the film, the door at the back of the room swished open, and he heard footsteps. His guest sat on a seat behind him, to his right. Without looking around, he raised a bucket of freshly-made popcorn, offering his guest some.

"Thanks for coming. Can't say I expected this, but how can I help?"

"I have client information I want to share," replied Maddox.

"What about?"

"BOrg and Ruiz."

"You'll be breaking your oath under the Bar Standards Board if you tell me what you know. Are you sure you want to do that?"

"I've never been so sure of anything in my life," she said. She was disappointed that she'd originally taken the Ruiz case for personal gain and career preservation, and her selfishness had now led to the death of her youngest brother, so she didn't care about the legality of what she was planning to do.

"Let's just say it's a debt of honour," and then she told Hibberd the story about the assassin.

"How did they find you?" he asked, when she'd finished.

"I... I don't know. I've been very careful. I've been using my Italian surname, I avoided using the internet, turned off my mobile and removed the SIM card, and I agreed with my mother that I'd use money I had sent her, via Western Union."

"Perhaps Ruiz traced your transactions?"

"No, I was very careful. I used a mixture of ATMs, bank branches, and post offices for several cash withdrawals from my bank account over a number of weeks, and never used the same Western Union facility twice. There is virtually no chance of him finding me that way."

As the film played in the background, the two of them sat in silent contemplation for a while until Hibberd turned to her:

"Thank you for reaching out and trusting me. As we're swapping information, you should know I'm working with Europol. We have intel that a man called Robert Kendrick is masterminding a takeover of BOrg, and he's using someone in London to help him. It's highly confidential and on a need-to-know basis, but as you're putting your career and reputation on the line, I thought you should know that Ruiz isn't the only person you might need to watch out for."

"Robert Kendrick?" interrupted Maddox, remembering the name.

"Yes. You know him?"

"I know of him. I met his wife during the Ruiz trial. He was reported as dead a year earlier, but she told me he'd faked his own death, and he was alive and well."

"Why did she decide to tell you that?"

"Her husband asked her to. She brought a piece of paper with her that I was supposed to show to Ruiz, but I never got there. Mrs Kendrick said her husband also wanted me to give him a message; something about how he could destroy BOrg and Ruiz, so he should leave him and his wife alone."

"Do you still have the piece of paper?" Hibberd asked eagerly.

"Yes, but it's in a safety deposit box."

"Could you show it to me?"

"Err, sure, but we'll need to be careful we're not seen." Maddox then had a question of her own. "A moment ago, you said Kendrick was plotting with someone in London. Any idea who it is?"

Hibberd didn't reply. He just stood and gestured for her to follow him. She deserved to know the truth.

Chapter 71

"Did your husband seem under any pressure lately, Mrs McCleary?" the special support officer enquired. Alessia just shook her head while her face was still partially buried in a fistful of tissues.

"Do you know if he'd been unwell, perhaps he'd been to see a doctor recently?" the second officer asked, looking up from Alessia to Mike. Again, Alessia just shook her head, but Mike spoke.

"He... he'd fainted outside a coffee shop a few weeks ago, but the doctor told him he would be fine after a few days' rest," he mumbled.

"And did he seem to be, to the best of your knowledge?"

"I... I think so," and he looked at his mother, who nodded in agreement.

"I'm sorry to ask, but did he seem anxious or was his behaviour unusual in any way?"

"I think we've all been anxious recently, especially my father. A long-standing problem at the bank had been weighing heavily on his mind."

Alessia looked up.

"H-how do you know about the bank?" she asked.

"He told me that day you and he had... had that argument. Said things had been a bit tense recently, and I offered to help."

"A problem with the bank?" asked the second support officer, seeking some clarification.

"Er, yes. My parents hadn't been able to access their savings for a couple of months," Mike explained. "The bank didn't seem able or willing to explain what had happened. Even when I went down to talk to them, they just blustered and tried to fob me off."

"Was it a worry, Mrs McCleary, not having access to your savings?"

"A bit, well… no, not really. We had enough to get by with our pensions, although I know Arlo obsessed about it."

"Is it still a problem?" one of them asked, looking at Mike.

"Er, apparently not. The bank manager called this morning to say everything had been sorted, although he still didn't explain why."

"So, it was something your husband was worried about?" checked the first support officer, glancing at her colleague.

"Yes, but not enough… not enough… not enough to make him…" but she couldn't complete the sentence before she buried her head in her tissues again and cried softly.

"Do we really need to continue with the questions?" begged Mike. It was hard enough for him to remain composed, so he realised just how difficult it must be for his mother.

"I am sorry, Mr McCleary, but it's often during the first few days after such a tragic event that we start to uncover what happened. I think, though, that we probably have enough for now," she said as she reached into her pocket and pulled out a card. "We'll pop back tomorrow, but if anything comes to mind in the meantime, or if you just want someone to talk to, please don't hesitate to call this number."

"Thank you, Officer. We will," replied Mike. He then checked on his mother before escorting the police to the door. Once they had gone, Mike returned to the lounge. Alessia sat, tissues in one hand and a framed photograph of her and Arlo in the other. It was from the last holiday they took to Malta, 10 years ago. She was smiling lovingly at it. Mike knelt next to her.

"Want a cuppa, Mum?"

"No, thank you, dear. Maybe a glass of water, though. I feel as if I've run out of water for my tears," and her face crumpled again as she stared at the photograph. He wrapped his arms around her and gave her a gentle hug, but after several seconds, his mother softly patted his hand, which was a sign he could let go.

"I'll go grab that water," he said, standing and then walking into the kitchen.

On the working surface near the sink, the police had left a small box of Arlo's belongings. They'd done the necessary forensics checks and saw no reason to keep them.

"A tea might be nice, actually?" Alessia called through.

"I'll bring you both. The water will definitely help," Mike replied, pushing the box to one side so he could get to the kettle. He filled it from the tap and placed it on its stand, flicking the switch on. As he did so, he glanced at the box again before taking the lid off and looking inside. It contained his father's watch, which had been a present from Mike as a thank you for all the support through MIT and while he was starting his career in Canada. His wallet was there too, along with a few coins and some oddities like a piece of garden twine and a bus ticket. Also in the box was a clear plastic pouch with his shattered mobile phone in it. The police said it was on the floor near where they had found his father. They assumed it had been smashed before Arlo took his own life, because of its proximity to a large stone that had some superficial scratches on it. The trace material on the stone matched the phone casing.

"Hmm," Mike chuckled at the apparent age of the smartphone, muttering to himself, "You always were one for a bargain, Dad."

The kettle boiled and Mike put two teabags in a teapot, before pouring the hot water in. As it brewed, he decided to take the phone out of the plastic pouch, but the back casing fell off as soon as he pulled it out. He turned it over, trying to reclip the back onto the phone. That's when he spotted the Kintaro logo on the SIM card inside. He narrowed his eyes as he tried to identify the version: it seemed to be a recent chip.

"Mum?"

"Yes, Michael?"

"How long has Dad had this phone?"

"Oh, that one is quite recent, but it's second-hand. Why?"

"No reason, just curious."

"He lost his other one, the one you got him. Such a thoughtful gift. He always used it to text me if he was out and was delayed, so I didn't worry... And for that bloody Twitter account," she sighed, before forcing a chuckle that was tinged with sadness.

"Twitter?" he called through to the lounge.

"Yes, he got into it while you were in Canada. I used to tell him off because he was obsessed with it. Always checking for things: don't know what, exactly." Inexplicably, Mike suddenly felt curious. An old phone, but with what looked like a relatively new Kintaro SIM card in it.

"Is it okay if I keep it?" he asked, turning the phone on.

"Fine by me. Any chance of that cup of tea, dear?" she queried, eager for some comfort.

"Yes, sorry. Won't be a moment." Mike slowly placed the teapot and cups onto a tray, glancing at the phone as the screen lit up. He picked the phone up, hoping there wasn't a PIN code to unlock the phone. There wasn't. Hesitantly and with a degree of trepidation, he tapped on the text icon, which then displayed just three conversations; one of which he recognised.

I'm sorry for what I've made you do.

> *Who is this? I think you might have the wrong number.*

It was the message he'd received the day production went live. As his mind tried to process what his father must have meant, he closed that text string and opened another one. It was his father begging someone to stop doing something, and it also referred to Mike:

My son signed the business deal!

Yes, he did. Thank you for your help.

"What the hell?" exclaimed Mike. The final conversation was dated the day his father had taken his own life. It only had three entries:

I'm ending this. You can't hurt me anymore.

I'm not sure what you think you can do to change things. Just do as you're told.

Arlo?

That was all he could find on the phone, but it was enough to make his brain scream because none of it seemed to make any sense.

He knew he needed to find out more about the SIM, but he was too tired and distracted to head to the Kintaro offices tonight, so he decided to head home and try to get some sleep. Maybe Tania would be there, and he could talk to her about it? Then, after some sleep, he would go to the office very early in the morning. It would be the perfect time as it would be empty, so he could do his research in peace and quiet. He just hoped he could actually sleep.

Chapter 72

The coffee shop was off the tourist route in Bucharest. It had waist-to-ceiling Palladian windows, with a wooden-beamed roof and dark hardwood flooring. The flooring was worse for wear, but it added to the character of the place. Hazy sun beamed in through an east-facing window, throwing a dusty shaft of sunlight into the shop. The barista was busy cleaning the glass pastry units that sat on top of the broad wooden counter, and a small bell that hung above the door jingled every time someone entered or left. Most were locals who preferred this off-the-beaten-track establishment and clearly had a rapport with the owner.

Robert Kendrick sat at a small table in the corner and stared around the room. He had only been in the city for a few hours, but he wanted to meet Apostu as quickly as possible, to seal the deal. He desperately needed to give The Broker some good news.

He felt a touch of melancholy as he watched two women, sitting on stools at the window-ledge bar, chatting without an apparent care in the world. Then there was the middle-aged couple who were at a table by one of the windows, surrounded by potted plants and holding hands. Whatever they were discussing was making him smile and her giggle.

I miss that, he thought, but the feeling went as quickly as it came. He had bigger things to deal with, because the third man in the scheme had called him last night with an update.

"Our investor called me yesterday. He told me the scheme isn't performing."

"The £64m investment isn't at risk," stated Kendrick.

"Fuck the money! He said he'd kill us if we didn't deliver," came the reply.

"Calm down. I told you when you first suggested this scheme that it would be bumpy," replied Kendrick, trying to placate his clearly panicked business partner.

As he ended the call and reflected on the news, a voice said, "Robert." It startled him out of his introspection, and he looked up to see who was talking.

"Simion, good of you to make time for a coffee," he replied, recovering his composure. After their coffee was served, Apostu updated him.

"Everything in the shop is ready to go on sale. I just need you to let me know when your buyer wants to place his initial order," he explained. This was the agreed phrase to say the BOrg operation was primed for when the production and distribution of the fraudulent chip was underway.

"I'm meeting the florist in two days' time, so we should have his order then," Kendrick confirmed, even though the investment from The Broker was clearly looking increasingly unlikely, but he couldn't let Apostu know that was the case.

"Excellent. To our future success," said Apostu, raising his espresso cup to toast their future. As Kendrick was about to respond, a delivery courier entered the shop and looked around. On seeing Apostu sitting with someone, she lifted the visor on her helmet.

"Mr Kendrick?" she enquired.

Yes," he replied innocently. She pulled open the flap of her satchel and smiled.

"I have a delivery for you," she said, pulling out a pistol and putting a bullet into Kendrick's skull.

Chapter 73

It was Sunday, and that meant a full roast dinner for all the family.

"Can you all hurry up, please; it's almost ready," shouted Cellier. Alice and Jack came thundering down the stairs, excited as always about the feast ahead. Her husband came out of the adjoining study and beamed at the table.

"Goodness, I love Sundays," he said as he saw the joint, a pile of hot Yorkshire puddings, veg, fresh roasties, and gravy. The cat also meandered into the dining room, as a Sunday dinner usually meant Jack and Alice would sneak small chunks of meat under the table for him while their parents weren't looking.

"Sit down, everyone," Cellier said as she placed two wine glasses on the table, and then asked her husband to carve the meat.

"Sure... but where's the knife?" he asked, looking around. The children looked too, but shrugged when they couldn't see it either.

Cellier sighed. "Sorry, must have put the one I was using in the dishwasher. I'll grab another." She marched through the kitchen doorway, over to the carving block, and pulled out a clean knife. As she turned, she jumped. Stood on either side of the kitchen door were two thugs she'd never seen before.

"Hello, Jenni," whispered one. "I hear you've been a bit rude to the boss, so he thought we should pop over and... you know, help calm things down a little. He doesn't like feeling disrespected." Cellier realised The Broker had sent them, as she'd sworn at him about Arlo McCleary's suicide.

"Yeah, well everything's calm now and we're all good, so can you two just piss off," she hissed, trying to show she was in control of the situation. The thugs smirked at each other.

"D'you kiss your children with that potty mouth?" asked the first one quietly, taking a step forwards.

"I'm officially shocked and offended," whispered the second, sarcastically. "We only came to have a chat, but maybe that's not going to be enough?"

"Oh no, you've offended Lenny. That's never a good thing," said the first thug. Just then, her husband shouted from the dining room.

"Hurry up with the knife, Jenni." She closed her eyes and took a deep breath, realising her attempt to be assertive had overstepped the mark.

"Look, I'm about to have Sunday dinner with my family. Tell the boss I'm really sorry, and I'll talk to him tomorrow. Alright?" The men looked at each other, softened their posture and smiled softly before Lenny's smile dissolved in an instant. He stared at Cellier.

"No can do. I'm afraid we're here to teach you some manners."

She looked from one man to another, assessing her chances, then held the carving knife out as a threat. "Leave my family out of this. This doesn't have to get nasty."

Both thugs took a step back, pretending to be afraid, but then nonchalantly pulled the side of their jackets back to reveal handguns in shoulder holsters. Cellier realised how quickly this could spin out of control, so she slowly placed the knife on the working surface, where the men could see it.

"Sorry," she said.

"Good girl. No one wants this to get all unnecessary, so let me explain what you need to do, and then let's go into the dining room and say hello to everyone." He leant forward and whispered something into her ear before gesturing for her to go into the dining room.

"What? No, please. It will…" Cellier gasped, but the man looked dismayed and went to pull his gun out.

"Alright, alright," she replied, a touch of panic in her voice while her brain tried to plot a way out of the horrific scenario.

"Jenni?" her husband called out again, wondering what was keeping her.

"Yeah, Mum, we're starving," shouted Jack, laughing at his own comment and then clapping his hands in delight as she walked into the dining room, but then his expression changed when he saw the two men walking behind her. One of them stayed next to Cellier, while the other walked around the table and stood behind the children.

"Darling, who… who are these men?"

"We're friends of your wife. Just popped in to say a quick hello, but don't worry, Mr Cellier, children, we'll be gone in no time at all," said the first thug, smiling warmly. He then turned to look at Cellier, expectantly. She swallowed hard. What they told her to do was horrific.

"Come on, Jenni, the food's going cold, luv," said Lenny. The children looked around at him, and then back to their mum.

"No," she blurted. "Sorry, but you really ought to leave. You'll... you'll miss your train, otherwise. We can catch up tomorrow, eh?"

The first man sighed and signalled to Lenny with a subtle nod. As everyone continued to look at Cellier, the second thug took a quiet step towards the children and pulled his jacket open just enough so she could see him tapping the handle of the gun.

"*Alright,*" she snapped in a growing state of panic, making her husband and children jump. She drew a deep breath and tore off a small piece of meat before pulling the large two-pronged fork out of the joint. She hesitated momentarily, swallowed hard, and then called the cat.

"Jasper?"

It dutifully wandered out from under the table and looked at the juicy morsel in her hand. She leant down and let the cat take the scrap before grabbing it by the scruff of the neck and lifting it up onto the table, pinning it down gently. Initially, the cat was submissive, but then it started to fidget and gently howl as she held it down more firmly. She held the fork tightly in her fist and took another deep breath.

"Jenni, what are you doing?" asked her increasingly worried husband.

"Mummy? Let Jasper go," pleaded Jack.

"Mum?" growled Alice, a little more assertively.

"Jenni, put the cat down. You're scaring the children... and me." She looked at her husband, then at the children, and mouthed 'I'm so sorry', before raising the fist with the fork in it above her head, ready to plunge the fork into the cat. As she swung her arm down, Alice screamed.

"Mum!!"

The thug next to Cellier reached out and grabbed her forearm to halt the downward thrust just inches above the cat. He smirked and nodded, letting her know she could release the cat and put the fork down. It sprang from the table and over to the far corner of the room, followed quickly by the children who raced from their seats to protect him. Her husband just stared, open-mouthed. He couldn't speak but had so many questions.

"That's self-discipline," said the thug. "Doing what you're told, whatever the consequence. We learned that in the army, didn't we, Lenny?" The second thug nodded, a little disappointed they didn't make her go through with it. He didn't like cats.

"Thank you," whispered Cellier in submission, as she stared at the floor.

"And that's manners," replied the thug. "We're not monsters, Jenni. We'd have never made you go through with it, but sometimes you need to remember who's in charge and how they can shape your future. Understood?" She was shaking with fright, but nodded her head again without looking up. The first thug then looked around the room and saw the children cowering in the corner, protecting the cat, her husband still staring at his wife in disbelief, and Lenny picking a few of the roasties from the bowl.

"What? I'm hungry," said Lenny, as he also grabbed a Yorkshire pudding and dipped it in the gravy.

"You're an idiot," said the first thug, before he turned one final time to Cellier and said, "Don't make us come back, will you." As she shook her head, the two men turned and walked back through the kitchen and out of the house. Cellier dropped to her knees and sobbed.

Even though her husband was still trying to process what the hell had just happened, he walked around the table and hugged her.

"It's okay," he said as he rocked his wife gently in his comforting arms. "We can talk about it later." After a few seconds, Cellier lifted her face to look at him. Her cheeks were wet from the tears, but there was now no fear in her eyes.

"We need to book a flight and a hotel right now, anywhere in the world."

"What?" exclaimed her startled husband. "We don't have that sort of money, and what about my work? What about school for the kids tomorrow?"

"Yes, we do have the money. We have more than enough," she said, unwilling and unsure how to explain her past and her wealth. That didn't matter right now, though; she was just desperate to get her family to safety.

Chapter 74

It was 4am, so when Mike shuffled into the Kintaro office, tired and bedraggled, the sleepy security guard on reception nearly fell off his stool.

Mike stumbled up to his office and logged onto the computer. He had barely slept the previous night, so he was feeling angry and irritable. He clicked on the icon for their warehouse database, which seemed a logical place to start tracking what had happened to the SIM in his father's phone.

"Right, Integrated Circuit Card Identifier number is…" and he read the tiny 20-digit number that was printed on the Kintaro SIM he had taken out of his father's old phone. He hit 'return' and, almost instantaneously, a box popped up on his screen stating the number couldn't be found.

"Got to get to Specsavers," he mumbled, squinting through tired eyes in an attempt to bring the numbers into focus. "Ah, okay, that's probably a 5, not a 6," and he re-entered the number correctly, but the same error message reappeared on his screen.

"What?" He drummed his fingers on the desk, deciding what to do next. He could check the number yet again, but it would probably end with the same result, so he decided to call Büggs and wake her up, so she could come into work to help.

"Everything alright?" she asked when she arrived and saw Mike sitting on a chair next to her desk. As she put her bag down and began to take her coat off, Mike growled in frustration.

"Thought you might get here a bit quicker." He stomped towards the door with no further explanation.

"You want me to follow you?" Büggs called out. There was no reply, so she picked up her bag and coat and shuffled down the corridor after him.

"Come in and shut the door," he said, standing behind his desk and fidgeting a little.

"Have... have I done something wrong?" she asked, slightly nervously.

"What? No! Why would you think that?" Mike challenged, unable to temper his fatigue and general irritation. He turned the computer screen towards her, which was still displaying the error message.

"I can't find something."

"What is it you're looking for?"

Mike took the SIM from his pocket and laid it on the desk.

"The warehouse stock trail for this."

She picked the SIM up and walked around his desk, implying he should step aside, which he did. She sat down and turned the computer screen to face her, before reading the number on the SIM and entering the details. She pressed 'return', but the stock record wasn't what she was expecting to see.

"That's odd," she mumbled.

"What's odd?" asked Mike.

"The shipment it was part of is logged as arriving, but the batch isn't recorded beyond that."

"Where the hell is it then?" he demanded. Again, she took a moment to calm down.

"I... don't... know... but just give me a minute, alright?" she replied calmly, although the staccato response did indicate her growing irritation. Mike recognised it as such and realised he was taking his frustration out on her.

"Sorry," he muttered quietly. "I'm just a little bit tired and—" but she cut across him.

"I know, and I'm sorry that you're going through something so terrible," she said softly. "Some of our smaller clients prefer to pay their own staff to load proprietary software, rather than use us, so although those shipments are logged as arriving, it never appears as part of our warehouse stock. If that's what's happened to it, it might be on what's known as the cross-docking log. That's where we list hardware coming in that we immediately load onto an outgoing lorry." She looked up at Mike, who seemed to be calm and paying attention.

"I know," he said. "It's actually cheaper for them if we buy the SIM and ship it than it is for them to buy it direct from the manufacturer. Volume pricing discount, basically." She nodded in agreement and kept on searching the database. Five minutes later, they had their answer.

"I don't get it," he said.

"Me neither," she replied, confused. "It's marked as arrived from the supplier, but then the batch of 50 it was in was marked as damaged. It never made it off the inward channel."

"Are you saying someone marked the SIMs as unusable?" checked Mike.

"Unusable and destroyed, yes. It's rare, but it happens."

"If that's true, how come one of them was being used in my father's phone?"

Büggs turned to look at him, wide-eyed. He hadn't explained where the SIM had come from.

"You mean you found this *active* SIM in your father's phone?"

"Yes," confirmed Mike.

"For it to be active, it would need to be loaded with the appropriate software. I wonder why the batch was marked as damaged and destroyed, then loaded with software?" Büggs replied, and she began typing again. A login number was listed against every transaction on the database, with a name listed against it, but the name for that batch had been electronically redacted.

"What are you doing, now?" he asked, as she logged out of the database front-end and entered a string of code.

"Even though the display is showing a redacted name, it's like when someone uses the 'number withheld' service on a phone. Although it hides the number from the recipient, the network provider always knows what number has been used and who it really belongs to, so they can bill for the call." She hit 'return' and a name popped up on screen. "Just like the system administrator in our stock management software knows who did what."

Mike stared at the name of the person who had marked the batch as unusable and destroyed. It was Bob Hall.

"I think we need to talk to him, first thing on Monday," said Mike. "He's got some bloody explaining to do if he's selling our SIMs for his own profit."

"How do you think one got into your dad's phone?"

"My mum said it was a second-hand phone. Maybe it was in there when he bought the phone?" he replied, although that still didn't explain the mysterious text conversations he had found.

The texts weren't his only priority, though. He'd been trying to call Yann Machendrie for the last couple of days, but there had been no answer. The money Machendrie had promised for this week still hadn't been deposited, and unless they received the cash injection soon, he didn't know how much longer Kintaro could operate.

PART 3:

ONE MAN'S LOSS...

Chapter 75 – early 2020

A visit to the fourth floor wasn't something Denton normally looked forward to, given it was usually because either his departmental budget needed further cuts, or because his crime statistics hadn't achieved the national standards. Today, however, he could hardly wait! Even though the information he had wasn't sufficient for an arrest and conviction, it was at least grounds for a search warrant, and that would feel like opening Aladdin's cave.

"Let's go over it one more time," he enthusiastically said to Jones.

"Is there something you're not sure about, sir?" she queried. They had pored over the details into the wee hours, so she was surprised if he felt he had any gaps in his case.

"No, I just love that feeling of success," he beamed, thrilled to revisit the evidence and re-live that moment of euphoria that he'd felt when they had catalogued and examined everything from Adrian Huxley's briefcase. Twenty minutes later, they had been through everything again, and the clock was showing it was only two minutes to his meeting with the DCI. If it hadn't been inappropriate, he could have happily hugged Jones. He triumphantly flipped his case folder closed, stood, straightened his tie, and then marched out of his office to head to the fourth floor.

"Come in, DI Denton," said the DCI when he rapped on her office door. As he walked in, a woman was sitting on one of the two chairs facing the DCI. She neither stood nor turned her head towards him, and the DCI silently gestured that he should sit. He did so, but the unknown woman's presence threw him slightly.

"Ma'am," he started, barely containing his excitement. "I'd like to update you on one of our current investigations. Hopefully you'll then be willing to approve a request for a search warrant."

"A search warrant for what, DI Denton?"

"We have reason to believe Matthew Berry, known locally as The Broker, is involved in a series of murders." As he was about to launch into the detail, he noticed the DCI glance at the woman next to him, so he paused.

"Is there a problem, ma'am?" he asked hesitantly, but it was the woman who replied.

"We need you to suspend that line of enquiry, Detective Inspector."

"S-suspend the investigation? I'm not sure I understand," he said. The woman gestured that the DCI could respond.

"I realise you may have a lead you wish to follow, but Berry is subject to a wider investigation, and I've been given strict instructions to support Europol," and she gestured towards her mystery guest, who nodded politely to Denton. "We do nothing that could compromise it. Is that understood?"

Denton stared at the DCI, then briefly turned his head to look at the woman, before returning his gaze to his DCI. He felt so incredibly deflated.

"Was there anything else, DI Denton?" the DCI asked, realising he would be disappointed, but she had her own pressures to deal with and instructions to follow. He paused to reflect on what he really wanted to say in response to her question, but knew it would be pointless or even counter-productive. He'd felt moments away from fulfilling a long-held aspiration to utter the words '*Matthew Berry, you are under arrest for...*', and yet now that had never felt so far away. He briefly closed his eyes as he gently rubbed his forehead, before standing and forcing a respectful smile at the DCI.

"No, ma'am, nothing else."

"Very good. Thank you, and please remember that this conversation goes no further. Understood?"

"Yes, ma'am," he replied. He gave the briefest of nods to the woman and then turned and stomped out of the office, muttering expletives under his breath.

Chapter 76

"He says he wants you there," explained Pritchard over the phone, having received a request from the minister that he and Hibberd meet him, again.

"You know how I feel about being summoned by him," replied Hibberd. Pritchard did know, but given Pritchard and the minister had shared their anxieties over Hibberd's alleged involvement in criminal activities for a number of months, and that there would be agents from the security services present, it was imperative Hibberd went. "But okay, I'll be there," added the reluctant Hibberd. He had expected this call as soon as news about Robert Kendrick's death had filtered through on the dark web, and knew the meeting was going to be an uncomfortable discussion.

Three hours later, they were sat in a hallway outside a parliamentary meeting room. The door to the room opened, and the minister stepped out.

"Good morning, Howard," he said, beaming as he held his hand out to shake Pritchard's, but there was only a begrudging glance towards Hibberd as he ushered them both into the room. As they sat down, the minister turned to welcome his other guests, who subsequently sat on the other side of the table. The minister turned his attention back to Hibberd and Pritchard.

"Gentlemen, thank you for your time this morning. I'm afraid we have some rather disturbing news to discuss. The two gentlemen to my left are from the security service."

Neither of the two said anything; they simply kept their gaze on the minister, who looked over to Hibberd and Pritchard, adding, "Over to you."

Pritchard had been up all night, preparing and refining his opening remarks. He had known Hibberd for three decades, but today was the day that their friendship would be shattered. He cleared his throat and took a deep breath before standing in readiness to address the minister and security duo, but the minister interrupted before he had uttered a word.

"Please sit down, Mr Pritchard. I'm inviting Professor Hibberd to speak." Pritchard was confused. Wasn't this *his* update meeting, and wasn't *he* the one leading the investigation into Hibberd? Slowly, he sat back down, watching as Hibberd stood and took a few steps away to his left to physically distance himself from Pritchard.

"Thank you, Minister. Part of my initial investigation into BOrg included a risk assessment of what would happen if Dennis Ruiz was arrested. One scenario was that someone might try to step into his shoes as head of the organisation. As you know, in 2017, Robert Kendrick was approached by someone with a proposition, given he played a key role for Ruiz, in BOrg."

Pritchard wondered why Hibberd had referred to Robert Kendrick by his forename. It seemed inappropriate, but he didn't have long to wait to find out why.

"That's how we learned Robert was flying in to meet someone in London and, although the surveillance team were unable to monitor the conversation between the two people, we know Robert met Mr Pritchard."

Pritchard's jaw dropped.

"You see, Howard, Robert Kendrick had agreed to support our investigation into BOrg, in return for immunity from prosecution and a new identity under the witness protection scheme. He had access to a lot of very useful information, but he knew Ruiz was clever and it wouldn't take long to identify the handful of people in his organisation who had access to it. We also agreed that Robert couldn't give the incriminating evidence directly to me, so we created our own web of deception."

The minister nodded and spoke: "As I recall, Professor Hibberd, you explained what you thought might be happening, so I was happy to support your continued participation in the joint initiative between Europol and GCHQ." It was at that point that Pritchard leapt to his feet.

"It's a lie! I'd agreed to go undercover to find out more about BOrg, and I know that you're the security threat," he scowled as he ferociously jabbed his finger in the direction of Hibberd. "All the minister and I have talked about these last few weeks was the evidence against *you*," but the minister had heard enough.

"Mr Pritchard, you've been... What's the word I'm looking for?"

One of the security service men said, "Played?"

"Yes, 'played'. Thank you," replied the minister.

"I don't understand," a confused Pritchard protested, as he looked at Hibberd again. "You showed me conversations between you and people on the dark web, including Senyor Fosc."

"Robert Kendrick was Senyor Fosc. We thought the dark web was as good a way to anonymously communicate as any," explained Hibberd. Pritchard closed his eyes as he tried to process what he'd just been told. "Robert was concerned that you were preparing to betray him to your key investor, someone nicknamed The Broker but more commonly known as Matthew Berry, to get a bigger slice of the pie. That's when he knew he'd have to stop messaging me, and I had to make you believe I was the traitor in the team."

"What?" checked Pritchard. His expression slowly morphed into one of realisation that he'd been duped. "The messages I got warning me about you being a gamekeeper turned poacher was actually from you?" he asked Hibberd.

"I needed you to believe I was the traitor, and you'd therefore assume you were safe," Hibberd replied as he walked around the table and stood by the minister. Pritchard couldn't hold his fury in any longer.

"No, this isn't true, you bastard!" Pritchard fumed, at which point the two security service men stood and strode around the table towards him. He stared at them, aghast, knowing where they would be taking him and what would happen. People accused of such a crime were tried behind closed doors, for fear sensitive information would put people's lives at risk, and then they were never seen again.

As they led Pritchard out of the room and through a private passageway, the minister smiled warmly.

"Thank you, Gary, I know that wasn't easy for you."

"Thank you for trusting me through all of this, Simon. I know you put your reputation on the line," he replied.

"At one point, I know you were worried that Pritchard was onto you," said the minister.

"I was, but that was the plan after all, wasn't it? To get him to think he'd framed me? I'm just glad you were there when I needed some reassurance that our plan had remained a secret," Hibberd replied, recalling his call to seek assurance a few days ago:

Don't worry; neither Pritchard nor Ruiz know about our plan. I'll deal with any unforeseen distractions. Let's just make sure we keep an eye on what Kintaro does, and we'll deal with the other distractions later.

"Time for a celebratory drink?" offered the minister.

Hibberd shook his head. "I'm due to meet someone nearby, to help bring closure for them. They've lost just about everything as a consequence of this investigation. I owe them my thanks and an explanation."

"Please let them know the British government also thanks them for their sacrifice, although..." and Hibberd finished his sentence:

"Although it can't and won't ever be acknowledged publicly."

After saying their goodbyes, Hibberd walked out of the House of Commons and across Lambeth Bridge to the Riverside Café. Waiting for him was Daniella Maddox.

"How did it go?" she said.

"As expected," he sighed.

"Does that mean it's all over?"

"I'm afraid not. Simion Apostu was the final link in the chain to finding the core infrastructure of the BOrg operation, and even though Robert shared a copy of the contract he signed with the man called Matthew Berry, it's not enough evidence to convict with. Berry never actually sent Robert any money, so while we could arrest and charge him on the intent, his defence lawyer would probably explain that he withdrew from the scheme when he realised it was criminal."

"But intent could still carry a custodial sentence," explained Maddox.

"It could, but we're after a much bigger fish than some gangland thug in East London. We don't want to scare Apostu or whoever is going to take over at BOrg, for fear we'll never find the billions they've stolen, or dismantle their operation. At least the client information you've given me means Ruiz never gets out. How are you feeling?" he asked, given Maddox would be automatically banned from practising law, as well as a potential target for the rest of her life.

"I'm not sure. I might return to my family in Italy, but even behind bars, Ruiz will still be able to get a message out, and I'll be constantly looking over my shoulder."

"If there's anything I can do to help, you know I will," offered Hibberd. Maddox nodded that she understood, and then she had her own request.

"There is one thing. I've brought the person with me that you asked to see. I think they, of all people, deserve an explanation of what's happened." She gestured to someone sitting alone at a table in the farthest corner of the decking, who, on seeing Maddox wave, stood and walked slowly over to their table.

"It's a pleasure to meet you," said Hibberd, as he prepared to share the truth about Robert Kendrick's role.

"Thank you," replied Stella Kendrick.

Chapter 77

The last few weeks had been incredibly traumatic for Mike, full of some fantastic highs but far too many desperate lows. From the initial high of being recruited as the Head of R&D at Kintaro, to the shock of Harry Sakamoto's death. Dealing with the demands of being thrust into the interim CEO role at a company on the verge of collapse, to then seemingly securing some lifesaving investment from Yann Machendrie, a man who claimed to be the uncle of his incredibly beautiful girlfriend, Tania, or whoever she really was. Both had disappeared, and he now had the heartbreak of his father's suicide and his mother's seemingly endless sadness.

Today, he had pushed his breakfast around his plate, rather than eating it. He was wholly focused on how to tell Kintaro's board and its 200 employees that he was going to have to put the company into administration. Without Machendrie's promised investment, they simply had no future. All those dreams destroyed and the lives of all those families thrown into chaos because he'd raised their hopes and persuaded some of them not to move on to other secure employment but to trust in him. Only the head of HR and one of his trusted managers knew what was going to happen today, which was why the two had been sequestered for a few days, working through the necessary paperwork and legalities required to make such an announcement to over 200 people.

Although sadness and a sense of failure occupied most of his waking hours, he also knew he needed to find out why Bob Hall had apparently stolen a small batch of SIMs, one of which had found its way into Mike's father's replacement phone.

"Good luck today, Michael," said his mother as she gently brushed his jacket with her hand. There was no dust or loose thread, but she just wanted to find a way to express her protective affection for her son. She knew nothing of what had really happened or of his plans for today, beyond the fact he had to tell people they had lost their livelihood. She didn't look up at him, and he knew she was fighting back tears, so a hug would have simply opened the floodgates for both of them. Mike had stayed at her house since his father's funeral, because leaving her alone would have felt like he was abandoning her. Besides, he only had an empty house to return to.

"Thanks," he said softly, trying to raise a smile that would take away a tiny piece of the sorrow his mother would now carry for the rest of her life. She had markedly aged over the last couple of weeks and seemed smaller and frailer than he had ever seen or could have imagined. She glanced up at him, but it was a fleeting glance, and then she tried to reassure him.

"It's not your fault, you know, this bankruptcy. You did everything you could. More than most probably, and your father would have been so very proud of you. He loved getting involved in the decisions you were making. I'd never seen him so focused," she explained encouragingly, but the intended kind words felt like shards of ice plunged into Mike's chest. Of course it was Mike's fault. Everything was his fault.

"I... I'd better be off," he said, holding her hands for the briefest of moments before turning and walking out of the door. He wasn't sure he could have held the guilt in for much longer, and he was close to losing the fight to keep back his own tears. He climbed into his car, took a moment, and then reached for his seatbelt as the engine of the Aston Martin growled into life. He let the satisfying noise sink in one last time, as he'd instructed the lease company to collect the car at the Kintaro offices later that morning.

Thirty minutes later, as he pulled into the company car park, he returned the wave of a few of the employees who saw him. His gut twisted as he imagined how they'd react when, in an hour's time, he'd tell them they all faced redundancy. Before that, though, he had asked Bob Hall to meet him in his office. Büggs had asked if she could join the meeting too, under the guise of providing technical support if Mike needed to show Hall the evidence on screen, although she was feeling slightly titillated at the idea of the meeting.

"What time is he due in?" she asked.

"In five minutes. Have you logged onto the system?"

"Yep, all ready to show him what we've found, if we need to," she replied. "Are you ready?" she asked in return. Mike nodded once, preparing himself for the confrontation, because that's what it felt like it was going to be. He knew he had to try to keep control of his temper, but every scenario he had imagined last night all led to some sort of physical intimidation of Hall. There was a knock at the door, which startled him. He looked around to Büggs as if to ask who it could be. She screwed her face up and shrugged.

"Maybe he's early?" she whispered.

Mike took a deep breath and then straightened his jacket and tie, before reaching for the door handle. He opened it, and there was Hall, sweating slightly as usual and holding his production clipboard tightly to his chest. Even though Kintaro was a leading-edge tech company, some of the more traditional things still felt appropriate to Hall. He had told Harry Sakamoto that he preferred paper to the iPads or tablets most of his managerial colleagues seemed to use.

"Come in," Mike said, trying his hardest to sound casual, but he wasn't sure it worked. He could feel the anger seething inside himself.

"I... I brought the figures for the last two weeks, as I... I wasn't sure what it was you... you needed to see," he explained nervously. He had been given no real context for the meeting. Mike gestured that he should take a seat, which is when he spotted Büggs. He was a little taken aback at her presence, but neither she nor Mike offered an explanation, so he sat down, glancing at her in his peripheral vision.

"Bob, I need to ask you about a particular batch of SIMs," Mike began.

"Er, sure. Which batch?" he replied as he started to flick through his production paperwork.

"It's not going to be on there," Mike explained, clenching his jaw slightly.

"Oh. Oh, er, well, I can go get..." Hall started to say as he rose from his seat, ready to go back to his office and search the archive for whatever period Mike needed, but Mike couldn't contain his growing frustration any longer.

"Sit down." Both Hall and Büggs stared at him in equal amounts of surprise and shock, but Mike

remained standing, his patience evaporating suddenly. *"Why did you steal a batch of 50 perfectly good SIMs?"* he growled.

"Mike?" Büggs said, in an attempt to calm him down, but he was past listening to reason. He had barely slept for the last two nights and didn't have the time or the patience to play any more games.

"W-what?" stammered Hall, looking at him and then at Büggs.

"Don't play innocent with me. I've seen the evidence on screen." Mike turned to look at Büggs. *"Show him."*

"I... I don't know what you're talking about," Hall pleaded, standing and backing away from his now crimson-faced CEO. Büggs stood as well, but she didn't move towards the computer as she was too preoccupied with an increasingly volatile and unpredictable Mike, who was now slowly walking around his desk and almost stalking Hall.

"You stole 50 SIMs, and one found its way into my father's phone. How?"

"Mike, I... I don't know what you're talking about," pleaded Hall, but Mike was now joining dots that he hadn't previously considered, let alone whether they were even real dots.

"Are you responsible for my father's death? Do you know about the messages he'd been getting? Do you want to explain it all to the police?"

"Mike," pleaded Büggs, increasingly worried that the situation was escalating out of control.

"The police? Why would you call them?" Hall begged. Mike was furious at his attempt to plead his innocence and was now within reach of Hall. Büggs realised this needed to be brought to end, now.

"Maybe it's time to make that call," she said, hurriedly.

"Yes, let's call the police. He can explain it to them," sneered Mike, but as he looked around at her, he realised she wasn't looking or talking to him. She was looking at Hall. Mike turned back to Hall, who now had a look of confident disdain on his face. Gone was the nervous, stammering employee.

"Yes, I think it probably is," Hall replied calmly as he reached into his pocket and pulled out a mobile phone. He pressed the speed dial facility and, within seconds, the call connected.

"It's me," Hall said, and then held the phone out for Mike to take. Mike was confused and looked at Büggs, who silently but assertively indicated he should take it. Now it was Mike's turn to be nervous as all the vitriol had gone. He slowly put it to his ear.

"H... hello?" he said, tentatively.

"Hello, Michael," came the reply.

Chapter 78

"Who... who is this?" Mike asked.

"You don't need to know my name. What you do need to know is Yann Machendrie is dead, but I actually hold the key to the multi-million-pound investment he proposed." News that Machendrie was dead shocked Mike, but oddly not as much as he thought it might. A nagging question in the back of his mind suddenly spilled from his lips.

"Were you the person responsible for my father's death?"

The Broker sighed. The answer was yes, indirectly, but he knew admitting that wouldn't help to progress his plan.

"I'm sorry for your loss. It was unnecessary and avoidable, but Mr Machendrie is no longer in a position to answer for that tragedy." Mike's head started to spin. He didn't know what was actually happening, or whether anyone else on the Kintaro team was involved, like Hall and Büggs. The Broker was starting to feel his patience wearing thin, though, so the silence had to be broken.

"Michael?" he said, attempting to get his attention, but Mike was still trying to process what was happening. He was supposed to be questioning Hall about the stolen SIMs, which Büggs had helped uncover, but she was in on the whole scheme?

"*Michael!*" he repeated, a little more forcefully. It worked this time.

"What?" Mike replied.

"Now I have your attention, let me explain the two options you have. Firstly, you can forget you ever received this call and interrogate Bob Hall and Penny Büggs if you want to. You can even call the police, but they will find nothing, you will have irked me, and your mother will receive several distressing photographs of your father in a compromising position."

"What?" exclaimed Mike, aghast at a seemingly irrelevant reference to his father.

"Be quiet and listen. I don't like to waste my valuable time," stated The Broker; his voice starting to sound irritated. As shocked as Mike was about the reference to his father and photographs, he did as he was told. There was something about this man's demeanour and tone that demanded silence.

"If you take that first option, you'll also have to tell everyone in your company that you've run out of money, correct?" Mike assumed that Machendrie shared Kintaro's finances with this man.

"What's my second option?"

"You continue with the plan you'd agreed with Machendrie, but you'll deal directly with me from now on. I should warn you that I'm a lot more direct than he would've been, but I also reward my employees: just ask the two who are in the room with you. You'll also be able to tell your employees that you've secured finances to save the company, and you'll be a hero. More importantly, your mother can continue to cherish the memories of her husband without them being sullied. I can only imagine what that would do to her, and you don't want to lose both of your parents, do you?"

Mike was suddenly furious. He wanted to tell this bastard that he'd make him pay for threatening his mother, but he knew it would be pointless. If he reacted to him emotionally, things could quickly escalate, and he now assumed Machendrie was dead because of this man, rather than it just being news that he had shared. The Broker allowed him the time to assess the implications of the two offers, but before Mike could respond, there was a knock at the door, and it opened.

"Hi," said the head of HR, who glanced around the room. "I'm not interrupting anything, am I?"

"Not at all," said Büggs, smiling as if they'd been having a friendly team talk, so he turned to Mike.

"Sorry, but it's time to brief the workforce. Are you ready?"

Mike hesitated, but deep down he knew which option he was going to take. He passed the phone back to Hall and followed the head of HR, but then stopped and looked back at them. His gaze flitted from one to the other before he turned and headed out of the room without saying another word. Hall put the phone to his ear.

"I didn't hear a response from him," said The Broker.

"Don't worry, he'll soon see he has little choice," replied Hall, looking over at Büggs to see if she agreed. She nodded to indicate she agreed with Hall's statement.

"Don't fuck this up," warned The Broker before ending the call. He then dialled a different number.

"Yes?" was the response from the recipient of the call.

"Kendrick is dead, but Apostu is in, and we're confident McCleary will be joining our scheme. What about your end?"

"The parliamentary minister believes that Pritchard is guilty and acted alone, so we're good to go," replied Hibberd.

"Very well. From now on, we only use pseudonyms. As agreed, I'll be Baloo, Apostu is Goldilocks, and McCleary will be Road Runner. Have you decided on yours?" The Broker asked.

"Just call me Alice," replied Hibberd.

Chapter 79

After explaining that she intended to break client confidentiality, Maddox needed to recover the files she had hidden. All through the Ruiz trial, she had contemplated this scenario and secretly copied certain documents and some of the transcripts, just in case.

"Where will you stay?" Hibberd had asked her at the meeting after Pritchard had been arrested.

"I don't know. I'll probably move from hotel to hotel, using cash rather than credit cards," she explained.

"Isn't that a little dangerous? You'll be visible at some point every day without knowing if anyone is following you or who'll be delivering food to your hotel room."

"I'm not sure I have any option. I can't go back to Italy, as that requires me to use my passport, which could be tracked, plus the documents I copied are safely stored here in England."

Hibberd assumed she would have placed them somewhere close to where she previously lived, in Yorkshire. "How about staying with me?" he proposed. She looked at him, unsure what 'with me' meant. "Don't worry," he said, seeing her trepidation, "I have a small farm, and there's a separate, self-sufficient wing in the house. You can even keep *me* locked out," he chuckled.

"Perhaps that would work," she replied. "Where is it?"

"Just south of a town called Harrogate."

Maddox knew where Harrogate was. It seemed a safe option, and she would be close enough to get to her files within an hour or so. "Deal," she said.

Now, several days after she had moved in, Maddox was preparing to make her first visit to retrieve a copy of the files. Hibberd had offered her the use of one of his cars, but they were all very conspicuous, so she declined. Instead, she took several taxis, spiralling towards her final destination rather than going straight to it. That way, if anyone was trying to follow her, she'd have a chance to confuse or lose them.

After the fourth taxi ride, she climbed out at an office complex. Wearing unusually bland clothing and a baseball cap, little make-up and her hair tied into a pony-tail, she readily blended in with the rest of the tenants. She had rented a small office under a pseudonym, and a friend had paid the monthly rent, no questions asked.

She slowly made her way up to the sixth floor, stopping to get out of the lift a couple of times on different floors, and then using the stairs to climb up or down before taking the lift again. She eventually reached her quiet corner office. On the door was a plaque stating this was the office of 'Orange Banana Publications', a name she'd made up one night after too many tequilas. Although the sixth floor was mainly empty offices, she checked the immediate area around her as she slid the key into the door before slipping inside.

In a corner of the room was a small desk, a cheap office chair, and a single fire-proof filing cabinet. The cabinet had a standard lock on the front, but she had had a high-security lock added to the side of the cabinet, out of immediate view. If anyone tried to force the drawer, powder and dye would be sprayed into the hanging files. She unlocked the cabinet and pulled the top drawer open, which held three copies of everything. Maddox then removed a pre-addressed envelope from her bag and took one copy of each document out of the drawer. She checked her watch.

"Damn, the courier will be here soon," she hissed, scolding herself for being so tardy. She had pre-booked a courier to collect the envelope and deliver it to Hibberd's London office address. "Get these in, seal the envelope, and..." she narrated as she got the package ready. She then ran out of the office, making sure the office door was closed, before heading down to the reception area.

"Hello, this package is from Orange Banana Publications, and a courier should be here shortly to collect it," she explained.

"Alright, Mrs Daniels. I'll make sure it goes," replied the receptionist. That was the pseudonym Maddox had chosen. She then raced back up to the sixth floor, not bothering to take the circuitous route she had taken when she first entered the office complex. As she reached the office door, she pushed it open and took a step inside, then froze.

"Hello, Mrs Daniels, or should I call you Miss Maddox?" said a man who was looking at the files in the cabinet that Maddox hadn't had time to lock.

"I'm sorry, but I think you have the wrong office," she replied as calmly as she could, trying to hide her Italian accent.

"I don't think we have. You look like the photo we were sent, and we followed you all the way from Harrogate. You didn't make it easy, though, so top marks for trying," and he quietly applauded in mocking admiration at the lengths she had gone to.

Maddox hesitated before turning to run back out, but the door slammed shut. Another man had been standing behind it.

"Leaving so soon?" the second man asked.

"What do you want?" Maddox asked, dropping the fake accent.

"Mr Ruiz says you've been a naughty girl," sighed the first man as he took all the copied documents out of the cabinet and put them into a bin bag. He then pushed the drawer closed and turned to face her.

"How did you know where I'd be?"

"That's for me to know and a question for you to take with you." She couldn't see it, but as she and the first man were talking, the man behind her silently drew a long-bladed knife from a sheath inside his jacket. "And Mr Ruiz doesn't like naughty girls."

Before she could try to do anything or scream, a powerful hand covered her mouth and the blade of the knife plunged into the back of her ribs.

Chapter 80

Mike pulled back into the driveway at his parents' house. He still thought of it as their house, even though the memory of his father's death cast a shadow over everything that had been 'theirs' for so many years. He eased his way out of the car, pulled his bag out from behind the car seat, and trudged to the front door.

"Is that you, Michael?" his mother called out on hearing the front door open and close.

"Yes, Mum."

She walked into the hallway and watched as her son took his jacket off and hung it on the banister post. He'd take it upstairs later. Ordinarily, she would have scolded him for making the hall look untidy, but not today.

"How did it go?" she asked softly.

"It didn't. I called the announcement off for another 24 hours. I needed some more time to think." He looked up at her, defeat in his eyes. The choice he was faced with meant either his mother was potentially at risk, or he'd have to live with the guilt of destroying two-hundred people's lives and dreams, as well as his own future prospects. Either way, he'd be spending the rest of his life looking over his shoulder for demons who were either hunting him or pulling on the leash that controlled him, and there would be the continued threat against his mother's wellbeing, even if he gave in to their demands.

"That sounds sensible, but you know you need to make a decision," she started to say, hoping to support and encourage him.

"*I know*," he snapped. Alessia flinched slightly, but she knew he must be struggling, given his father's death and the pressure of such a momentous decision. "Sorry," Mike said. "It's been a tough day, that's all," he said. "Tell me about your day," and he tried to brighten his tone, realising he was being a little sullen and selfish.

"Your Aunt Doreen called."

"From New Zealand?"

"Yes."

"That's nice. What did she want?"

"To offer me the chance to finally go visit her. Your father never wanted to fly, and, to be honest, he and his sister never really got on. I don't know that I want to…" but as she spoke, the news gave Mike a spark of inspiration. Could the call from a distant relative provide him with the breathing space he needed and his mother with a degree of safety? Surely, even the thugs involved in this fraudulent scheme wouldn't go hunting for an old woman on the other side of the world? "… but it seems-" his mother was still explaining, when he interrupted her.

"You should go."

"Er, what?"

"Yes, it's a wonderful opportunity and just the change you need."

"Well, I suppose I could have a think about it," she mused, but Mike wasn't interested in delays and reflection. Whenever his mother took time to think about doing something, she rarely actually did it.

"No, no thinking. It will be perfect for you, Mum. Let's get you on a flight for tomorrow."

"Tomorrow? But I'll need to..." but Mike was having none of it.

"Is your passport still valid?"

"Yes, but..."

"And you don't need jabs for New Zealand, right?"

"I don't think so, but what about..."

"No, no, Mum. No thinking. I want you to call Aunt Doreen and tell her you're going. If you don't decide right now, I know you; you'll still be thinking about it in a month, and you know Dad would have agreed with me." He strode over to her, put his hands on her shoulders and gently but firmly turned her back into the lounge. "I've got a call to make, and then we'll get a seat booked for you. You call Doreen right away. Okay?"

"I... I suppose so," she said, actually feeling a buzz of excitement at the speed this was all happening.

Mike left his mother in the lounge and leapt up the stairs, three at a time, heading into the small home office he'd set up since his father's death. He glanced at a framed photo of him that sat on the desk.

"Love you, Dad," he whispered, before picking up the phone and turning his computer on. The phone was answered after a couple of rings.

"Hi, this is Addison," said the CEO of the Californian start-up that Mike had spoken to a few days ago.

"Addison, hi. This is Mike McCleary. I know you said your offer was time-bound, but I just wondered..." he started to say, but he heard a sigh on the other end of the line.

"Aww, Mike. I'm sorry, but we signed a deal yesterday. I'm afraid the offer is no longer on the table. I'm sorry, man."

Mike knew it had been a long-shot and thanked Addison for taking his call, wishing him the best of luck with the new venture. He tossed the phone onto the desk and then slumped into an armchair he'd put in the office, exhaling in disappointment. With that option off the table, he wasn't sure what to do next.

As his mind and mood both sank into gloom, he snatched the remote for the small television mounted on the wall, and switched it on. He needed a distraction from the cacophony in his brain, although he wasn't really watching or listening to what the news reporter was doing and saying: something about the latest data breach at an online retailer and asking for the views of a purported cyber expert. Something then clicked in Mike's brain.

"A cyber expert," he mumbled to himself. He thought about the idea for a few seconds before jumping out of the armchair and racing over to his computer. It was already open at his preferred search engine home page, and he began to type furiously. "Professor Gary Hibb... ah, there you are." Within seconds, hundreds of entries appeared about his old MIT professor, the man he'd seen on television a few days ago when he was in the Kintaro office. He found his contact details and sent him an email. Minutes later, a reply pinged.

'Dear Mike. How lovely to hear from you after such a long time. I'd be delighted to discuss your mysterious conundrum, but could we talk tonight, as I've just started a new venture and need to meet with my new business partner about something. Did I read that you work at a company called Kintaro, now?'

Chapter 81

Denton sat at his desk, surrounded by what felt like the biggest pile of administrative paperwork he had ever had. How he hated his job. It was almost a week since he'd been told to suspend his investigation into The Broker, and his mood had rarely lifted since.

As he took yet another file from his to-do pile, there was a knock at the door. It was Janine, the CID team's civilian administrator. It was a growing trend to use civilians in what were deemed as non-specialist roles.

"Thought I'd take some of these files off your desk," she explained, waiting for approval to enter his office. Denton wearily gestured for her to come in. She turned to grab her trolley and pushed it into the office. He had over 20 folders ready for filing, and to see the pile disappear off his desk was surprisingly satisfying. He looked up and smiled at her as she placed them on the top shelf of the trolley, and then she smiled back.

"Now, where do you want these new ones?" she asked, lifting a pile of at least an equivalent size from the bottom shelf of the trolley. His face dropped. "Sorry," she said, and he nodded that he understood her sentiment was genuine, but he couldn't bring himself to tell her it was fine.

"Just there, on the 'to-do' pile, please, Janine."

She placed them in the tray, making sure they didn't topple over, such was their size, and then pushed her trolley out again. She reached for the door handle and started to close it, but a hand rested gently on the glass, and a woman's voice could be heard. It had a slight but definite accent, although Denton couldn't quite place it.

"It's alright, I need to go in," the woman said, and she pushed the door open as Denton looked up. If he was miserable before she arrived, he was downright testy now. It was the Europol officer that had been in the DCI's office a few days ago.

"Detective Inspector, may I have a moment?" Denton slumped in his chair and gestured for her to take a seat opposite his desk. "I realise our first meeting was a little disappointing for you."

"Just a little," he replied, trying not to clench his teeth.

"Well, perhaps I can make a better impression today?"

"Feel free to try. I doubt you could make a worse one." He glanced at the pile of files, which suddenly looked far more appealing than talking to her.

"You realise that we are on the same side, DI Denton. Just because what I needed didn't allow you to request a search warrant, that doesn't mean you should feel you lost."

"Is there something you've come to say other than to gloat?"

The woman understood his irrational emotion, but she wasn't here to pander to it. She stood and said, "Would you come with me, please?" Denton assumed it was rhetorical, so he stood, lazily pulling his jacket off the back of his chair, and followed her out of the room. As he did so, he saw Jones standing nearby.

"What's going on, Jonesy?" he muttered, as they followed the woman across the CID room and to the lift.

"I don't know. I've just been told I need to attend a meeting."

Two floors down, and in an area that Denton and Jones had never seen or used, the three of them stopped at a door. An electronic keypad blocked their entry, but the woman entered a six-digit code, and the door unlocked. The room had no windows, so two fluorescent tubes provided a stark and sterile blanket of white light. Sitting at the far side of a desk were two men, with their DCI standing to one side.

"DI Denton, DC Jones," said the DCI.

"Ma'am," they replied. They then looked at the two men, neither of which Denton recognised, but Jones thought she'd seen one of them somewhere before but couldn't recall exactly where she knew him from.

"Please take a seat," the DCI requested. Denton and Jones glanced at each other, equally unsure of what was about to happen.

Chapter 82

The DCI took a step forward and introduced the two men.

"This is Professor Gary Hibberd, and this is Michael McCleary, the interim CEO of a company called Kintaro. They have some information, and I thought you might like to hear it," she explained before turning to Hibberd. "Professor?" she said, inviting him to speak. Jones nodded to herself as she recalled seeing Hibberd's name and photo in several newspaper articles after the Ruiz trial.

"Good morning to you both. I believe you've already met Senior Agent Peeters from Europol?" and he gestured to the Europol officer. "She shares some common ground with all of us, despite what you might have felt last week, but I have some good news. I won't bore you with the details; suffice to say we feel we now have sufficient evidence to charge a large group of people with criminal activity... including Mr Matthew Berry."

It took a few seconds to sink in, but a wave of euphoria began to sweep through Denton. Under the desk, he subtly clenched his fist in celebration, but as he did so, doubt then arose in his mind and smothered the elation.

"How?" he asked, worried that this was too good to be true.

"Mr Berry has been the subject of a year-long Europol investigation. It was an extension of the Interpol joint-venture we'd already completed on someone called Dennis Ruiz," Peeters explained.

"Ruiz was the cybercriminal I told you about when we were investigating the Lottery Ticket Murders," whispered Jones. Denton vaguely remembered the conversation.

"One of Mr Ruiz's main lieutenants, Robert Kendrick, provided us with enough incriminating evidence to prosecute Mr Ruiz in return for anonymity, immunity from prosecution himself, and a new identity. Mr Kendrick also confirmed that someone in the British government was complicit in supporting his plan to become the new head of Ruiz's criminal operation, BOrg. That person was Howard Pritchard, the Director of GCHQ," explained Hibberd. "Part of their plan was to recruit Mr McCleary as Kintaro's Head of Research and Development so they could manipulate him into producing a chip that enabled data theft on an unimaginable scale. Oddly, it was an idea Mr McCleary had reflected on when he was a student at MIT, although his thesis was about how to defend against such a scheme rather than create it. I came across his thesis because I was his interim professor for the final few months of his course. Although the idea was to place him into the Kintaro team, when the CEO died after an accident at home..."

"Which we no longer think was an accident," interjected Peeters.

"Mr McCleary was subsequently manoeuvred into the interim CEO role, with Kendrick agreeing to act as an opportunistic investor. He used the pseudonym of Yann Machendrie and had to work with a woman who called herself 'Tania'. We don't know her real name, but she'd been hired to connive her way into Mr McCleary's life. She pretended to be a love interest when they met in Canada, as well as then pretending to be the niece of Machendrie," concluded Hibberd.

"Okay, but what's all this got to do with Matthew Berry?" asked a now slightly subdued Denton.

"To ensure the continuation of the BOrg operation, Kendrick needed funds. We jointly created a sophisticated business case about how to get the fraudulent software into the market on a Kintaro chip. Kendrick decided to take the idea to Berry, who had the ego as well as the appetite to facilitate the funding."

"And did he fund it?" asked Denton hopefully. Hibberd smiled and turned to Mike McCleary.

"Yesterday, we received £1m from a shell company in Dubai that Matthew Berry co-owns. He told me he'd personally authorise the payment three days ago," Mike explained.

Denton's hope evaporated. Surely that was something Berry's solicitor would immediately ask the court to dismiss as circumstantial evidence and propose the theory that one of Berry's co-owners must have been responsible. "I'm sorry, but the defence will tear that apart," he scoffed.

"We have the text conversation between Berry and Mike recorded," Hibberd announced.

"Wait, how did you capture and verify it? Matthew Berry isn't stupid enough to just send him a text."

Peeters stepped in, "Have you heard of EncroChat, Detective Inspector?"

"I have, yes, but it's a secure communication system."

"It's not widely-known yet, but in 2019, a joint operation between UK, French and Dutch police broke into EncroChat's sophisticated encryption service. The company had provided approximately 60,000 criminals across Europe with a modified Android phone for about £1,600 each. The devices allowed fully encrypted conversations, text messages, and images to be sent from one device to another. The devices also have a 'kill' capability that allows the user to wipe all the content on their device, or it automatically wipes if an incorrect PIN code is entered too many times, destroying any evidence it might hold. Thanks to the joint operation, though, we now have the capability to access all text messages through their servers in France."

"The authorities broke through their layers of security and dropped some malware onto their server. Ironic when you think about it," said Hibberd. "Thankfully for us, Berry provided Mike with such a phone so they could communicate securely, or so he thought. When Mike called me last week, we agreed he should help us gather enough evidence to charge Mr Berry."

"What's in it for you, Mr McCleary?" Denton questioned.

"Those bastards were probably responsible for my father's suicide," explained Mike. "And they threatened to hurt my mum if I didn't comply."

Hibberd picked up the story again. "Mike asked Berry when he should expect to see the promised investment. Berry told him not to worry about the details, but Kintaro would receive a £1m loan from a company called Ashton, James, and Proctor. It was intended to be the start of a much deeper investment in Kintaro."

The company name sounded familiar to Denton. "Wasn't Ashton, James, and Proctor the crypto-currency company Dr Pickett allegedly invested £475,000 with?" he asked as he turned to Jones for confirmation.

"Yes, it was."

Peeters spoke next. "We were still gathering the final pieces of information last week, which is why we needed you to withdraw your request for a search warrant. We didn't want to scare Mr Berry, and it meant we could cast our net a little wider and a lot deeper."

Hibberd smiled. "We also received a file from the lawyer who'd previously represented Dennis Ruiz, which will now allow us to locate and dismantle a significant part of the BOrg operation. There will be a series of dawn raids tomorrow, across the whole of Europe, related to cybercrime and fraud. We thought you might like to come on one particular raid," he said as he looked up at the DCI.

She smiled back and, turning to Denton and Jones, said, "Be here at 4am tomorrow, ready to raid Matthew Berry's offices and home. I've already got the search warrant you wanted approved. We'll even let you arrest him if you like?"

Denton didn't know whether to run around the room cheering, to repeatedly thump the table in celebration, or to hug Jonesy in relief.

Chapter 83

At precisely 5:30am, the door to The Broker's offices was smashed open. Its frame exploded, and glass shattered, with splinters of wood flying in every direction. Twenty members of the Metropolitan Police's armed unit, SCO19, poured in, shouting, "ARMED POLICE, ARMED POLICE."

At exactly the same time, four police vehicles screeched to a halt in the driveway of the Berry family home. Denton and Jones jumped out of one of the cars and followed the lead squad, who were armed with a sledgehammer. No-one had guns on this raid though, given they knew innocent children were probably in the house. The door was stronger than most traditional residential ones, but after three swings of the hammer, it was hanging by a single hinge: its lock now skidding across the polished marble floor and thudding into the bottom of the sweeping staircase.

"POLICE, POLICE, POLICE."

Mrs Berry woke and shrieked before jumping out of bed and running to her children. One was already screaming, while the other two were sobbing as they hid under their quilts. The Broker was also momentarily confused, aroused unnaturally from a deep sleep. He glanced down at the bedside unit where he kept a loaded pistol, but as his mind cleared, he realised what was happening and that any resistance would be counter-productive when it came to his interview at the police station. Denton appeared moments after two officers had found Berry and called downstairs.

"Matthew Berry," Denton started, trying to suppress a smile of satisfaction. "I'm arresting you on suspicion of extortion, conspiracy to murder, kidnap, money laundering, and aggravated assault. You do not have to say anything, but it may harm your defence if you do not mention, when questioned, something which you later rely on in court. Anything you do say may be given in evidence." The two of them stared at each other for several seconds as the officers cuffed him, but the silence was broken when his wife stormed out of her children's bedroom.

"*What the hell is going on, Matthew?*"

"I don't know. It's all a mistake. I'll be back for lunch. Call Michael, will you?" he asked her calmly, referring to his solicitor. As he was being led away, Denton then introduced himself to her.

"I'm Detective Inspector Denton from the Metropolitan Police."

"I know who you are," she muttered, trying to hide her anger and frustration as her children clung to her arms and legs. "What the hell is going on? All my husband ever does is help you people, and now you smash your way in here, scaring my kids half to death."

Denton remained calm, speaking matter-of-factly to her. "Your husband is under arrest, Mrs Berry, and I have a search warrant for the house. I need you and the children to get dressed, please. DC Jones will stay in the room with you."

"What? We don't need no-one watching us dress, thank you very much."

"Sorry, but DC Jones must be present," he insisted, gesturing that she and the children should lead the way for Jones.

Scores of other coordinated raids took place all over the United Kingdom that morning, as well as on mainland Europe. All of them timed so that no-one being arrested could warn any of their colleagues or contacts that they should flee. Scores were captured and tens of millions of pounds in cash and drugs were recovered, but one man did avoid arrest. Shortly before a raid on his apartment, Simion Apostu received a text:

This is not a fire drill. You have 15 minutes to get out

He always had a grab-bag ready; in case a client asked for an urgent meeting at short notice. It was perfect for one, maybe two nights away, but the text meant he would be leaving his Bucharest home and possessions, forever.

As predicted, the Poliția Română subsequently arrived and raced into the apartment block. He watched them from an apartment across the street as its elderly owners sat shaking in fear of the man who had forced his way into their home at gunpoint.

Five minutes later, the task force commander accepted that he had escaped, and ordered his men back to the station. The quiet street then slowly returned to normal, except for the two officers positioned outside the apartment block's main entrance. Anyone who approached the door was asked for their identification before they could enter or leave. Apostu glanced back at the couple, who hadn't moved an inch, before he retrieved his phone and responded:

Safe

Back in his Harrogate home, Hibberd read the message and smiled before returning to review some of the paperwork Maddox had sent to his London office. He had given most of the contents from the package to the police as evidence, but not before removing a handful of documents that contained relevant and detailed information he needed. The doorbell rang. He was expecting two people today, and he knew who this would be because his second guest had a key. He walked down the long hallway and unlocked the door to meet his first guest.

"Good morning. Thank you for coming. Please, come in," Hibberd said warmly.

"Thank you," replied Mike McCleary.

"Straight down the hall, second door on the left. Please, make yourself at home and I'll bring us some tea."

Mike walked slowly down the hallway, admiring the décor as well as the pictures on the wall, before accidentally entering the first door on his left; Hibberd's home office. Somewhat surprisingly, there was no computer in the room. A high table and several stools stood in the middle, with light cascading in through several windows in the sloping roof. The longest wall had pinboards and a wipeboard, all with various diagrams and articles on. He then turned and meandered over to the table, perusing the paperwork that Hibberd had laid out.

"I'm sorry, but I seem to have run out of biscuits," came a voice from the hallway. Seconds later, Hibberd walked past the room Mike had mistakenly walked into. He saw Mike take a step back from the table. "Wrong room," Hibberd said, quickly putting on a pleasant, warm smile as if it wasn't a problem, but it faded just as quickly. He bowed his head and made the decision to talk to Mike in that room instead of the small library down the hall. Hibberd walked over to a small, round table that stood by the side of a recliner chair and placed the tray on the table.

"Mike," he sighed, "I really wanted to talk to you before we showed you this room, but we might as well stay in here now."

"We showed you?" questioned Mike. Just then, a key slid into the front door lock, and they both heard it open and close.

"Yes, 'we'," replied Hibberd before calling out, "We're in the office," to whoever had just entered the house. When the person came into view, Mike took a step back.

"What's she doing here?" Mike asked.

"Thought you were going to wait for me?" said Büggs, looking first at Hibberd and then at Mike. "Hello, Mike," she said.

"I said what is *she* doing here?" an increasingly nervous Mike asked.

"Relax, Mike. Penny is part of my team."

Mike looked over her shoulder, expecting to see Bob Hall enter the room as well, but there didn't appear to be anybody else there. He glanced at Büggs and then glared at Hibberd.

"There's no-one else, Mike. It's just you, me, and Penny," assured Hibberd. "We wanted to talk to you about Kintaro and what we want you to do next."

"I... I thought..." but Mike felt totally confused, so he decided to stop talking.

Twenty minutes later, Hibberd had explained Mike's proposed role in, and the risks associated with, Hibberd's ongoing undercover investigation into BOrg.

"And if I decline?" asked Mike. Hibberd just shrugged his shoulders. "I... I need to think about it," Mike continued.

"Of course, but don't leave it too long, Mike. I've not got a lot of time to waste. Either you're in, or you're out," was Hibberd's reply.

"I'll... I'll call you," were the last words before Mike turned and headed out of the house.

"What do you think?" asked Büggs. "Do you think he believed you?"

"I'm not sure, but he's a smart guy. He just needs a little time."

"We don't have time. This needs to be seamless, or someone will suspect."

"Let him be for 72 hours, and then we'll press him for his answer."

"What about some assurance?" proposed Büggs.

"I was just thinking the very same thing," replied Hibberd.

A few days later, two hundred miles away, Alessia was packing her final belongings into a box, ready to be shipped to storage. Mike had been unable to get her on a flight to New Zealand as quickly as he'd hoped, but after a series of long and surprisingly frank discussions between them, she decided that perhaps the trip was just what she needed. The house continued to remind her of Arlo, and although she fondly recalled the decades that they had spent turning this house into the most wonderful home, it now felt depressing to be here. Consequently, she decided to sell it, with a possible move back to Malta. She still had family there to help her grow older gracefully or, knowing them, possibly disgracefully. She laughed at the thought. Mike said he would handle the estate agent and the viewings so she could head off on her new adventure. As she wrote 'photographs' on the box with a thick black marker, one of the removal men tapped on the lounge door, breaking her moment of reflection.

"Sorry to disturb, but we've almost finished," he said. "Just wanted you to have this. We found it in the shed, behind some empty plastic pots." He held out a notebook.

"Thank you," said Alessia, taking the notebook from him. She assumed it was filled with some gardening nonsense, and her eyes began to fill with tears as she imagined Arlo sat in the shed, scribbling a shopping list for maintaining the lawn or writing down just how high the sweet peas were that week. He loved keeping lists about the most obscure things that he would tell her about as they sipped their afternoon cup of tea.

"I've got nearly double the number of tomatoes growing compared to this time last year," he would proudly announce, showing her his notes. "Reckon it's the new feed I'm using, or maybe it has been a bit warmer this summer?" he'd say, questioning his own assumptions. She would always reply with words, or more likely, sounds of encouragement when in fact she wasn't really listening, but he seemed oblivious to her indifference. She sniffed as she fought back some new tears but found herself smiling at the memory.

"Oh, you silly, lovely man," she whispered to herself as she opened the notebook to see what his last entry was, but it was nothing that she could have imagined. "Who is Jane?" she mumbled, recalling that was the name on the back of the envelope she had received that contained the photograph of the murdered girl. The doorbell rang. She dropped the notebook onto the chair, intending to look at it later, and walked to the door.

"Morning," said the postman. "So, you ready for the off?" he asked, a sad smile on his face.

"Good morning, Ian. Yes, yes, I am. Thank you for being so lovely. We always enjoyed getting post, rather than this silly email nonsense that everyone does nowadays, and you've been a wonderful and reliable postie, whatever the weather," she said, pulling an envelope from her apron pocket and handing it to him. In it was £20 as a sign of her gratitude.

"Aww, thank you Mrs McCleary. Well, here's your last delivery from me. Have a safe journey, and we'll miss you around here," and he handed her a few letters and a small, padded pouch. After saying their goodbyes one more time, Alessia closed the door and browsed the mail.

"Junk, bill, junk, and oh yes, the sodding society wedding invitation from the Argyles. No thank you very much," and she threw that straight into the bin. She then ripped open the pouch. Inside was a phone and a post-it note. On the note, it said:

Turn me on. You'd be mad not to

AUTHOR'S NOTE

Scammer (noun)
DEFINITION: *a person who commits fraud or participates in a dishonest scheme to gain money or possessions from someone.*

This book has been nearly 3 years in the making. One of the hardest things throughout that time was trying to keep some sense of *'what it will be like for someone reading the story for the first time'*, because I've probably read parts of it over 30 times. I've included, excluded, re-included, and re-excluded multiple characters and scores of chapters, changing approximately 40% of the content over the last 9 months, but hopefully I've got there now!

From a storyteller's perspective, the idea that all our data could be stolen and used without us knowing gave birth to this book, and truth can be stranger than fiction. From a technology perspective, everything in this book can already happen and, every now and then, the media carries stories about stolen sensitive data. Whether all the news stories are entirely factual rather than sensationalised is unclear, but the technology to mirror a smartphone, for example, allowing you to see exactly what the owner of the phone is seeing on their screen, has been around for years. The social media question examples in this book are also real, fraudulent methods to compile a jigsaw all about you, but is mass data fraud on an almost unimaginable scale, possible?

Gemalto was an international digital security company providing software applications, as well as secure personal devices such as smart cards. It provided 49% of the market with chips used in ATM cards, credit cards, and had a foothold in the markets for electronic passports, ID cards (including for the US Department of Defence) and contactless payment technology, generating €2.969bn in revenue, in 2018. According to documents leaked by Edward Snowden, the American NSA and British GCHQ infiltrated Gemalto's infrastructure to steal SIM authentication keys, allowing them to secretly intercept and listen to the conversations of tens of millions of mobile phone users. While Gemalto investigated and denied the breach, Gemalto issued a press release on February 25, 2015 saying there were "reasonable grounds to believe that an operation by NSA and GCHQ probably happened". The company denied that the government agencies gained access to any authentication keys, but doubts still remain. If it was true, just how much data could be collected?

Please don't have nightmares, but don't be fooled into thinking someone really wants to know how far a Facebook message can reach or is asking you to tell them what year you were born in *without telling me*. Every bit of data is part of a jigsaw, and there are plenty of people out there who don't care about you, as long as they can get access to your money or, more importantly, your data. Money can be spent once, but data can be sliced and diced and used many times, as real people have discovered. The fictitious character, Stephen Attwell, is based on real crime victims.

Finally, thanks for investing your hard-earned money to purchase this book and investing your valuable time to read it. I hope you enjoyed it and are looking forward to BOOK 4 – *The Horologist.*

www.ingramcontent.com/pod-product-compliance
Ingram Content Group UK Ltd.
Pitfield, Milton Keynes, MK11 3LW, UK
UKHW011459081125
464823UK00005B/19